OBSESSION

OBSESSION

Claire Lorrimer

This first world edition published 2013
in Great Britain and the USA by
SEVERN HOUSE PUBLISHERS LTD of
19 Cedar Road, Sutton, Surrey, England, SM2 5DA.

British Library Cataloguing in Publication Data

Lorrimer, Claire
  Obsession.
  1. Triangles (Interpersonal relations)–Fiction.
  2. Widows–Fiction. 3. Nonbiological mothers–Fiction.
  4. Great Britain–History–Victoria, 1837-1901–Fiction.
  I. Title
  823.9'14-dc23

ISBN-13: 978-0-7278-8324-7 (cased)

All Severn House titles are printed on acid-free paper.

Severn House Publishers support The Forest Stewardship Council [FSC],
the leading international forest certification organisation. All our titles that
are printed on Greenpeace-approved FSC-certified paper carry the FSC logo.

MIX
Paper from
responsible sources
FSC® C013056

Typeset by Palimpsest Book Production Ltd.,
Falkirk, Stirlingshire, Scotland.
Printed and bound in Great Britain by
TJ International, Padstow, Cornwall

For Charlotte, Tom and Arthur with very much love and my thanks. C.L.

PROLOGUE

January, 1860

'Bessie, I can't wait to tell you. I've met him . . . the man I want to marry . . . I've fallen in love and he's the handsomest man you've ever seen . . . and he smiled at me . . . and he asked Papa why he'd kept such a pretty daughter hidden in the schoolroom and wanted to know how old I was and . . .'

Harriet broke off, too breathless with excitement to continue.

The rosy-cheeked, freckled face of the gamekeeper's eldest daughter was smiling as she helped the fifteen-year-old girl out of the pelisse jacket and dress she had been wearing for luncheon in her father's shooting lodge.

'Papa said that because I behaved so well at the luncheon, I might act as his hostess tonight at dinner,' she continued, 'so I want to wear my prettiest dress, Bessie.'

She sat down at her dressing table in her chemisette and regarded her reflection in the mirror.

'If only I was pretty!' She sighed. 'My mouth's too big and my nose is too short and I just wish I had blue eyes like my sisters. Hazel isn't a proper colour at all!'

Never having heard Harriet pay any attention to her appearance before, her maid hastened to reassure her. ''Course you're pretty, Miss Harriet. Haven't I told you, you would grow up prettier even than those older sisters of yours?' She reached for the silver-backed hair brush and began to untangle the young girl's chestnut curls, adding: ''Cept when you's all messed up playing with the little ones down the farm.'

Harriet laughed. 'But you know I love playing with the children,' she said. 'I'm going to have at least ten of my own when I get married.'

Her face was glowing as she jumped up from the dressing-table stool and, grabbing hold of Bessie's arms, waltzed her round the room in her chemisette and pantilettes.

'He's staying for the night!' she said. 'So I'll see him again, and Bessie, I heard *his* father invite Papa to join him for grouse shooting in Scotland in the summer and I'll be sixteen by then and maybe Papa will take me with him.' Her face fell as she released her maid and sat down on the bed. 'I just *wish* they didn't live so far away from Sussex!' She sighed. 'He said Leicestershire is nearly two hundred miles from here!'

A minute later, she was smiling again.

'He said they had come on a train which was much, much faster than a coach and asked me if I'd ever ridden on one, Deerskeep Manor not being near a railway station, and he said he was sure I would enjoy it as it goes so quickly.'

Bessie put away the discarded garments in the wardrobe and brought over the new dimity dress with cornflower-blue bows which her young mistress would wear that evening, saying: 'You've not yet told me who this young man is you say's going to be your future husband, Miss Harriet! Any road, I reckon you's much too young to be having such fancies.'

'Charity was only eighteen when she got engaged, so I'm not too young. I'm sixteen next birthday, Bessie, and he and his father are staying here tonight so you can help Mary take up the hot water jugs when they are changing for dinner and then you can see for yourself how handsome he is . . . oh, and his name is Brook, Brook Edgerton, and his mother died like mine but his aunt brought him up. He went to Rugby which is a boys' boarding school and he has been to Jamaica because his family have sugar plantations there, and . . .'

'You's going to be late down to dinner if you don't stop chattering!' Bessie interrupted as she fastened Harriet into her hooped petticoat and then into the new dress, shaking out the layers of flounces that decorated the full skirt. She then fetched a lace collar, and a clean ribbon for Harriet's hair.

It was a long time, she thought, since she had seen her young mistress so animated. It was the first time that the young girl had ever been permitted to attend a shooting party luncheon as only the wives of the guns and servants who carried the food to the shooting lodge were normally present. Training to be a lady's maid, Bessie had never been one of the household servants who attended these lunch parties.

Harriet sat down once more at her dressing table whilst Bessie braided the back of her hair, entwining it with the blue ribbon and then anchoring it securely into a smooth knot with a pearl pin, and started once more to regale the maid with further descriptions of the luncheon, and of the handsome Brook Edgerton.

'He's Sir Walter Edgerton's son,' she elaborated. 'He's been abroad these past three years and he told me he was twenty-four years old.' Finally running out of breath, she came to a halt.

Bessie shook her head. 'Best you stop thinking too much about the young gentleman,' she cautioned as she completed the arrangement of Harriet's hair. 'If he be as handsome as you say, like as not he'll have found himself a wife long afore you's old enough to be wed.'

Harriet sighed. 'I just wish I was older now!' she repeated wistfully. 'I'm tired of people saying, 'Goodness me, all your sisters married and you still a little girl!'

She paused for a moment, her expression thoughtful.

'I suppose if my sisters hadn't been so much older than me, I would never have been allowed to have you as my friend, Bessie.'

Nor would she herself be so blessed! the older girl thought, recalling the beautiful sunny day some ten years ago when she had first set eyes on the little girl from the manor. Miss Harriet had been leaning over the farm gate watching her as she came out from her house with a plate of scraps for the hens. Their cottage had been given to her father by Harriet's father, Sir Charles Drake, when he had employed him as his gamekeeper. Bessie was the eldest of his eight children.

Although in the past she had often seen the family from the big house in church on a Sunday, Bessie had only very occasionally caught sight of the youngest girl as she came out of church, her hand held by the Drakes' nanny.

On a bright spring afternoon, Bessie had been astonished to see the five-year-old child unaccompanied, although she knew the nanny had recently left Sir Charles' employ in order to go to Ireland to look after his eldest daughter's babies. A governess was now in charge of Miss Harriet, the one remaining child.

According to Bessie's mother, the woman, having first been

employed when Miss Una, the eldest of the young ladies was only six, was well into her sixties now and ready to retire, but Sir Charles had begged her to stay on as his motherless youngest would be feeling the loss of her familiar nanny and might need the security of someone she knew to give the little girl lessons in the morning and supervise her daily routine.

Sir Charles had agreed that the governess should enjoy a rest in the afternoons after settling the child with suitable activities not requiring adult supervision. These were of necessity indoor occupations, and Mary, the nursery maid, reported that she often saw the little girl looking wistfully out from the schoolroom window, and heard her say how much she wished she could spend the afternoon outside picking blackberries or strawberries in the summer, or that she had a friend with whom she could play.

It was on one such day when the sun was dancing on the white pages of the book Harriet was tired of reading, that she had crept quietly down the servants' staircase, past the butler's pantry and out through the garden door.

She had known at once where she was going – across the lawn, through the vegetable garden and down to the gamekeeper's cottage. She had heard the parlourmaid say that the gamekeeper, Mr Benson's Labrador had birthed thirteen puppies, and that he intended to keep the most promising two to train as gun dogs.

Agog to see them, Harriet had slipped out of the house unnoticed.

Although Bessie's numerous brothers and sisters ran all but wild round their yard and the nearby farm, the older ones looking after the younger, she knew from her mother's accounts of the days when she'd worked as a parlourmaid at the manor that the young ladies were never allowed to go out of doors unsupervised. Their late mother, Lady Drake, had been extremely protective of her offspring, but after she had died in childbirth Sir Charles had taken no interest in nursery affairs.

By the time Harriet was old enough to escape from the school-room that spring day, Bessie, the gamekeeper's eldest daughter, was fifteen years old and more than happy to show the little girl where to find the hen's eggs, how to feed the ferrets and, best of all, she took her to play for a while with the lively pack of golden-haired puppies. With natural hospitality, she invited Harriet into the kitchen to sample her mother's home-made scones and freshly baked bread still warm from the oven.

Mrs Benson threw up her arms in distress when Bessie explained Harriet's presence and the child confessed that she'd not had permission to leave the house.

'Lawk's-amercy!' she'd gasped. 'Whatever can you be thinking of, Bess? Now take Miss Harriet straight back to the manor, quick as you can. Like as not they'll all be out searching for her!' She'd glanced at the kitchen clock on the mantelpiece above the range and looked even more anxious. She had turned then to Harriet, adding: 'It's not that I'm not wanting you here, Miss Harriet, but . . .'

'But I like being with Bessie!' Harriet had pleaded. 'I want her to be my friend. I haven't got any friends!'

Mrs Benson had shaken her head, her expression compassionate, as she'd said gently, 'It wouldn't be proper, Miss Harriet.'

The same words were repeated by Harriet's governess when the distraught woman caught sight of the somewhat grubby figure of her missing charge standing in the big hall of the manor, and heard the child's rebellious voice insisting that she be allowed to spend time with Bessie when she wanted.

'And I SHALL go there!' she'd stated, not a little frightened as she heard herself rebelling outright for the first time against a grown-up's ruling.

The day had ended with one small tearful child standing in front of her father in the drawing room. A quick look at his bewhiskered, unsmiling face had undermined her confidence.

'Miss Perkins has told me about your escapade this afternoon,' he said, 'for which very serious misdemeanor she wishes me to punish you. However, I do not intend to do so as I understand you were never actually forbidden to leave the house on your own.' He cleared his throat, touched quite unexpectedly by the child's likeness to her dead mother. 'However . . .' he repeated, '. . . I have my suspicions that you were aware of such an embargo. No matter! You are quite old enough now to have the ways of the world explained to you – or perhaps I should say the way society expects us to conform to its rules. You may sit down.'

He waited until the little girl was sitting facing him in an

armchair which looked far too big for her small person. He
cleared his throat a second time, unsure suddenly how to explain
the somewhat complicated division of the populace in simple
enough fashion for the child to understand.

'It's like this,' he began. 'The population is divided into three
main classes depending on their parents' status. We, people like
ourselves, belong to the upper classes, who employ people to
look after us and our properties; then there are the people in
trades or businesses, who are in the middle classes, and then
those who serve us. They belong to the working class. These
classes do not mix with us – er, that is to say with ladies and
gentlemen like ourselves. We do not as a rule speak to lower-
class people unless it is to those to whom we give orders such
as our servants or the tradesmen and craftsmen who provide our
needs and we pay them to do so.'

Harriet had regarded her father wide-eyed. She herself talked
happily to all the servants in and out of doors. Her father's words
did not make a lot of sense, nor did they answer the important
matter on her mind.

'Yes, Papa,' she said, hoping to please him, 'but why mustn't
I be friends with Bessie? I haven't got anyone to play with except
that stupid boy who comes with the vicar's wife when she calls,
and silly Cousin Jane who screams when she sees a spider. And
I'm bored of Miss Perkins's lessons and the books she wants me
to read and I know she only does it to keep me from bothering
her when her legs hurt!'

Sir Charles regarded the pretty but rebellious face of his
youngest daughter – the unwanted after-thought who had been
responsible for his wife's death – and wondered if the child
apprehended what he had attempted to explain to her about the
strict divisions of the classes. He attempted a more forthright
explanation, saying, 'That girl who took you under her wing this
afternoon . . . Benson's daughter, I gather . . . well, as you know,
Benson is my gamekeeper so he works for me and therefore he
and his family belong to the working class. As I told you, they
are quite separate from us and it would be against the rules for
you to visit them socially. Do you understand?'

Harriet shook her head. 'I just want Bessie to be my friend,
Papa! I know Miss Perkins is old so it's not her fault she doesn't

like doing the things I want to do, and there's no one for me to play with and Bessie showed me how to feed the chickens and where the squirrels build their homes called drays and . . .'

As he continued listening to all the harmless enjoyments of his errant daughter's afternoon, her father found himself questioning his own dictates. Benson's wife had been their senior parlourmaid before she had left to marry him and, as a consequence, she should know the social boundaries. It was highly unlikely that his small daughter would suffer any harm or disrespect in the company of their offspring.

Thus it was, Sir Charles decided that such visits could do Harriet no harm whilst she was so young. Having relented, as much for his own need to be free of the problem, as for Harriet's sake, he was obliged to send for her disapproving governess and inform her that Harriet might be permitted, whenever she had no lessons or piano practice to perform, to spend an afternoon twice a week visiting the Bensons.

Ten years had passed since that day, and by now the two girls had grown close despite the difference in their ages and social standings. Harriet regarded Bessie as a friend, but despite Harriet's wish to be called by her Christian name, the older girl never forgot what she knew to be her place. Being trained now by the housekeeper as a lady's maid to Harriet, this allowed the two girls to spend some time together in Harriet's room.

Whilst Bessie was assisting Harriet to get dressed, Sir Charles's valet was also busy laying out his master's evening clothes and thinking him unusually silent. As a rule, Sir Charles would have been either enthusing or complaining about the day's bag, but his thoughts were not on the afternoon's beat – they were centred upon his young daughter. He had been surprised when, having half-heartedly agreed to permit her to join the ladies for luncheon in the shooting lodge to see how ably she had conducted herself, he had noticed how much time his friend, Walter Edgerton's, son had spent chatting to Harriet, and questioned how the young man's attention could possibly have been captivated by so young a girl. As his valet slipped his black tailcoat over his frilled white shirt and waistcoat, he decided that Edgerton's boy would make a good match for her in a few years' time.

Whilst such thoughts were occupying her father, Bessie was

fastening a pearl locket containing a picture of Harriet's mother round her neck. Harriet, still euphoric, was saying breathlessly,

'If I can't marry Mr Brook Edgerton when I'm old enough, I'll have to be a spinster like poor Miss Perkins for the rest of my life, as I won't marry anyone else!'

Much later that night, as Bessie helped her into bed and bade her goodnight, Harriet decided to add her poor old governess to the list of people in her nighttime prayers. Her last thought before falling asleep was a prayer for herself – that she would be placed somewhere near the handsome Brook Edgerton again soon, before he forgot all about her.

ONE

'**M**y dear chap, are you quite sure you know what you're doing, eh?'

Sir Walter Edgerton regarded his only son over the top of his spectacles.

'See here, Brook,' he continued as he took a cigar out of the box on the table beside his favourite large studded leather armchair, 'I've nothing against her . . . pretty little thing . . . but you say she is only seventeen.'

Brook got up and went to stand with his back to the fire where he could better observe his father's face. His own expression was slightly ironic as he said gently, 'I believe you told me, sir, that Mama was only eighteen when you married her.'

Sir Walter harrumphed and took time to cut the end of his cigar and light it before replying. Then he said, 'Your mother had come out by then – done her season; knew a bit about adult conventions.'

The hint of a smile crossed Brook's handsome face as he asked, 'What kind of conventions do you have in mind, sir?'

Sir Walter paused, his round, florid face wrinkled in thought. 'Dash it, Brook, you know perfectly well what I mean – keeping house, entertaining, social calling, that sort of thing.'

Once again, Brook's voice was gentle as he replied to his father: 'I am aware that Harriet is very far from being a sophisticated woman of the world, Father, but I propose to engage an experienced housekeeper to take care of domestic trivia. As for Harriet being . . . unsophisticated, I think you meant . . . yes, that is true, but ever since she turned fifteen years old her father has allowed her to act as hostess when – on the few occasions – he entertained formally, and he went to great pains to assure me that Harriet's manners were as appropriate as they were

charming, and so I have no qualms about her qualities or suit-
ability to be my wife.'

Sir Walter shook his head. 'No need to get on your high horse,
m'boy – only wanting to make sure you know what you're doing.'
He drew a long sigh which threatened to tip the ash off the end
of his cigar. 'Fact of the matter is, I'd thought once or twice that
you and Denning's sister might make a good match. Know who
I'm talking about? Paul Denning – the railway chap – has his
widowed sister living with him. Nice-looking woman – speaks
a bit better than he does. Had a better education, I suppose . . .
you'd never know she was – well, not exactly top drawer. She
has money too.' His face lit up as he gestured towards Brook.
'Denning inherited the fortune his father made in the railways.
Bought some shares m'self. Told you to do so, didn't I?'

Giving Brook no time to reply, he continued, 'Denning has
none of his own flesh and blood, so like as not he'll leave his
ill-gotten gains to his sister, the widow. I gathered she was not
yet thirty – so about the same age as you, m'boy!'

Brook was smiling. 'Not exactly "ill-gotten gains", sir. Mr
Denning wisely had the foresight to see how the shares were
likely to rise. However, rich as he is or his sister might be, it is
little Miss Harriet Drake I happen to be in love with. It may
interest you, sir, to know that when I proposed to her, she told
me she had fallen in love with me when she was only fifteen
years old. If you recall, I had just arrived back from Jamaica that
January and Sir Charles was short of a gun for his weekend
shooting, so you took me with you.'

Sir Walter frowned. 'Young, maybe, but not too young to set
her cap at you?'

Brook laughed. 'No, Father, she gave no inkling of her feelings and was quite charming company. She only told me how
she had felt at our first meeting once I had declared myself to
her. I'm quite sure you will love her when you know her better,
Father. She is delightfully innocent, sweet-natured but intelligent.
If she can be said to have any fault, it is that she is, so she tells
me, very impetuous. If there is something she feels should be
done, she will wish it to be done yesterday rather than tomorrow.
I find her enthusiasm for life quite enchanting, and I believe she
will make me an excellent wife.'

Sir Walter sighed. 'I suppose you are more than old enough to know your own mind, young fellow.' He sighed again and then frowned as an uncomfortable thought struck him.

'I suppose there will have to be quite a few changes here, won't there, when you get married? I confess that after your mother died, I rather let Firlbury become a bachelor establishment. Remember when you were a boy, you used to complain that you had umpteen uncles but no aunts to spoil you! A young wife will want a few females around, I dare say . . .'

Smiling once more, Brook interrupted. 'Having grown up here, I am well aware of your preference for the bachelor nature of your life, sir, and I am of the firm opinion that it is only right that it should remain so. However, as you say, Harriet and I will want young people to visit us, and we have agreed we shall have a large family of children, so I don't think, large as this house is, that sharing Firlbury Manor with you is a good idea for any of us. I have, therefore, instructed the agent to buy Hunters Hall. It is a very attractive old house situated only an hour's ride from here, so we can visit each other as often as we chose. Do you know it, sir?'

Diverted from his son's matrimonial intentions, Sir Walter nodded. 'Certainly do! Used to belong to the Harewoods. Dashed shame Harewood losing all his money the way he did. Always said gambling was a fool's game – gets to be an addiction. Poor Alice Harewood had to take the children to Shropshire, I think it was, to live with her parents. I thought the place had been sold to pay the debts!'

'It was, sir, but the new owners only stayed there a month or two – too isolated for them, I was told. It's been empty ever since, so the asking price is a lot lower than it should be. I think Mama would be pleased to know to what use I am putting all that money she left me.'

For a moment or two, Sir Walter did not speak; then he tossed his half-finished cigar into the fireplace and, nodding his head, turned to look at his son.

'Seeing you've got it all settled, m'boy, I'd best go along with it.' He cleared his throat and, leaning over, pulled hard on the rope to summon his butler.

'Bring up a bottle of the 'fifty-five!' he instructed the servant, and turned to give Brook an impish smile. 'Good excuse for a tot or two of the Perrier-Jouët, eh? Your mother always used to deplore the drinking of alcohol before luncheon! You make sure you set the rules in your home, m'boy. Start as you mean to go on, I say. Far too easy to play second fiddle when marriage is a bed of roses for the first year or two.'

Brook laughed. 'I think you have forgotten what you were deploring earlier, sir. My darling Harriet is ten years younger than I am and I cannot envisage her ever overriding my wishes.' His expression softened further into one of affection.

'I'm sorry to disappoint you in the matter of Mr Denning's widowed sister, Father. If, as you say, she is an attractive woman with money, I'm sure it won't be a problem for her to find a second husband.' His eyes twinkled. 'Why don't you marry her yourself, Father?'

Sir Walter shook his head vigorously. 'The last thing I want is a woman fussing round me. Besides, half the time you can't make them out. With men, we all know where we are – call a spade a spade, eh? I have more than enough companionship with my friends.'

His father did, indeed, have a great many long-standing male friends, Brook reminded himself as he finished his glass of wine and rang the bell to order the coach to be brought round to the front of the house in readiness to take him to the train station. It was his intention to go down to Sussex and call to see Harriet the following day. He couldn't wait to tell her that his father had raised no objection to the marriage or to them living elsewhere after their wedding. He would also surprise her with the news that he had heard that morning from the land agent to say his offer for Hunters Hall had been accepted. He wanted to see if she would be as eager as he was to see their future home.

As the train steamed its way speedily towards London where he intended to spend the night in his club, he felt a brief moment of anxiety lest the lovely old house he had chosen for them did not meet with her approval. It did not cross his mind that, being as deeply in love with Brook as she was, Harriet would happily have lived with him in a tent in the Sahara Desert so long as he was there beside her.

* * *

A year later, disregarding the two lines of servants waiting on the front drive to greet them, Brook lifted his young bride into his arms and carried her across the threshold of Hunters Hall. Mindful of the astonished faces of his waiting staff, he kissed Harriet before setting her on her feet and walking her back down the steps. Holding her hand, he effected the introductions: first, the upright, immaculate figure of his new butler, Fletcher, who he had been fortunate enough to inherit from the previous owners of Hunters Hall. The family had left for Shropshire leaving not only Fletcher but most of their former staff behind them for the young newly-weds. These included the appropriately named Mrs Baker, the cook, a middle-aged, experienced Scotswoman, and a number of junior servants – housemaids, footmen, kitchen maids and, not least, the necessary lower orders as well as the outdoor staff. Only two of the staff had arrived with Brook and his wife: his valet, Hastings, and Harriet's lady's maid, Bessie. Each of them had accompanied the couple on the month's honeymoon which had followed their wedding.

Following their betrothal Brook had taken Harriet to see Hunters Hall, the beautiful old house which was to become their home. Since then, during the long months of their engagement, it had been redecorated and furnished.

At that time, Harriet and Brook had stood hand in hand in the big hall deciding where the portraits should be hung, what colour she would like for the furnishings and which of the forty rooms they would select for their bedroom and dressing rooms. Whenever Brook had been able to escape the notice of the decorators, he had drawn her into his arms and kissed her. She thought those kisses the most exciting thing in the world, but that was before Brook's lovemaking on their honeymoon. With his gentle teaching, she had learned how wonderful the days and nights of love could be.

Today, the start of their life together as a married couple, Harriet was enchanted once more by the loveliness of the house basking in the warm, summer sunshine. She was delighted by the smiling welcome of the staff as they bowed or curtsied as Brook introduced them.

On the journey up to Leicestershire from London, Brook had been a trifle apprehensive, unsure how his young wife would cope with a household of strange staff and the responsibility of seeing that everything was to his liking. However, Harriet herself was full of confidence; besides which, Bessie had learned well enough during her years of service at Deerskeep Manor to know how a big house was made to run smoothly, and would be there to offer advice to Harriet should she need it.

Brook now tucked his arm through Harriet's and guided her back indoors while the footmen unloaded their many pieces of luggage from the second coach. Mr Fletcher, the butler, approached his new master.

'I've taken the liberty of instructing Albert to carry hot water up to your dressing room, sir, as I thought you would want to refresh yourself after the journey, and one of the maids will be bringing water to madam's dressing room.'

He took Brook's top hat and travelling overcoat and, turning, said, 'May I bid you and madam welcome, sir, and Cook has asked me to tell you she has taken the liberty of preparing a *poussin* for your evening meal with apricots and peaches from your glass houses to follow, not being sure what time you would arrive home to give her orders.'

Having thanked Mr Fletcher, Brook guided Harriet up one of the two wide curving staircases towards their rooms. Brook pressed her hand in his, saying, 'It seems as if we might be well satisfied with our new employees. I could tell that they are going to be delighted to serve you by the admiring look on their faces – and how could they not? Why, even Father, who had it in mind for me to marry that rich widow who attended our wedding, has quite fallen in love with you and intends to call on you as soon as we are settled.'

He drew her into their bedroom and, barely waiting for Bessie and his valet, Hastings, to depart, put his arms round her and said gently, 'You know, my darling, I never imagined married life could be as wonderful, as perfect as this. Had I done so, I would have married you years ago.'

Harriet returned his kiss, laughing. 'So you would have had a silly little child for your bride. You forget, Brook, I am only eighteen now. Not so long ago I was still in the nursery!'

Brook kissed her again. 'Then I would have emulated some of those royal kings in the past who sometimes became betrothed to children still in their nurseries – for dynastic reasons, of course. Oh, Harriet, my dearest, do you think we can always be as happy as this? I wake up in the mornings now thinking how fortunate I am that there is nothing – nothing at all I want that I have not got!'

Harriet reached up and touched his cheek. 'I feel as you do, Brook, but what of all those children you told me you wanted when we were drifting down the canal in Venice in that lovely gondola? Four boys and five girls, if I remember right. All the girls were to look like me and I said I wanted all the boys to look like you. That's when you said nine wasn't really enough: that if we had a dozen we would never run out of children to look out for us in our old age.'

Brook laughed. 'Yes, we agreed a large family! At least I can then be sure that as you will be so busy having all these infants, you will never have time to run away and leave me.'

Harriet regarded him, wide-eyed. 'Leave you? But why ever would I want to do that, Brook? I love you. I would never ever love anyone else, or want to be without you.'

'Nor I without you, my dearest,' Brook said. Then added with a smile: 'Have you forgotten telling me how you had imagined when you were a child that your prince would have golden locks and blue eyes like Cinderella's prince in your storybook, and here am I with dark hair and brown eyes – the very opposite of Prince Charming!'

Winding her arms round him, Harriet laughed. 'Only because I imagined all princes looked like the one in the storybook.'

Brook broke away from her embrace. 'I will not be answerable for my actions if I have you in my arms any longer. At this moment, I wish we had no servants at all who might appear at any second and be shocked to find us half-clothed on your bed. I'm seriously frustrated, my dearest! We have not made love since last night and the way I feel . . .'

He broke off as his valet knocked on the door and, without waiting for a reply, came in with two large bath towels over his arm.

'I think Bessie has your bath water ready for you, madam,' he said to Harriet. 'She said to tell you she was afeared it would get cold if . . .'

Breaking free of Brook's arms, Harriet said quickly, 'It's all right, Hastings! I'm just leaving.' She hoped that she was not looking as disappointed as she felt. Her sister, Una, had warned her on the eve of her wedding to Brook that not every wife enjoyed their husband's bedtime approaches. Having lost their mother at Harriet's birth, Una, her elder sister by twelve years, had taken on the role, and had admitted she did not particularly welcome her husband's visits to her bedroom, most of which invariably led to the birth of another child.

At the time, Harriet's reply had been that everyone knew how totally devoted the queen had been to her husband, Prince Albert – so much so that she was unwilling to come out of mourning for him even though it was now two years since he had died. Surely she wouldn't have loved him so much if she had not been happy to fulfil such duties? Harriet had no doubt whatsoever that she and Brook loved one another every bit as devotedly as the royal pair, or that she would ever tire of any demands Brook might make. Since Una's warnings the blissful five weeks of their honeymoon travelling in Italy could not have proved more adequately how totally they had been unfounded. Once Brook had initiated her into the pleasures of their bodily union, she was only too willing to repeat them whenever Brook so desired.

Later that evening, as they sat one each end of the large, candlelit mahogany dining table, and the last of the excellent meal had been cleared away by the footmen, Brook drew a long sigh.

'I suppose we shall have to do our duty and issue invitations to our neighbours to dine with us. I am far from being an unsociable person, as you know, Harriet, but I really don't want to share you with anyone!'

They both smiled.

'We will entertain them as seldom as possible,' she agreed, 'but I know I am required to make calls, and that I shall receive them.'

Brook nodded. 'Fortunately, there are not that many big houses near enough for too many calls. Leicestershire is hunting country and in the hunting season the lodges are full, but that does not continue all the year round. Nevertheless, there is one family we must invite as soon as we are settled here – my father's friend, Paul Denning and his sister, who is widowed. If you recall, they gave us that hugely valuable Venetian glass-footed bowl. Goodness knows what we are supposed to do with it, but we cannot ignore such generosity.'

'Are they the family your father refers to as The Railway Entourage?' Harriet asked, smiling. 'He said Paul Denning was an excellent shot which is why he always invites him to his shooting parties, but that they had only become socially acceptable because of their wealth.'

'There is a widowed younger sister, a Mrs Felicity Goodall,' Brook replied, 'but I've only met her once.'

'Is she the one your father wanted you to marry?' Harriet asked. When Brook nodded, she added curiously, 'What was she like, Brook? You never told me.'

Brook laughed. 'Because I don't think I've ever given the good lady a second thought,' he said. 'I suppose I do remember she was not uncomely,' he added truthfully, 'tall, quite sturdy but small-waisted. I'm not knowledgeable about women's clothes but she seemed reasonably fashionable. I do remember now – her voice was a little loud, possibly because she was an accomplished singer. I seem to recall her entertaining the gathering with one or two operatic arias, and getting a lot of applause.'

Harriet felt herself relaxing. It had disturbed her in an inconsequential way when, at the time of her engagement, Brook had referred to Mr Denning's sister as his father's choice of wife for him. Jealousy, she reminded herself, was an unpleasant and in this case, a thoroughly unjustified trait.

She forgot all about Felicity Goodall who, had he not first met herself, might have been here in her place as mistress of Hunters Hall.

Unaware of Harriet's thoughts, Brook continued to sip his port and talk about their nearest neighbour. 'With the huge expansion of the railways, Denning will quite likely end up a multi-millionaire, and doubtless receive a knighthood into the bargain. Being the snobs we all are, despite his low birth, he'd then be a much-wanted guest! At the moment, Father told me, they tend to be shunned by the county.'

'Then all the more reason we should invite them here,' Harriet said. 'I wouldn't want us to shun nice people who you like just because other people do. They must be very lonely.'

Touched by his young bride's kindly thoughts, Brook did not disillusion her by saying he thought it highly unlikely Denning's sister would remain lonely very long. The one time he'd met her he'd found her very far from being a 'grieving widow' or a 'shy violet'. She was flirtatious – some might say forward – with any male guest who addressed her, even himself. It was not just the way she wore her clothes. There was something about her which drew men to her: had them wondering – as indeed, had he – what she would be like in bed without the constraints of her clothes. Despite her obvious attractions he'd had no inclination whatever to respond to her attempts at flirtation.

It was a strange thing, he thought now, how he had never been tempted by the thought of marriage before he had fallen in love with Harriet three years almost to the day since that shooting weekend in Sussex shortly after he'd arrived back from Jamaica. He'd recalled the charming young immature girl he'd met on his visit to Deerskeep, playing the part very seriously of an accomplished hostess. It had surprised him to discover on his second visit that she was no longer a child, and that, at the age of seventeen had blossomed into a lovely young woman.

Although Harriet was not beautiful in a classical way, her vivacious manner combined with a contrasting youthful shyness had instantly drawn him to her side. Openly monopolizing as much of her time as he could, he had been intrigued by her avoidance of the usual party chit-chat, and the way she'd answered his questions intelligently. No one could have been more astonished than he was when, quite suddenly, she had looked directly into his eyes and said, 'When Papa told me you were coming to the shoot today, I supposed that you would almost certainly be married and might bring your wife with you. I am so glad you didn't!'

'Didn't what?' he had asked her. 'Bring my wife?'

'No!' had been her reply. 'I meant get married!'

Almost immediately, before he had recovered from his astonishment and thought of a reply, she had said matter-of-factly, 'It means that there is still a chance for me. You see, I made a promise to myself that if I couldn't be married to you, I would never marry anyone else.'

Seeing the look of utter confusion on his face at such outspokenness, quite suddenly she had laughed and, putting a small gloved hand on his sleeve, had said, 'Please don't think I am trying to make fun of you, or some such. You must remember that I was only fifteen years old when we first met, and of all Papa's friends I had never met a handsome young man like you. Last thing before I went to sleep, I would ask God in my prayers to please hurry up and make me older more quickly and find a way to help me meet you again. I was very romantic, you see. I'd read far too many romantic poems – granted mostly with my mouth full of bonbons I had stolen from the dining room!'

Suddenly, they had both been laughing, and then equally suddenly, he had realized that he wanted nothing better than to spend more time with this delightful, unspoilt, unusual young girl who, flatteringly, had been telling him she had fallen in love with him, albeit not seriously.

Although he had spent as much time in her company that weekend as convention allowed, he had returned home and told his father he had met the girl he intended to be his wife. Now, only little more than a year later, they had returned from their honeymoon as deeply in love as it was possible for two people to be.

Brook stood up and went round the table to put his hand under Harriet's arm and help her out of her chair. 'It's time we retired,' he said gently. 'We have had a long day and a tiring journey . . . and . . .' He broke off but Harriet was certain what he meant. The pressure of his hand on her arm, the look in his eyes, left her in no doubt that he wanted to make love to her. As always, her body sprang to life in response.

Such was their love-making that first night in their new home that, three months later, Harriet realized that she was going to be able to give Brook the first of the many children he wanted – and that she wanted, too.

TWO

1864–1865

Harriet lay back on the heap of soft white linen pillows and touched the empty space in the big four-poster bed, an ache in her throat as she struggled to keep the ever-ready tears at bay. The nurse, dozing in the chair by the window, fussed if she caught her weeping. After the first disappointing miscarriage Harriet had heard the doctor say it was perfectly normal for a mother to grieve if she lost the baby she had been carrying, but this was the third occasion and this time the baby had survived long enough for her to know it had been a son.

Harriet now thought despairingly of the son Brook so much wanted when she had first become pregnant after their honeymoon. Although she had conceived again soon after, she had lost that one too, and before it had been possible to know if it would have been a boy or girl. Now she feared that, having miscarried for the third time, something must surely be wrong with her.

The threatening tears dried on her cheeks as with her eyes closed, she relived the magical moment when Brook had asked her to marry him, and the moment she had first set eyes on him when she had been only fifteen years old. Tall and broad-shouldered, his dark hair matching the colour of his dark brown eyes.

Harriet now drew a deep sigh – her bitter disappointment at this third miscarriage momentarily forgotten as memories of their courtship, Brook's proposal and her father's open admission that he could relax now the youngest of his five daughters was off his hands, flooded her memory. There had been no single stumbling block. Brook's father was a baronet and after his death Brook would inherit the title.

After their wedding, Harriet now reminisced, Brook had taken her to Italy for their honeymoon – first to Rome, then Florence, Sienna and finally Venice. Brook had laughingly insisted that every day they should see one – if not several – famous sights, to let their families know they had not spent all their time in their luxurious hotel rooms where he could make love to her. She must have conceived for the first time on the night of their return from honeymoon, Harriet realized. Recalling Brook's pleasure when she had first told him they were to be parents, Harriet drew another long, tremulous sigh, her eyes filling once more with tears. Brook had assured her, like the doctor had, that young and healthy as she was, she would soon conceive again, but she had lost that baby, too.

Tears began once more to drip down her cheeks as she thought how bravely he had received the news and insisted that she was in no way to blame; that possibly he was responsible for carrying out his lovemaking so passionately. Since then he had moderated his ardour and she was forced to see herself as a failure as his wife.

Downstairs in the big, book-lined library, a cheerful fire burning in the fireplace, Brook sat opposite his father as both tasted the brandy Brook had told the butler to bring up from the cellar. Sir Walter Edgerton nodded his bald head, his pale blue eyes glinting approvingly as he regarded his son. For one thing, Brook was and always had been good-natured. He was also what he called 'a damn good shot', and a good fisherman, too, who made excellent use of the well-stocked trout stream running through the grounds of the estate. Sir Walter had lost his wife and two daughters in an epidemic of smallpox which, miraculously, he and his only son had escaped. As a consequence, he and the boy had become very close – perhaps even more so as he had never remarried.

'Sorry to hear the, er . . . news, m'boy!' he said, when Brook told him of the distressing ending of this third pregnancy. His heavy jowls shook as he coughed, clearly embarrassed. 'Not something to talk about, really, but I recall your mother once saying the same thing had happened to one of her sisters, and that she'd gone on to have five healthy offspring.' Relieved to have got this attempt at sympathy off his chest, he added more cheerfully: 'Might be a good idea to tell young Harriet, eh?'

Without waiting for Brook's acknowledgement, he went on in a far more convincing tone: 'Happens with dogs, too, you know!

You remember that black Labrador bitch, Jem? Best retriever I ever had, but hopeless breeder. Only litter the old girl had, half of 'em were too weak to survive. Still, you never know, do you? Daisy here . . .' He patted the old gun dog lying as always by his feet, 'she lost her first – same as Harriet – and went on to produce thirteen pups. Good noses, all of 'em.'

He paused whilst Brook, amused rather than annoyed by the older man's analogy, refilled his glass. 'Tell you what, Brook,' he said, his eyes bright with enthusiasm for the idea which had just come into his head. 'One of Daisy's blood line – a nice young bitch – has just whelped. Hitchins told me only last week that we'd have to find a home for one of 'em – gun shy, you see. Now why don't you give young Harriet a dog? Great comfort dogs, you know, and retrievers are gentle animals – good with youngsters, obedient, that sort of thing.'

His face grew even redder as he warmed to his idea. He was essentially a very kind man if lacking much in the way of brains – 'upstairs' as he was wont to say, tapping his forehead.

'Best thing for a female in her condition. Hitchins is a know-ledgeable fellow and he says that when a ewe or a nanny goat throws a dead one, he gives it one from the others that have had two. Something to look after, don't you know!'

Brook did not know whether to be insulted by his father's comparison of his beloved wife to an animal, but he knew he meant it kindly. Besides, giving Harriet a puppy was not such a bad idea – it would keep her busy when he couldn't be with her. That was not very often but he did spend time assisting his father when their bailiff, Bates, had a problem on the estate. There were, too, the seasonal shooting parties to which Harriet was invited, but he had not thought the bumpy coach ride a good idea whilst she was carrying a child.

'Yes, thank you, sir – splendid idea!' he told his father. 'I'll talk to Harriet about it.'

Sir Walter looked pleased. 'I'll get that stable lad, Billy, to bring the pup for you to see.' He chuckled. 'That boy has got a way with animals – he can do anything with horses. Cats like him, too. Can't stand them m'self but Hitchins said we had to have 'em to keep down the vermin.'

He broke off, drained his brandy glass and gave Brook a boyish grin as he said, 'Your mother was always telling me I go on talking so long I forget what I began with. Quite right, too! Now, what was I saying?'

He took out his watch, and without waiting for Brook's reply, said, 'Better get a move on – I mean to go up to London this afternoon and see my banker in the morning. I'd best get off home now.'

Brook went over to the fireplace and pulled the rope, calling one of the servants to bring his father's horse round to the front door.

As soon as his father had disappeared down the long drive, Daisy following close behind, Brook went upstairs to see his wife. She had fallen asleep and the nurse was tip-toeing round the room tidying the various medicines and paraphernalia round her patient's bed. She looked sympathetically at the handsome young man standing in the doorway. She had perforce seen the distress and sympathy on his face when he'd first been allowed into the room after the unhappy miscarriage. He had held his sobbing wife in his arms so tenderly that, surprising herself, tears had come into her eyes.

Regardless of the nurse's presence, Brook had lent his cheek against Harriet's and told her that he loved her and that what had happened was unimportant – that they would soon have another baby, 'Two, three, fourteen . . .' he'd added in the hope of making her smile through her tears.

The doctor had given strict instructions that his patient was not to have any visitors for at least two days other than her husband, who should stay no more than five minutes at a time, but now, for the first time in her long life as a nurse, the woman found herself disobeying a doctor's instructions. She had not been able to bear to part them as Brook had rocked Harriet gently in his arms.

'There'll be another one on the way afore long, sure as ducks is ducks,' she said later to Cook as she accepted a welcome cup of tea in the big, busy kitchen. 'Like two lovebirds, they were! Wouldn't surprise me one bit if she don't end up with a dozen or more.'

What the nurse had no way of knowing was that Fate had other ideas.

THREE

I t was a beautiful spring morning and, for the first time since her miscarriage, Harriet's former joy in her life had replaced the months of depression. Worrying continuously about her, Brook had decided to indulge her further by dismissing the nurse who he had insisted must remain to oversee her recovery long after it was necessary for her to do so.

Harriet had disliked the way the woman fussed over her all the time, even, on occasions, interrupting her evenings alone in the drawing room with Brook, saying, 'Time you were in bed, madam!' and, 'Tut-tut' when Harriet protested she was not in the least tired and had no wish to retire.

Holding her hand, Brook would look anxiously at her and at the implacable face of the nurse, and say reluctantly, 'My darling, much as I have been enjoying our conversation, I think you should do as Nurse says, otherwise you will never get your strength back!'

It was useless for her to protest that she felt perfectly well again, that she wanted to stay with Brook with whom she was more in love than ever. In the daytime when he was busy somewhere on the estate, or out shooting or fishing, silly as she knew it to be, she missed him.

On occasions, Jenkins, their coachman, would drive Brook to London to his father's offices in the city in order to be brought up to date with the situation in Jamaica where his family owned a vast and profitable sugar estate. Shortly before Brook's marriage, Sir Walter had handed over to him the responsibility for the running of the estate. During the three years Brook had spent on the island after he'd left university, he had learned everything necessary for good management of the sugar plantations and his promotion had earned him an increased allowance which enabled him to fulfil more than adequately his future duties as a husband and, he hoped, father.

Brook disliked the days and nights in London apart from Harriet as much as she did, but in view of her pregnancies – and subsequent miscarriages – he had ruled against taking her to London with him. Whilst there he stayed at his club for as short a time as was necessary before hurrying back to Hunters Hall and his beloved wife.

Harriet had assured him that he had no need to worry about her when he was away, that as the youngest daughter with four much older sisters, she'd grown up as if she were an only child. Bessie, she told him, would always be on hand if she needed anything. Bessie, she said, had always assisted her mother with twelve younger children and, although older than herself, she was not only capable but totally devoted to her. As children, she explained, she had been permitted to spend much of her spare time with the older girl despite Bessie being the daughter of her father's gamekeeper. Bessie was familiar with all her needs and was as necessary to her as Brook's valet, Hastings, was to him. But for Bessie, she confessed, she might have felt even more lonely than she did when he was away.

They did not have many close neighbours and Hunters Hall was quite isolated. Brook's friends, who he invited to enjoy his sporting occasions, either came on horseback or travelled over the rutted country roads in their coaches. Consequently, the formal half-hour visits by their wives were not, understandably, undertaken very often. The vicar's wife came up from the rectory in the village once a week on foot, weather permitting. She was a middle-aged, strait-laced, childless woman who, having come upon Brook and Harriet in an unconventional embrace near one of the statues on the terrace the summer they had moved in after their marriage, had made it clear to Harriet that she thought in her position that she needed to be far more circumspect.

Brook did not object to his wife's fondness for her maid. He was aware that Bessie thought the world of him. She seemed unusually intelligent and had imitated Harriet's lady-like manners. He also approved of the fact that the cheerful girl never, to his knowledge, forgot her position, and had made the transition to lady's maid with very little difficulty. She was popular with all the other servants, even the meticulous housekeeper, Mrs Fraser, whose habit it was not just to find fault but to look for faults in those beneath her. It was partly Bessie's cheerful company as well as his own which Harriet had needed to help her recover from her grief at the loss of her third baby.

The sunshine on this beautiful spring morning had raised Harriet's spirits as, with Brook's hand holding hers, they strolled down to the rose garden. Brook, however, was far from carefree as he tried to find the courage to tell her what must happen in the near future. It was news he had no doubt would wipe the contented smile off her face. She had discarded the bonnet that females wore when the sun shone as it did now; her dark curls tumbled about her pink cheeks, and the loving, happy smile on her pretty face caught at his heart. He loved her so very much, and had been even sadder for her obvious suffering than for his own when she had lost their third unborn child. Now it was he who was obliged to distress her – something he would have avoided at all costs had it been possible.

'Sit here beside me for a moment, my love!' he said as he seated himself on the stone seat near the fountain. The roses newly in bud were, he thought, at their loveliest. He drew Harriet down beside him and, putting his arm round her waist, said gently, 'I'm afraid I have something to tell you that will not please you. I am going to have to leave you for a little while.'

Harriet's face paled, and her heartbeat quickened as she asked, 'But why, Brook? Tell me quickly before I become even more anxious.' She reached up and touched his forehead. 'That frown frightens me!'

Brook tightened his arm round her waist and drew her closer against him. He knew it was unseemly to be having such thoughts in the daytime in such a public place, but he felt the customary rush of desire for her and it was all he could do not to carry her up to their bedroom and make love to her, he thought to himself wryly. There were very few occasions when seeing her, touching her, even watching the smile light up her face, that he did not thank the good Lord for allowing him to find her, and for her willingness to marry him. He had no doubt that they were the most blessed and happiest of couples.

'As you know, I was in London last week,' he said, 'and I suppose I should have told you on my return that things are not going well with my plantations. It seems the sugar cane

is not producing as it should; but, even more worrying, there is
ongoing trouble with the workers. My London agent told me
that the fellow he'd despatched to look into the trouble last
autumn returned saying the fault almost certainly lies with
Herbert Banks, our estate manager. He feels unable to take
responsibility for what is occurring.'

He paused for a moment, unhappily aware of the look of
distress on Harriet's face. 'My father wishes me to go out there
as soon as possible,' he resumed quickly. 'Much as I shall hate
leaving you, my dearest, I cannot refuse to do so. I hope very
much that it will not be for long. The sea voyage will be ten
days, and I trust I shall be able to deal with the problems within
a month.'

He paused once more before taking Harriet's hands in his. 'I
hate the thought of our separation as much as you do, but as the
only son who will one day inherit the properties, I have no
alternative but to take my father's place as he has requested.'

Harriet's expression was one of dismay as she whispered, 'Oh,
Brook, I shall miss you so much. I miss you even when you go
to London for a few days!'

'And I you, but every cloud has a silver lining, as my old
nanny so often said. Father intends to increase my allowance
again on my return. We live quite happily on what I now receive,
but if we are to have the large family we both desire, then we
will have many more expenses, will we not?'

Too close to tears to trust her voice, Harriet nodded.

'The time will pass, my darling,' Brook continued. 'Perhaps
you could arrange to stay with one of your sisters? Or might you
invite your father to visit you here? I do not like to leave you
here entirely on your own.'

Harriet sighed. 'Have you forgotten, Brook? Papa is now
confined to his bed. As to my sisters – Hope, as you know, is
married to an army officer and has accompanied him to India.
My sister Charity has been forbidden by her doctor to have visitors – not even the vicar – because her three children have scarlet
fever. That letter which arrived last week was from her. The
children are being given quinine and mutton broth and beef tea
to swallow, as well as twice daily baths and a mixture of ammonia
and ether. Richard, the eldest, is recovering slowly but the

youngest, Vaughn, is very ill. As you can imagine, the last thing she would want was a visitor – even a sister.'

'I'm sorry to hear of this,' Brook commented, 'but did I not meet your other sister at our wedding? Una, is it not?'

Harriet nodded. 'Yes! She is married and lives in Ireland. But I would not want to travel so far lest you could return earlier than you now expect.'

Much as Brook wished to comfort her, he was honest enough to say that there was very little – indeed, no hope – of that happening. The sea voyage to Kingston would take at the very least ten days; the journey up into the hills another day. If, as he suspected, he would have to replace Herbert Banks, he might even have to go back down to Kingston to find a suitable fellow who would be better able to cope with the problems. Even the English newspapers had referred to the severity of the unrest in Jamaica, and not a month passed that his worried London agent did not warn him that the situation was worsening every day.

Longing to comfort his young wife, he said, 'Then why not invite Una to enjoy a sojourn here at Hunters Hall? If she cannot leave her children, I would suppose that Bessie could manage to look after them. Did you not tell me once that she looked after a large number of her younger brothers and sisters?'

Not wishing him to consider her deliberately negative, Harriet nodded silently rather than reminding him that, unlike herself, Una had successfully given birth to yet another baby a few weeks previously, so would not consider a journey to England.

Ignoring the fact that one of the gardeners might come upon them, Brook kissed her and said, 'You can be sure, my love, that I shall not stay away from you for one single day longer than I must.'

Harriet kept her tears at bay until she was alone in her bedroom with Bessie, who did her best to comfort her, saying, 'Hush, now, Miss Harriet! Was it not one of your poets you told me of who said, "Absence makes the heart grow fonder"?'

Harriet smiled through her tears. 'Yes, but Shakespeare, the greatest poet of all, wrote that "parting is such sweet sorrow". Not that I can think of any sweetness in it lest it be the prospect of Brook's homecoming.'

'Happen you should go with him,' Bessie suggested as she ran a brush comfortingly through Harriet's hair before starting to prepare the dinner gown her young mistress would wear that evening.

'Dearest Bessie, even if it were possible, Brook would not want me with him on such an occasion. I do not want to remain here in this big house, lovely as it is, without him here. I wish it had been possible for Una to visit me with the children as my husband suggested.'

Bessie sighed, and then her face brightened. 'So why do you not visit her?' she enquired. 'Happen it would be a fine adventure for you to travel to Ireland!'

Harriet smiled and then sighed. 'My sister wrote last summer that she would so enjoy our company if we could pay them a visit and her husband, Sir Patrick, said that the journey was not hazardous.'

'Then you should go, Miss Harriet. What better way to pass the time whilst the master is away?'

Appealing as such an idea was, she hesitated. There was the faint possibility that she might be pregnant once again. If it proved to be so and she undertook the journey to Ireland, and were to have yet another miscarriage, Brook would not forgive her for taking such a risk; nor, indeed, would she forgive herself. It was not just to please him that she had been so desperate for a child, but for herself, too. She had always – even as a young girl – looked forward to the day when she would be a mother, and her adoration for Brook had added to her need to have a child – his child.

Their family doctor had once told her after one of her miscarriages that irregularity of the monthly cycle was by no means uncommon so, although this had been the case, she had no other reason to suspect she was with child again. She was neither sick nor faint, as had been the case on the last three occasions that she'd been carrying. She felt so well and always ready for Brook's lovemaking. In these past months since her last miscarriage she'd felt no tiredness and was happy to walk for hours with Bessie in the woods and lanes whilst Brook worked in his study writing letters. She and Bessie would watch the new-born lambs and calves in the fields; watch the trout rise in the river flowing through the meadows, the ducklings and cygnets following their parents, one behind the other. Sometimes she would take her shoes off like the farm children and paddle in the shallow water amongst the beautiful dragonflies darting amongst the water lilies which had spread from the beautiful lake in the garden.

Brook had promised to take her to Paris for a holiday as soon as she felt strong enough and, laughing, she had told him he fussed too much about her and assured him that she was quite back to normal good health.

Because of his protectiveness, she had refrained from telling him of the vague suspicions she nurtured very occasionally about her condition. He had been unable to hide his disappointment when she lost the last baby and she had not wanted to give him unnecessary cause for further concern. She knew already of his longing for a son – a boy he could teach to ride, to fish, to shoot, and to whom he could teach country lore so he would one day love Hunters Hall as much as he did himself, the home the boy would one day inherit.

Occasionally a letter from Una would arrive; the last said that she and Patrick were delighting in the safe delivery of yet another male baby. Brook had laughed at Patrick's somewhat ribald postscript that if they could keep up the good work, they might manage a whole platoon! Una always ended those letters saying, *I so wish you could see our brood, dearest Harriet.*

Harriet always wrote back saying she would indeed love to meet her nephews and nieces but it would not be easy to drag Brook away from his much-loved home and the many sporting parties which took place both at Hunters Hall and on their neighbours' estates.

'It will be so lonely here without him!' she said sadly to the older girl who was now laying one of her several trousseau evening gowns on the bed. 'I wish I were going away too, and that I did not have to live here without him.'

'Hush now, Miss Harriet!' Bessie said as she placed a pair of long evening gloves beside the dress. 'If you go down to dinner with a doleful face like that, you'll upset the master and no mistake! Like he said, you should visit Miss Una as surely you'd enjoy being with them.'

Harriet nodded. 'I know I would, Bessie, but Dublin is a long way across the sea.'

'Is it so far away then?' Bessie asked as she removed Harriet's day dress and slipped the deep magenta silk dress over her head and her arms into the puffed bishop sleeves.

'Indeed it is!' Harriet said. 'It would mean a long coach ride to the port of Liverpool, with a stop overnight on the way, and then maybe another night in Liverpool before sailing across the Irish sea in a ferryboat to Dublin. Then there would be a further coach journey to Ballsbridge Street where my sister lives. That means travelling for at least four days!'

The colour on Bessie's round, rosy cheeks deepened. 'And what is wrong with that, surely!' she said, using her mother's Sussex dialect. 'How many times did you use to tell me afore you was wedded of all the adventures you was going to enjoy when you'd be grown up! Just because you'm married now, I reckon as how the master would be pleased to hear you wasn't going to be a-grieving whilst he's gone.'

As Bessie fastened an amethyst and pearl pendant on a gold chain round Harriet's neck she was mindful of the fact that it was only a few months since her young mistress had recovered from the depression which had followed the loss of the third baby she had been expecting.

Three months was not really such a long time, Harriet decided. Brook would be back in time for her birthday. Even the thought raised her spirits, and Bessie remarked on her sudden change of mood when, her toilette completed to Bessie's satisfaction, Harriet went downstairs to join Brook in the drawing room.

He was, as usual, impeccably attired in his black superfine dress coat with velvet facings and black waistcoat. She noticed with pleasure that he was wearing the set of pearl shirt studs she had given him, and his hair, with a centre parting, was brushed flat. He had also fastened a single diamond pin into the folds of his cravat, enhancing his aristocratic good looks. Harriet's heart missed a beat as he strode across the room to greet her. Regardless of the footman's gaze, he took her hand to his lips and told her how truly beautiful she looked – especially so this evening, he insisted. The sorrowful look had gone from her eyes and now he had every hope that she had come to terms with his enforced absence.

Sitting down on the sofa with her hand still clasped tenderly in his own, he avoided the topic of his impending departure and said, 'I am now going to confess to you that, as you know, this evening we were to have had the Reverend Hobson and his tiresome wife to dinner. On coming out of church two Sundays ago, I was cornered by the unctuous Hobson, saying that he and his wife had seen so little of you these past weeks they were really looking forward to calling on us again.' Brook laughed mischievously. 'It was an obvious hint to be invited to tea or something! I felt obliged to ask them to dine with us.'

He smiled at her tenderly. 'However, I have been so concerned about having to leave you – and I was certain you, too, do not feel up to facing their company, so it is to be hoped the good Lord will forgive me for telling the poor fellow that we are obliged to postpone any further invitation because now our cook and three of the staff are indisposed with an infection whose name I had forgotten!'

'Brook, that is very naughty of you!' Harriet said, laughing. 'Just suppose you were married to Mrs Hobson, you would be as bored as he most probably is by her endless complaints about their parishioners. And I, myself, would be even less well able to tolerate his incessant biblical quotations. The two of them were probably greatly looking forward to a change from each other's conversation. Besides, Brook, sooner or later we shall have to have them here.'

Brook returned her smile. 'But not for some considerable time, my darling, as I won't be here with you to receive them.' His smile faded. 'You are not too unhappy about my going away?' he enquired.

Harriet had vowed on her wedding day never to lie to him or deceive him, but now, suddenly, she knew that if she truly loved him, she must do so.

'Please don't concern yourself, Brook,' she said quietly. 'I have recovered from the shock, and Bessie will help me find a way to pass the time. If the weather stays fine I shall pay calls upon our distant neighbours who all left their cards whilst I was indisposed. That will certainly keep me busy! Twelve weeks is not so very long, is it? You will be home before the summer is over.'

'You should call on Denning and his sister!' he suggested. 'Paul was most concerned for you when I took him to see the new automatic pheasant feeders the other day. His sister sent that extravagant hamper of fruit, most of which I think I ate!'

Hearing Harriet laugh, Brook breathed a sigh of relief. He had been minding Harriet's distress at his forthcoming departure far more even than his own. As Harriet had pointed out, he would not be leaving her for very long and their reunion would be the greatest joy.

His thoughts were interrupted by the footman announcing that dinner was served. Taking Harriet's arm, he led her into the brightly lit dining room not doubting that the evening would end with him showing her, in other ways, how much a husband could love his wife.

FOUR

1865

H arriet was counting the days until Brook's likely return but as yet she had had no letter advising her of the date. When at last a letter arrived with the breakfast tray Bessie now always brought her in the mornings, she was so happy to see it she nearly knocked the tray over as she waved the letter in the air. Her eyes shining, she scanned the first page. Bessie's smiles as she looked at her young mistress' excited face changed to alarm as she saw the colour leave Harriet's cheeks and her hands holding the letter start to tremble,

'The master's not ill, is he?' she asked anxiously.

Harriet shook her head. Tears now trembled on her cheeks as she whispered, 'He isn't coming home . . . not yet . . . not for weeks and weeks . . .' She broke off, the tears of disappointment now flowing. Bessie removed the breakfast tray from her lap and handed Harriet a handkerchief.

'Don't upset yourself so!' she said. 'The master wouldn't want to see you crying like this!'

Harriet blew her nose. 'I know, Bessie!' she whispered. 'But he won't be coming home for MONTHS . . .' Her voice rose. 'Not for four months – maybe even six . . .'

She broke off, the tears flowing again. Bessie regarded her anxiously. Six months – half a year . . . It was a very, very long time.

She found another handkerchief for Harriet to replace the wet one, wondering as she did so how she could possibly find something comforting to say.

'Does the master say what's doing out there to keep him, Miss Harriet?' she asked.

In a choked voice, Harriet replied, 'The man who was managing the plantations has been shot and killed. There's been trouble amongst the Jamaican people and it's gone on despite the slaves being given their freedom thirty years ago. Brook says his workers are all loyal, but the plantations are at risk and he will have to find a new manager and see him settled in and make sure the danger has passed before he dare leave the country.'

'Six months is an awful long time!' Bessie said, sighing. Then her expression brightened as she added, 'I'm sure as how he'll come back just as soon as ever he can, Miss Harriet, I never did see a husband as devoted to his wife as what the master is to you!'

Harriet attempted a smile. 'Even four months more without him is almost more than I can bear to think about!' she said. 'I miss him so, so much!'

'I know you does, Miss Harriet but . . .' Bessie had another thought. 'You've the time to make that visit to Miss Una now. You said as how it was too long a journey to go for a short while: now you could stay for several weeks, couldn't you?'

Harriet drew a deep, shaky sigh. It was small consolation, but she could do as Bessie was suggesting. Una had been so disappointed when she'd declined to go before. She would take Bessie with her, of course. She had always wanted to go abroad again ever since her honeymoon. If they left for Ireland at the beginning of October she could stay at least six weeks with Una and still be home long before there was any chance of Brook's return.

Bessie replaced the breakfast tray in front of Harriet and went downstairs to get her a fresh pot of hot chocolate. Dry-eyed now,

Harriet ate her breakfast as she considered the implications of her proposed absence from Hunters Hall. There were a number of invitations she had accepted which would now have to be refused. Harvest festival was in a week or two's time and a basket of fruit and vegetables from their garden would have to be taken to the church for the parish. There was a garden party too, and she would miss the annual cricket match on the green. Brook usually took part while Harriet gave the prize to the winning team. She had also agreed with Felicity Goodall to spend a few days at her brother, Paul's, house in London next month and go to an opera and a concert with them. That, too, would have to be cancelled or postponed.

Although nearly ten years older than herself, Felicity had proved to be a welcome companion in Brook's absence. Brook had suggested before he left that Felicity Goodall's desire to be included in their coterie of friends might have something to do with the Denning family's ambitions to raise their social status as they were still not accepted by all their neighbours, such as Viscount Harrogate and his wife and Lord and Lady Bancroft. Nevertheless, Harriet had begun to liken her to one of her older sisters who, regrettably, she seldom ever saw now because of their busy lives in distant parts of the country.

When Bessie returned, Harriet was dry-eyed as she discussed with her how they would travel – not by one of the new trains, she said, because not only would they have first to go by coach to the nearest railway station at Leicester, but the train's carriages would be cold and dirty. They would travel in their own coach.

'We can stop on the way and spend a night at one of the inns,' she said. 'You could go down to the village this morning, Bessie, with Jenkins, and find out more details about such a journey. I will write to my sister and advise her of our arrival . . .'

When Bessie had left, Harriet lay back against her pillows, thinking of the letter she would write that morning to Brook. She must not let him know how upset she was, but write of her plan to go to Ireland. She would also go up to the nursery with Bessie and pack a basket of toys for Una's many little ones – toys she had bought when she thought that she herself would be having a baby, and which she had hidden away after that first miscarriage.

There had been that moment about a month before Brook's departure when she'd thought she might have been pregnant again. She noticed she had put on a little bit of weight, but Brook always insisted on having all his English dishes and following them with cream trifles and cook's chocolate truffles with macaroons and whipped cream from the farm, as well as insisting upon spoiling her with her favourite violet creams, so it was small wonder her waistband was tight. However, she had no signs of the morning sickness which had beset her throughout those past pregnancies, and although she had been momentarily sad to realize this was not now the case, she thought it was perhaps as well, since Brook would not be there to share her hopes for the survival of the next baby. At least now, she reflected, she could undertake the journey to Ireland without risk, something she would not otherwise have done.

Four weeks later, Harriet and Bessie departed in the comfort of the well-sprung coach, leaving Hunters Hall behind them. The household staff had been instructed to make an early start on the spring cleaning whilst she was away so that everything would be pristine and orderly by the time Brook returned. The clothes the two travellers needed on their visit were packed and strapped securely to the back and on the roof of the coach. Harriet's dressing case was placed on the seat by Bessie for safekeeping.

It was a cold, blustery morning as they set out early on to the road to Derby. It was their intention not to stop there but press on to Ashbourne for the night. Jenkins had every confidence in the horses, and knew of the various stops they would have to make to exchange them for fresh ones. After a night in the Green Man, a well-respected coaching inn, they would have another long day travelling to Knutsford, where they would spend the night in the Rose and Crown, and then the final leg to Liverpool.

Reaching Ashbourne by nightfall, they stopped at the Green Man and were glad of a hot meal brought to them in a private parlour and afterwards a comfortable bed. Both Harriet and Bessie were a little stiff after sitting for so long on the otherwise trouble-free first day of their journey. Bessie shared Harriet's bedroom, sleeping in a truckle bed at the foot of the large four-poster.

They breakfasted on slices of ham – cured by the landlady

herself, they were told proudly – devilled kidneys, and hot bread freshly baked that morning, and were joined by a woman on her own also travelling to Liverpool. Harriet invited her to ride in their coach but she said she preferred to go more quickly by train, even though it was less comfortable.

They were obliged to make another stop when one of the horses went lame, but arrived safely in Liverpool the following evening without further mishap. Having missed the evening ferry, Harriet said they would sail for Dublin the following morning.

The St George coaching inn was bustling with travellers, a mail coach and three private coaches having not long since arrived. However, the landlord said he had one remaining bedroom he could let Harriet and Bessie occupy, not the most comfortable as it was over the tap room, but warm from the fire below. He assured Harriet there would be a hot meal available and that there would be no difficulty next day obtaining a hackney cab to take them and their luggage to the docks. This being the case, Harriet told Jenkins and the groom that they could return home as soon as they pleased.

Despite the noise, clatter of dishes, and smoky atmosphere in the rather dark, low-beamed dining room, the food was hot and well cooked, and, never having eaten or stayed in such a public place before, Bessie enjoyed the experience. Harriet found it not dissimilar to the coaching stops she and Brook had made on their honeymoon, although the food had been very different and the quantity of it not so hearty as that now provided by the landlord's wife.

That night, as Bessie helped Harriet out of her clothes and they prepared for bed, she was agog with excitement. Tomorrow, she said to Harriet, she would sail across the sea for the first time in her life – indeed, she had never seen the sea before. She looked anxiously at Harriet as she tucked her into bed and prepared to blow out the candles.

''Tis terrible noisy!' she commented, listening to the chatter and laughter from the tap room below. 'They's having a few too many glasses of ale if I'm not mistook!'

Harriet laughed. 'Believe me, Bessie, I am tired enough to sleep through anything!' she assured her, little knowing that were she to do so, she might not be alive the next morning.

FIVE

1865

B essie was the first to awake. She sat up, rubbing her eyes and coughing. She could see through a gap in the curtains that it was still pitch dark outside and, normally a very sound sleeper, she wondered if it was her coughing which had woken her.

That was the moment she smelt smoke. Clambering out of her truckle bed, she ran across the room in her bare feet to look out of the window. To her surprise, there was no sign of a fire. Turning back to the room, she saw it – a thin drift of smoke coming up through a gap in the oak floorboards.

For a minute, she stood staring at it, wondering if she was dreaming, and at that moment, the shouting began: 'FIRE! FIRE!', followed by the sound of pounding feet on the staircase and a woman screaming.

Wasting no more time, Bessie hurried to Harriet's bedside and shook her shoulder. 'Wake up! Oh, do wake up, Miss Harriet!' she urged. The smoke in the room was intensifying and it seemed to Bessie that she could feel heat on the soles of her bare feet.

'Oh, please, please hurry, Miss Harriet,' she begged. She reached for Harriet's dress and mantle, fearing as she did so that there might be no time to rescue all her petticoats.

Wide awake now, and aware of the smoke, Harriet instructed Bessie to see to her own clothing as, ignoring her cashmere stockings, she struggled into her buttoned boots. Neither girl was now in any doubt that the fire below was a serious one. Outside the window they could hear shouts and see buckets being carried from the water butt by the stables, and ladders put up to the windows.

Bessie dressed quickly, her voice shaking as she said, 'I'll see if it's safe to go downstairs, Miss Harriet. I don't fancy you having to climb down one of them ladders!' Not least, she thought, because her mistress had no underclothing on. Shoving her feet into her boots and not waiting to tie the laces, she hurried to the door. Somewhat to her surprise, only a slight haze of smoke was drifting up the stairs. The fire, she thought, must be down below in the dining room on the opposite side of the building. Men and women were emerging from their rooms and were hastening down the narrow staircase. Seeing Bessie hovering on the landing, one of the men stopped and said, 'Best make haste, miss. This place is built of wood – it'll go up like tinder if it gets a hold.'

Then he disappeared down the stairs. Bessie hurried back into the room and pulled Harriet away from the portmanteau into which she was attempting to pack some clothing alongside the presents she had brought for Una.

'Leave it, Miss Harriet!' she said. 'We can get everything later once they've put out the fire. We've got to be quick.'

With Bessie holding tight to her arm, Harriet hurried after the men and women down the wooden stairs. The smoke was stinging their eyes and causing them to cough continuously. As the man had warned, the old inn was entirely constructed of oak, and whilst its former occupants now stood shivering in the cobbled yard, they watched the flames reach the roof and heard the sound of horses' hooves clattering down the cobbled street bringing a fire engine and firemen. Despite the men's efforts to quench it by throwing water on to the flames, it soon proved impossible to save the building.

The heat from the blaze was intense, but Harriet was shivering as she pulled her blue plush mantle more tightly around her. Bessie, she saw, was weeping. She put an arm round her. 'We may have lost our belongings, Bessie,' she said gently, 'but we have not lost our lives. See over there – it's the landlord's wife. She will tell us of the nearest inn we can go to . . .'

She broke off, realizing that in the haste of their departure, she had not brought the most important item of all – her purse. *They were without money*. Then, her heart beating swiftly in relief, she remembered the sovereigns Bessie had insisted upon sewing into the hem of her dress. She had laughed when Bessie insisted on doing so, saying her father had told her it was never safe to travel anywhere without a hidden amount of money to pay for the journey home.

'We'll be perfectly safe, Bessie!' Harriet had said. 'It's not as if we will be crossing the ocean to America, which has not long since been in the thick of a civil war.'

With a frightening crash, the roof suddenly collapsed inwards and sparks shot high into the air. There was a horrified shout from the onlookers.

'We can't stay here,' Harriet said, shivering in spite of the scorching heat from the burning building. 'This is such a big, busy city – there must be another inn close by. We should make our way now before others have the same notion and hire the rooms before we get there. Tomorrow, at first light, you can come back to see if any of our valises have been saved, which I fear is most unlikely. If not, Miss Una will provide us with everything we need when we arrive tomorrow. Thanks to your father's advice, we have enough money in my skirt to pay for a room and for our ferry passages, and we will be safe with Miss Una by nightfall.'

They stayed for a short while longer, watching the firemen trying ineffectually to contain the blaze lest it spread to adjacent buildings. In their scanty attire, the warmth of the fire was welcome as a cold breeze had arisen which was fanning the flames. One of the other occupants spoke to them, bemoaning the disaster, and who had, like themselves, lost his belongings.

'I think we should not remain here a moment longer!' Harriet repeated quietly to Bessie. 'We will walk until we find a likely inn to take us in.'

At first, they were obliged to force their way through the crowds who had gathered in the street to gaze at the fire. Above the roar of the flames and the crash of falling wood, they could still hear the whinnying of the frightened horses being led from the stables on the opposite side of the cobbled courtyard. The sounds followed Harriet and Bessie as they turned into a less crowded street. Here, the gas in the street lamps had been turned lower, and Bessie shivered, saying, 'I think we should go back to the main street, Miss Harriet. It is quite deserted here, and there is no sign of an inn.'

Harriet sighed. She was feeling very tired and retrospectively distressed by the recent frightening events, and knew that it would take them at least another ten minutes to retrace their steps to the main thoroughfare. She agreed with Bessie that this narrow, poorly lit backstreet was an unlikely place to find the refuge they were seeking. Had it been daytime, she thought, they could have asked passers-by for directions, but there was no sign of life other than the sound of a dog barking in the distance.

They were not far from the turning when without warning three shadowy figures suddenly appeared from the darkness and approached them with arms uplifted in a threatening manner.

'Give us yer purse!' one said in a coarse, guttural tone.

'And yer jools!' barked another with a jeering laugh.

'We haven't got any money or jewellery!' Bessie cried.

'We've lost everything in the fire – the one you can see glowing in the sky over in the next street!'

The arm she now lifted to point to the conflagration was without warning brutally hit down by one of the three assailants as he tried to make certain that she had nothing hidden on her person. The thieves now began swearing as they discovered that the two females they hoped to rob were without property of any kind.

Harriet stepped forward between Bessie and the man who was threatening her. 'Don't you dare hit my maid again!' she commanded. 'She was telling you the truth. We have nothing but the clothes we are wearing, and this . . .' She took off her wedding ring and handed it to him. 'Now leave us alone or I shall shout for a constable. We saw one just now walking towards the fire,' she lied.

It was the last thing Harriet would say before she fell to the ground as a heavy blow thundered into the back of her head. When she regained consciousness, she was lying in the gutter. Blood was beginning to congeal from the wound in the back of her head and was colouring her clothes. A burly constable was trying to lift her to her feet. He blew his whistle for assistance and shook his head, assuming that the bedraggled young woman was one of the many who walked the streets of Liverpool, plying their trade more often than not to sailors. There was no sign of Bessie.

When further help arrived, it was decided Harriet should be taken in an ambulance to hospital, but then, realizing it might be overflowing with casualties from the fire, they began to doubt if

would be room for this woman. Concerned about the amount
 ̶d she was losing, from down her legs as well as from her
 ̶y reached an agreement that, the hospital being too far
away as well as over full, the best hope for her survival would be
the nearby Convent of the Sacred Heart, which was not ten minutes
distant. It was well known that the nuns there take care of anyone
in need – even a streetwalker. They were renowned for caring for
the poor and destitute, even harlots like this young woman who
was without proper clothing and appeared to have no money.
Clearly she had been robbed of any she might have had upon her
person. Knifings, robberies and drunken fights were commonplace
during their night-time shifts patrolling the maze of dark streets
bordering the docks. This was undoubtedly one of them.

It was three-and-a-half weeks before Harriet recovered from the
coma she had been in. She opened her eyes to see a tall, slim
woman in a nun's habit standing at the foot of her bed, watching
her. Beside the bed was another nun, round-faced with kindly
forget-me-not blue eyes, who was holding a cup of water to
Harriet's lips.

'So you were right, Sister Brigitte!' the first one said. 'Your
patient has finally recovered her senses!' Her voice was quite
harsh, and without knowing why, Harriet felt a stab of fear. Then
the one who had been addressed as Sister Brigitte gently wiped
her mouth with a white napkin and smiled as she asked, 'Are
you feeling a little better, dear?'

'My head hurts!' Harriet whispered. 'And my stomach!'

'Not to be wondered at!' said the tall nun, her mouth tightening. 'God punishes those who sin as he thinks fit.'

Not sure what she meant, Harriet closed her eyes and drifted
back – not into her previous coma, but into a deep sleep. When
she woke again, the room was in near darkness, only a single
candle giving a glimmer of light from a table by the window.
Above it, Harriet saw a framed picture of Jesus on the Cross.
Somewhere at the back of her mind she recalled seeing a nun
– two nuns. The room, bare of anything but necessities, was
unfamiliar, as was everything around her.

She called for Bessie, who she knew would explain things to
her – why she was here and what they were doing in this strange

place, but no Bessie answered her call. Instead, the tall, thin nun came into the room and stood by the bedside.

'Please, can you tell me where I am?' Harriet asked. 'And could you kindly call Bessie for me?'

Ignoring Harriet's request, the nun came closer to the bed. 'You may call me Sister Mary Frances,' she announced. 'I am in charge of the infirmary in our Convent of the Sacred Heart, and you are very fortunate indeed to have been found and brought here. Sister Brigitte has remained at your bedside every night for the past three weeks. We have all been praying for your recovery if such was God's will. Frankly, we thought He was going to take you, but Doctor told us there was a chance you would come out of the coma you were in.'

She turned to pick up a note book from the bedside table. 'If you feel well enough, perhaps you would kindly answer a few questions. That . . .' she pointed to Harriet's dress hanging on a hook on one of the walls, '. . . that . . .' she repeated in a tone of disgust, '. . . is the only garment you were wearing when you were found, other than your cloak.'

She stared down at Harriet, her eyes steely as she continued, 'We reached the conclusion that you had probably been thrown out of one of your customer's houses for not carrying out the ungodly duties for which you were being paid; that they beat you over the head to punish you. Young women like you,' she added scornfully, 'must know the risks you take when you decide to ply your trade on the streets. You will consider yourself fortunate, I imagine, to be rid of your poor, innocent baby?'

Unable to make sense of what Sister Mary Frances was saying, Harriet stared up at her. Was this a dream, she asked herself before saying, 'What baby? I have no baby!'

'No, young woman, you miscarried the unfortunate child that was in your womb.'

'You mean I have had another miscarriage?' Harriet said faintly, now sure that she must be dreaming.

'Yes, a miscarriage!' Sister Mary Frances said scathingly. 'Did it not once occur to you, when you plied your disgusting trade, that you might endanger the innocent life of your unborn child? You truly deserve whatever punishments God chooses to mete out to you, young woman . . .'

Harriet stopped listening. There was only one conscious thought in her mind – not that this nun seemed to think she was a harlot but that she'd had a miscarriage and must, therefore, have been pregnant when she left home despite her certainty that this had not been the case. When *had* she left home? Why? Where was Brook . . .?

Her mind came to a halt as a fresh set of anxieties beset her. She remembered now that she and Bessie had been on their way to Ireland – to stay with Una. If she had known for certain that she was once more carrying Brook's child, she would never have risked a fourth miscarriage – not when both she and Brook had begun to wonder if they would ever have a live son or daughter. It was not even that her figure had changed or that she had noticeably put on weight.

If it was true that she had had an early miscarriage, she must never tell Brook. He would be angry that she had risked losing yet another baby by journeying so far. She closed her eyes, but the nun's sharp questioning fought through her desire not to listen.

'Who are you? What is your name? Who is this Bessie you called for so often? Do you not know who fathered your child? Why else were you trying to get money? Was the man not willing to have the finger pointed at him? I want some answers, young woman. You are here because we are sworn to Pity and Charity, but it tries me that with our limited resources we must be charitable to wicked young women like you . . .'

As Harriet now drifted back into sleep, she heard another voice – a quieter, gentler one saying in a soft Irish brogue, 'She is still very poorly, Sister Mary Frances. I think we should allow her to sleep now. I will sit with her, and when she wakes up, I will give her some food. Then, when she is stronger, I will question her for you.'

In the days that followed, it was the kindly Sister Brigitte in whom Harriet longed to confide, but she dared not mention her name or where she lived. If the nuns were ever to find out, they might – almost certainly would – ask Brook to send them money for the care they had been giving her. He would learn of her miscarriage brought on by her own unwillingness to remain at Hunters Hall alone. She could not expect him to believe – indeed, she could barely do so herself – that she had shut her mind to the possibility that she may have been with child in his absence. If she were totally honest with herself, there had been *some* tell-tale signs but she had ignored them, assuring herself it could not be so since she had none of the usual discomforts she'd suffered in the past. What saddened her most of all now was that Sister Brigitte told her that her unborn child had been a boy – the son Brook had so much wanted.

Memory of the fire and the thieves' attack slowly returned in full, but she made no mention of it to either nun, lest they somehow traced her name through the landlord of the inn where she and Bessie had stayed. Knowing Brook could never discover what had occurred, her only certainty was to go on insisting that she had no memory of events. All Harriet told them was that she had a sister living near Dublin whose name she could not recall but with whom she would go to stay when she was well enough; that although she could recall the short route from the port to her sister's house, try as she might, she could not recollect its name either.

After several weeks, a doctor came to examine her and told the nuns that the wound on her head had healed and she could, therefore, leave the convent as soon as she felt strong enough to do so.

Harriet now revealed through necessity the existence of the coins, undiscovered by her assailants, sewn into the hem of her dress. As Sister Brigitte unstitched the hem for her, Harriet pondered yet again over the unexplained absence of Bessie. Surely, she told herself, if Bessie had managed to run away from the thieves who had attacked them, she would by now have found her way somehow to Harriet's side? The two policemen, who Sister Brigitte told her had carried her to the convent that fateful night, would have been able to tell Bessie what had happened to her. Was it therefore likely that she had been more seriously hurt or, God forbid, killed?

At night Harriet found it hard to sleep, fearing that some other dreadful fate had overtaken her faithful maid. It brought fresh tears to her eyes when remembering that it was thanks to Bessie's insistence upon hiding the money in her skirt that she could still pay for her passage to Ireland. Sister Brigitte had reassured her that only a small amount would be deducted for her keep and care.

Sister Brigitte tried to soften the harsh words Sister Mary Frances used whenever she visited Harriet's sick room. The gentle Irish nun had realized from Harriet's speech that before her fall from grace she had come from a well-to-do family. She wondered if the unfortunate girl had brought disgrace on them by running away from home. Why else, she pondered, would a well-bred girl like Harriet have need to earn money on the streets? And if she were not earning a living that way, why did she not deny it? Sister Brigitte had asked all her fellow sisters to pray for Harriet, and to dedicate a special Mass to fallen young women like her. Sister Mary Frances, conversely, gave Harriet a prayer book and a book about the saints to read, whilst bemoaning the fact that Harriet was not of the Catholic faith and would not go to Confession, so would remain unpardoned.

Once again, it was the kindly Sister Brigitte who counteracted such lectures by telling Harriet that God was kind to sinners, and that if she prayed for forgiveness, He would grant it even if she was not of their faith.

Harriet hated deceiving this caring little woman, but she dared not relinquish her pretence that she had lost her memory, despite the horrifying thoughts they had about her. For them ever to know her name meant that she could be found to be Brook's wife, and he would learn the truth about the miscarriage she need never have had. She would do anything to prevent that, even if it meant letting the nuns continue in their delusions. Often she was unable to check her tears; the fact that she had lost the baby boy who would have been Brook's precious son as well as hers hurt even more painfully because she herself had caused it. She longed to be able to confess the truth to her kindly carer, who kept assuring her when she found her weeping that it was not her fault that she had miscarried. The good Lord, she said, gave life, and it was His to take away as He thought fit. Harriet must not feel that she was being punished by God for trying to earn a living on the streets.

SIX

1865

I t was early on a surprisingly warm, early November morning when Sister Brigitte escorted Harriet on to the ferry boat tied up at Clarence Dock. The kindly nun, pink-cheeked and flustered, said for the umpteenth time, 'You shouldn't be travelling on your own, child. I know you think you can manage, but in that lovely gown we have mended and laundered for you, you look quite the lady who should be travelling with a maid. Are you quite sure you still cannot remember who you are? Looking after you as I have, I feel sure you are accustomed to such attentions.'

Harriet's heart doubled its beat. Despite having begged the nuns to enquire after Bessie, who she had referred to as a friend, there had been no news of any kind. According to Sister Brigitte, there were accounts every day in the *Liverpool Daily Post* of thefts, assaults and drunken fights, but as Harriet did not know the name of the alley in which she and Bessie had been attacked, it had proved impossible to discover what had happened on the night of the fire.

The thought which from time to time crossed Harriet's mind – that Bessie might have been killed by their attackers – filled her with distress, which added to her guilt over the loss of the baby she'd not known she was carrying. Part of her longed to be able to write to Brook and let him know what had transpired, but she did not dare risk the withdrawal of his love for her, or, indeed, want him to be worried and upset by what had befallen her when there was nothing he, at such a distance, could do about it.

Sister Brigitte was approaching an elderly lady with a great deal of luggage, about to board the ferry. A chill wind was blowing and Harriet shivered in her velvet mantle as she watched the two women talking. Beside her, another woman who appeared

to be her maid was instructing one of the crew members as to
which of the portmanteaux he must take to her mistress' cabin.
For a few moments Sister Brigitte remained in conversation with
the passenger, during which they both turned to look at Harriet.
Then the nun returned to her side.

'The lady's name is Lady Cavanagh,' she told Harriet, adding
happily, 'and she has agreed to keep an eye on you during the
voyage. She will ensure that her maid sees you safely into a
hansom cab when you dock at Dublin Port. It is to be hoped
your cabin is not too far from theirs. She will look for you there
from time to time to ascertain you are all right. I told a little fib
– I said you were a governess on your way to a new position.'

She gave a sigh. 'I shall have to confess the lie,' she said with
a wry smile, 'but I expect Father will give me as many penances
as necessary to ensure God's pardon!'

She still looked worried, wondering whether with Harriet's
loss of memory of her sister's name as well as her own, she
would really be able accurately to recall the route to her relative's
house. Privately, she had disagreed with Sister Mary Francis that
Harriet was a 'fallen woman' whose dire situation had been
brought about by a love affair disapproved of by her parents, and
that she had run away with the unsuitable gentleman who had
deserted her, thus forcing her on to the streets. This suspicion
was reinforced by the number of times, whilst in her coma, that
Harriet had called for someone whose name had sounded like
Luke to 'come back' to her.

Now, despite Harriet's assurance that she could clearly recall
the route to her sister's house, Sister Brigitte still doubted if her
patient, whom she had grown fond of these past weeks, would
ever in fact arrive safely. Mother Superior had refused to allow
her to travel with Harriet to Ireland, so she had taken the precau-
tion of giving her the name of the convent in Dublin where she
must tell the cab driver to take her if she became lost.

She now clasped Harriet's hands, saying, 'May God go with
you, child, and keep you free of sin.'

There were tears in Harriet's eyes as she watched the warm-
hearted nun who had taken such limitless care of her, often
throughout the long nights, walk slowly down the gangplank and
disappear amongst the milling crowds of sailors, dock workers

and people on the jetty. She turned to find Lady Cavanagh staring at her.

'Your nun told me you had been very ill,' she said. 'I hope you will not feel ill during our passage to Ireland. It can be very rough at times, you know.'

Harriet smiled. 'It is kind of you to ask,' she said. 'As it happens, I am a very good sailor. Two years ago I crossed the English Channel in a gale, and . . .' She broke off, aware that mention of her husband and their honeymoon might arouse this woman's curiosity, and cause her to ask awkward questions such as why she was without her maid or, indeed, her husband or a relative to escort her.

'I do assure you that Sister Brigitte was worrying about me quite unduly,' Harriet said. 'Please do not let me delay you as I am sure you want to get settled in your cabin. I will find a steward to show me to mine.'

Seeing the older woman hesitating, she added, 'If I should have need of assistance, I can ask for his help, but thank you for your kind offer.'

Relieved that the young girl sounded so self-reliant, Lady Cavanagh departed to her cabin with her maid. A steward appeared to take Harriet to her cabin. Having deposited her few belongings in the small space available, she decided to find a sheltered spot on deck. A passing sailor opened out a deck chair for her and she settled down to watch the crew making preparations for departure. The sight brought back memories of similar occasions on her honeymoon and a deep pang of longing for Brook.

Her thoughts were distracted by the crowds of men, women and children pushing past her on their way down to steerage below deck. All were loaded with luggage for the journey. It was a full half hour later that she heard the sound of the boat's engines throbbing as the steamer prepared to leave the dock.

A number of passengers were now braving the cold and were standing at the rails waving to their friends or relatives who had come to see them off. It was not long, however, before the steam packet had left the shelter of the dock walls and was heading out into a choppy sea.

Harriet could look down to the lowest deck, where the

passengers were competing to take possession of one of the wooden-tiered bunks lining each side of the cramped interior. The only light came through the open hatchways. The noise of people talking and children shouting or crying was deafening as families climbed into the bunk beds which were stacked to the ceiling above in three tiers. Although Harriet's cabin was tiny and there was only standing room beside the bunk, she did at least have the much-needed privacy she wanted.

She unpacked her few belongings from the parcel Sister Brigitte had given her, and then the box containing food and drink for the journey – bread, cheese, fruit, a flask of milk, tea, a piece of cooked mutton wrapped in cheesecloth and a small packet of oatmeal to make porridge. The nun, who had travelled by steam packet many times, told her she could heat water to make the porridge in one of the two galleys at either end of the deck.

Afraid that the steerage passengers unknown to her might include pickpockets or thieves, Harriet decided to conceal her belongings beneath her wooden bunk before attempting to go back on deck and find the galleys to make herself a hot drink. It was a great blessing, she told herself, that as a child she had been able to watch Bessie's mother in her kitchen as she had never in her life in her own home made so much as a cup of tea – Mrs Kent, the cook, disliked any unnecessary family invasions of her kitchen.

She took from her pocket the copy of *The Life of the Saints* given to her by Sister Brigitte and read for a little while before deciding to go up on to the top deck to get some hot water for a cup of tea and some fresh air. The weather had deteriorated, and a cross wind was causing a marked swell. Several passengers were already being seasick. It was strange, Harriet thought, that she should feel no discomfort from the swell when she had been so plagued by early-morning sickness during her past pregnancies. The thought brought a sudden sting of hot tears to her eyes as she allowed herself to remember the boy baby who had failed to survive – something she had tried very hard not to do when she was in the convent. She had pushed the grief to the back of her mind, concentrating her strength on the difficulty of deceiving the nuns about her lost memory. Uppermost in her mind ever since she had regained consciousness following the attack upon her and Bessie was that she must not let Brook know she had undertaken the journey to Una's in her condition lest he never forgave her. But for the fire at the inn and the attack upon her, she might have kept the baby. He must never know the truth; it was the only way she could save what mattered most in the world to her – Brook's love.

Now, as she mingled with the crowd on deck who were trying to get to one of the galleys to cook the food they had brought with them, she closed her eyes, wishing above all at this moment that she had Bessie with her. Bessie had always managed somehow to make her feel happier when she was downcast: to convince her that things were never as bad as she feared. Even when she had suffered the previous miscarriages and the doctor had suggested she might never be able to carry a child full-term, Bessie had shrugged off the suggestion, insisting that babies survived when God and Nature intended, not when a doctor decreed.

Would Bessie have tried to stop her travelling to Ireland if she'd known how many months into her pregnancy she'd been? Harriet wondered now. Almost certainly she *would* have done so, but not wishing to forgo her sojourn with Una, Harriet had said nothing to Bessie of her vague suspicions. This time, the loss of her baby was entirely her own fault.

Her thoughts were interrupted by the appearance of her supposed guardian, Lady Cavanagh's maid.

'M'Lady asked me to make her apologies but she is so over-come by sea sickness, I have to stay with her and cannot assist you, miss. She is very sorry.'

Harriet shook her head. 'Please thank your mistress,' she said, 'and assure her that I am well and can manage quite satisfactorily on my own.'

Looking relieved, the maid hurried away, wishing only that she was anywhere in the world but on this rolling, heaving vessel crossing the Irish Sea.

The storm worsened and some of the more stalwart passengers left the queues for the galleys, struggling to hold on to the rails as they succumbed to sea sickness. Those who had cabins had disappeared to the sanctuary they offered.

There was a sudden noise beside Harriet and she turned to see a woman sitting down heavily on the bench beside her. She held a crying baby in her arms and four young children came to stand beside her. Her face was white and pinched with the cold, as were the faces of the children. Although shabbily dressed, there was nevertheless a look of refinement in their pale, thin faces. Their clothing looked worn but the mother's speech was educated, tinged with a slight Irish accent as she spoke to them.

The children were silent – unlike the baby, who was making a sound like a kitten mewing. There was a desperate look of appeal in the woman's exhausted face as she looked up at Harriet and said, 'Please forgive me for addressing you. I can't think what else to do. I am at my wits end, you see and . . .' Her voice suddenly broke; tears filled her eyes and overflowed down her cheeks. 'I saw you with one of the sisters coming up the gang-plank,' she murmured. 'You were smiling at my little boy and helped him up to the deck. I thought then how kind you were and . . .'

As she broke into silent tears once more, the children turned to stand more closely beside her, clutching her skirts, their faces anxious. The baby's whimper turned to a choking cry.

Harriet was uncertain how she should reply to the stranger, who repeated in a trembling voice: 'Please forgive me for disturbing you! The baby is only two weeks old and very weak . . .' Her voice broke and tears rolled down her cheeks as, yet again, she apologised.

'Don't cry, Mama!' the eldest of the children said gently, patting her shoulder. 'It will be better soon.'

What would be better soon? Harriet asked herself. Was the baby ill? In need of a doctor? Why was this woman travelling by herself with no husband to take care of her? She had said the baby was only two weeks old – she shouldn't be travelling at all. Perhaps it was crying because it was hungry? Had she no cabin to go to where she could feed it in privacy?'

She put an arm round the woman's shoulders and felt her heart jolt as she glimpsed the tiny white face of the infant. Memories of her recently lost child engulfed her. With an effort, she pulled herself together and enquired:

'Is your little one ill? I could find the purser for you and see if there is a doctor on board . . .'

'No, not ill!' the woman said, her tears drying and an expression of utter hopelessness on her face. 'He is hungry but I don't have enough milk for him.'

As if this fact was something for which she herself should be blamed, she added: 'My husband died before the baby was born. He was only thirty-six, but the doctor said he'd had a heart attack. We had no warning, but I expect it was the worry, you see.'

The words now started to pour from her as if a dam had burst. Her husband, who was called Michael Lawson, had been a clarinettist. This unfortunate woman was living at her home in Donegal, where by chance they'd met and fallen in love. The stumbling block to their marriage was that she was from a staunchly Catholic family, and he was an English Protestant. Her father, she told Harriet, had flatly refused to give his permission for them to marry. Although only twenty years of age, Joan had eloped with her lover. Back in England they had been quietly married.

At first, all went as well for them as could be expected, considering that Michael Lawson had been disinherited by his own family when he'd eloped, and the only money the pair had to live on had come from his earnings as a musician employed irregularly by an orchestra. After the birth of the first two children, she told Harriet, the young man was obliged by his desperate need for more money to find extra work playing for a quintet employed at the Assembly Rooms in Bath whilst afternoon tea was served to the well-to-do residents and visitors to the spa.

Two more children had arrived and, shortly after, disaster struck once again when the orchestra was disbanded. It was the constant worry about their desperate need of money which had brought on his heart problems, his widow Joan now repeated, as it was when she'd told him that yet another baby was on the way that the worry had proved too much for him. Sinking their pride, the couple had each written to their families asking for assistance, as they were now close to starvation. Michael Lawson's family did not even reply: Joan's mother had written to say she was doing her best to persuade her husband to relent, and agree to allow Joan and the children to return home.

'I dared not tell my mother how many children we'd had,' she concluded her sad story. 'As if four was not enough, now there is the new baby . . .' Tears started once more to roll down her cheeks, much to the consternation of her two eldest girls. Managing to control her emotions, she whispered: 'My father will say that it is God's punishment for marrying out of our Faith! Perhaps he is right to say so, as I put my love for my husband before anything else.'

'So your father has relented and you have a home to go to!' Harriet said, but the woman shook her head.

'I had no further letter from my mother so I do not know if I am to be allowed back. I am praying he will take pity if not on me at least on my children. My husband had no savings, you see. All I had after paring for his funeral and our debts was the money for our fares today. If . . .' Her voice broke. '. . . If my father will not allow me home, we will have to go to the workhouse.'

Before Harriet could exclaim she paused and lowered her voice to a whisper that the children could not hear. 'You will think me wicked – unworthy of God's pity,' she said, 'but when I gave birth to this baby a month after Michael's death, I wished it would die, too. Michael loved his children, but we had agreed we must control our love for one another and have no more. This baby . . . may God forgive me . . . neither he nor I wanted. Now I can no longer feed it and my children have eaten only some stale bread since we left our lodgings. If my father will not take pity on us, we will have no choice but to go to the workhouse,' she repeated.

'Oh, no, not that!' Harriet said. Her father had given her a book for her sixteenth birthday by the popular author Charles Dickens which had described the dreadful life of those destitutes who ended up in a workhouse. It was inconceivable that a woman of gentle birth like this young mother should be forced to go to one with her innocent children.

'I have a little money – not very much, I'm afraid, but I can spare a little,' she said. 'Perhaps your eldest girl could go to the galley and see if there is something for you all to eat. As for the baby – did you tell me you cannot feed it yourself?'

Her companion shook her head. 'I give it what I can,' she said, 'but it is not enough. He should have a wet nurse but . . .' Momentarily her voice trailed away. Then she said, 'I found a bottle for him but . . .' she pointed to the infant now fast asleep in her arms, '. . . now I do not have enough milk with me to last until we reach Dublin.'

She was trembling, and quickly Harriet took the baby from her. When the eldest girl, who had managed to reach the galley, returned with half a loaf of bread which she had begged from another passenger, she proceeded to distribute amongst the younger ones. She offered some to her mother, but the woman shook her head. She was, Harriet realized, very close to collapse as her daughter confessed she had not been able to get milk for the baby.

The infant had woken and was staring up at Harriet from blue eyes which looked huge in its tiny, pinched face. Her heart melted. His mother, she thought, had wished he'd never been born, and it now looked likely that he would not survive the journey and starve to death. With the loss of her own baby coming to mind, Harriet felt close to tears herself.

She reached quickly into the small purse the nuns had given her containing the last of the coins retrieved from the hem of her dress. Sister Mary Frances had declared them enough to pay for her fare, and the hansom cab she would need to take her to her sister's.

It now crossed her mind that were she to give some of this last money to the eldest girl in the hope that the girl could find someone to sell her some milk, she would be taking a risk of being stranded penniless in the city of Dublin were her sister, unexpectedly, to be away from home. Dismissing the thought and with no further hesitation, Harriet told the girl to go in search of milk for the baby that, if possible, would be sufficient to last for the whole crossing. Someone might be willing to forgo their own need if the child offered more than the half penny the milk would cost.

The distraught widow dissolved into steady soft weeping, her self-control undermined by her gratitude to Harriet, the unknown stranger who had taken pity on her. For the moment at least, she and her children were surviving, and she tried not to think of the approaching time when she would have to face her father. He was a deeply religious man who had not minced his words when he'd warned her that she would never be allowed in his house again if she married her English suitor. Even if he were to soften his stance and accept her back if she resumed her religious dictates, she feared he might not accept the children of her Protestant husband.

Most worrying of all was the advent of her last baby, born posthumously but whose conception had occurred while she was living 'in sin', as her father would declare it. Were he to refuse to accept the baby, she might have to put him in an orphanage.

It was now clear to Harriet that the mother's self-control had been undermined by her story as, trembling, she gave way once more to tears. When the eldest girl returned with a pitcher of milk Harriet could see that the shaking woman was in no state to fill the baby's bottle, still less to feed it. Despite having never done such a thing before, instinctively Harriet fulfilled both tasks and within minutes the infant was sucking hungrily.

When at last the bottle was empty, unexpectedly he opened his eyes again and looked directly up at her. Harriet's heart lurched with a jolt that was as intense as any emotion she had ever felt before. She could feel the warmth of the tiny body against her arms and, instinctively, she clasped the baby closer to her breast.

The child's mother had stopped crying and the hint of a surprised smile lit up her face as she said, 'You have a way with babies, don't you? This one has hardly stopped crying since I gave birth to him. Maybe the poor little thing has somehow sensed the grief I felt when my husband died: or have you already learned how to nurse them? How many children do you have?'

Harriet caught her breath. When she could speak, she related as briefly as she could her ongoing history of the miscarriages, and confessed she had lost her last baby only two months previously. With tears in her eyes, she said, 'Perhaps your baby senses how greatly I longed to hold one in my arms.'

The mother's face was questioning as she sighed, saying, 'Life can be unjustifiably cruel at times, can it not? Here am I wishing this last one had never happened, and you – you so sad because you do not have one of your own.'

She turned to look at her daughter standing silently in the doorway, and drew a long, tremulous sigh. 'The children have been so good – so very good since their father died! So many nights they have gone to bed hungry. There was simply no money for wholesome meals once Michael's funeral expenses were paid. He had kept from me the fact that he'd had to delve into our savings after the end of his employment in the orchestra. To tell you the truth, neither of us were very experienced where our finances were concerned. We had both been brought up in affluent households where money simply wasn't discussed unless it was about the price of a new horse, or the demands for better wages for the workers.'

She paused briefly before asking, 'Would it be impertinent of me to enquire if you, too, have suffered some financial mishap? I noticed when you came on board that you had no luggage. You were standing with a wealthy-looking lady and her maid, but did not accompany her when she disappeared below deck.'

'No, I am on my own,' Harriet admitted. 'I am going to stay with my sister who has an Irish husband and lives in Dublin. My personal belongings and money were stolen by thieves the night I arrived in Liverpool, and the nuns very kindly took me in and nursed me. I was in a coma for some time, during which I suffered a miscarriage.'

'That is very sad,' her companion said, 'but you will be well looked after, I'm sure, with your sister.'

Harriet looked at her anxiously. 'I do very much hope you will be safely reunited with your family.'

The woman nodded. 'I am praying they will give me sanctuary, but if my father refuses to have Michael's Protestant children . . .'

She sounded close to tears, and Harriet said quickly, 'I'm sure you are worrying unduly. From all I learned from the nuns when I was in the convent, the Catholic religion requires their followers to be charitable.'

She paused, remembering Sister Mary Frances' stern face and bitter disapproval of what she had called Harriet's 'fall from God's grace'. If the father of this unfortunate young woman applied her attitude to his daughter rather than the kind, sympathetic attitude of Sister Brigitte, he might indeed feel he could not accept the offspring of a Protestant father.

The baby stirred in her arms, once again opening his eyes to gaze up at her, and her heart melted. How could any mother be expected to hand over a tiny baby like this one to be brought up in an orphanage? Or, indeed, any of the children who, until now, had been remarkably quiet and well behaved.

As it was nearing the evening Mrs Lawson and her children went down to steerage to make sure they had suitable bunks for them all to sleep in. When she returned, she held out her arms to take the sleeping baby from Harriet. Without warning, the infant's face screwed up and he started to cry – a long, unhappy wail that tore at Harriet's heart. Although she knew it was stupid to imagine the baby did not want to be parted from her, the realization did not lessen her anxiety.

His mother drew a long, unhappy sigh. 'I know I am to blame for this!' she said in a near whisper. 'I think the poor child somehow knows that I wished – may God forgive me – that he'd never been born . . .' Her voice dropped almost to a whisper. 'I can never love him; he will always be a reminder of my dear husband's death.' She drew in her breath and added: 'You will think me wicked – and I may well be so – but if my father insists, I will place this baby in an orphanage.'

Harriet remained silent, her heart twisting in unexpected grief at the cruelty of Fate. Here was this unfortunate, unhappy woman prepared to give her baby son away, and she, herself, bereft because she had lost the baby she and her beloved Brook had so much wanted.

The following morning, when Harriet awoke, she looked for the mother and children when she went on deck to one of the two galleys. She needed to heat water to make the porridge Sister Brigitte had given her. There would be enough, she decided, for her to spare some for Mrs Lawson and her children, but there was no sign of them. From the open hatchway to the steerage deck came a foul stench of unwashed bodies and vomit, doubt-less due to the lack of toilet facilities down there. She was still trying to bring herself to descend to the steerage deck when the eldest girl appeared with the baby in her arms. They were approaching the Irish coast and one or two of the passengers were watching from the rail for sight of Baily lighthouse at the entrance to Dublin Bay.

The little girl looked anxiously at Harriet. 'Mama asked me to ask you if you could carry the baby when we disembark,' she said. 'Jimmy, our littlest, is too weak to stand having been sick so often and she says she will have to carry him and I am to hold on to Peggy and Jack.' The words continued to come out in a rush as if they had been carefully memorized. 'Mama said to tell you she wouldn't have asked the favour 'cepting she knows you don't have any luggage so could you hold the baby for her?'

Harriet smiled. 'Of course I will!' she said unhesitatingly, holding out her arms for the baby. 'Doesn't he have a name?' she enquired.

The child shook her head. 'Mama said we would have him christened when we reached our grandparents. She was too busy, you see, after Papa died and she had to sort out all his papers and such.' Her eyes filled with unshed tears when she added huskily: 'I loved my papa very much. He used to sing to us, and before we had to sell the piano he played lovely music and we danced and he promised when he was rich that we would have lessons on how to dance for the ballet. He . . .'

She broke off to wipe the tears now falling down her pale cheeks.

'I'm so sorry about your papa!' Harriet said quickly. 'But I'm sure you will be very happy with your grandparents. Now please assure your mama I will take great care of her baby. I expect I will probably disembark before the steerage passengers, so I will wait for her where she will see me when you all arrive. If I can find a waiting room, I will remain where I am whilst you search for me.' She smiled at the young girl and told her to look in the pocket of her cloak, which was draped over the edge of the seat on which she had been sitting.

'You may take one of those pennies,' she said gently, 'for being such a help to your poor mama.'

A smile replacing the tears on her face, the little girl departed and Harriet sat down once more on the seat, her arms cradling the baby. He was no longer whimpering, and seeing his wizened little face she rocked him gently and wondered how so young an infant could survive the journey with all its discomforts.

It crossed her mind suddenly that perhaps it would not live, and she was filled with a sudden fierce desire to prevent such a tragedy. The girl had left the feeding bottle but it was empty. Harriet stood up, a look of determination on her face. Someone on board must have milk to spare now they were so soon to land and she had money still to pay for it.

Wrapping her cloak around the infant, she hurried along the

deck where the queues for the galleys had almost disappeared. Then she caught sight of Lady Cavanagh's maid, who looked pale and tired. She greeted Harriet with an apology for not having visited her as had been promised, but explained that she as well as Her Ladyship had been ill throughout the journey, and only now that they were in calmer waters did she feel able to take food or drink. In her hand was a pitcher of milk.

Harriet felt a sudden irrational desire to wrench it from her but managed to keep her voice quiet as she pleaded to be given some, explaining that she was caring for another passenger's baby who was only two weeks old and might die if it was not fed.

The maid looked surprised as she stared briefly at the tiny, pinched face of the baby. 'You're more than welcome to most of this,' she said. 'Her Ladyship thinks it might be a whole day on dry land before she can keep food or drink down her. We shall be home, at Castle Killbray, just outside Dublin by midday, so all this will not be needed. Give the bottle to me and I will give some of it to you.'

Five minutes later, Harriet sat in her cabin watching the colour return slowly to the face of the starving infant. She remembered suddenly Sister Brigitte's comforting words when she had been recuperating. 'The Good Shepherd always watches over his flock', she had said, adding that He would bring comfort to those who believed in Him. Was it possible that she, Harriet, alone and childless, had been sent to help his unfortunate mother?

Far from sure whether or not she was being unduly fanciful, Harriet continued nevertheless to care for the unwanted baby until the ship docked in Howth harbour on the northern edge of Dublin Bay. She went as promised to the waiting room where she sat down on an uncomfortable wooden bench and awaited the arrival of Mrs Lawson and her children. Staring at the clock above the ticket office, she began to feel uneasy when an hour had passed and there was still no sign of them. At first she wondered what could have detained them, but as the crowd of passengers dispersed and eventually left her the sole occupant but for a porter, she was shocked by a sudden thought that the woman was not coming to collect her baby.

Another half hour passed and a porter came into the waiting room and approaching her, touched his cap and said, 'One of the passengers with a heap of youngsters gave me this letter for you, madam, said as you'd be dark haired, tall as herself and nursing a babe, and you'd be waiting here for her. Well, there not being a soul here but yourself, I'm thinking as how this must be for you.'

Her hand trembling, Harriet thanked him, unfolded the piece of paper and started to read.

> *If you can find it in your heart to do so, please forgive me for what I am about to do when we land. May God forgive me, but I can never love the baby nor could I afford to keep him if my parents will not allow my children and me to return to the safety of their roof.*
>
> *I am now praying that, as you seem so kind a person, and so caring with my poor unwanted child, that you might think of him as God's replacement for the baby you so recently lost. If you are horrified by this thought, please take him to the orphanage in Dublin, which was my intention before I met you.*
>
> *You may think this cruel and irresponsible of me as I know you only as Harriet and neither your surname nor where you live. Perhaps it is best that way as if you did decide to raise my child as yours, you can be assured that I can never find you or ask you for further help.*
>
> *Whatever you decide, I will never forget you or cease to thank you in my prayers for your great kindness to me and my children.*
>
> *May God bless you.*
> *Joan Lawson*

It was several long minutes before Harriet could come to terms with what she had just read. The woman's suggestion was, of course, ridiculous. She could not possibly undertake such a responsibility, least of all without Brook's agreement. Even if she wanted to agree to such a crazy notion, he would not be home for at least another twelve weeks. The baby would have to go into an orphanage. Mr Dickens' heart-breaking story of an orphan called Oliver Twist came unwanted into her mind.

She looked down at the baby in her arms, who seemed to be staring back at her. The bone structure of his little face was delicate, and she was reminded that both the mother's family and that of his musical father were of gentle birth. What would happen to such a fragile infant in the harsh rough and tumble of an orphanage?

Her heart jolted as she realized suddenly that she might just consider taking a live new-born baby in place of the one she had lost, and were it not for her certainty that Brook would veto such an idea, she could . . . would welcome it. Having held him in her arms and fed him, she cared for him; how could she now bring herself to abandon him to an orphanage where, sickly as he was, he might not even survive?

'Are you wanting a hansom cab, missus?' asked the porter who was still standing in front of her unnoticed. 'There's one awaiting outside for a fare.'

Slowly Harriet got to her feet. The porter reached down for her basket and she followed him out into the bitter cold of a November day. Suddenly, she was longing quite desperately for the warmth of her sister's house and the welcome she knew she would receive. The infant started crying – a thin, sad wail – as she climbed into the cab and gave the driver Una's address.

'Hush now, baby!' she said as she settled him on her lap. 'We will be warm and well cared-for soon. There is no need for your tears. My sister will look after you until we decide what to do with you. Just stop crying, please.'

As if the infant understood what she was saying, he suddenly looked up at her with what Harriet swore later was the hint of a smile.

SEVEN

1865–1866

B y the time the hansom cab arrived at the door of Una's beautiful home in Ballsbridge Street, on the outskirts of Dublin, both Harriet and the infant she was holding were in no state to be received. The few towelling squares that were on the child had long since been soaked. Shamefaced, she paid the driver and, holding the basket with her few belongings as best she could, rang the front doorbell.

After one look at Harriet's bedraggled figure and the now wailing baby in her arms, the footman told her sharply that Her Ladyship was not at home and he was unsure when she would be back.

Harriet started to explain to the disbelieving servant that she was Una's sister when someone approached from behind him. For a single moment, Una's nanny stared at Harriet and then, smiling in delight, she pushed the footman aside and pulled Harriet gently into the hall.

'Lord save us!' she exclaimed. 'Whatever has befallen you, Miss Harriet . . . and the baby . . .?'

She reached out and took the wailing infant from Harriet's arms, her face taut with shock. As the footman closed the big front door, she gasped, 'Surely to goodness you aren't on your own, Miss Harriet! Have you no maid? No nanny?'

Harriet burst into tears, partly from exhaustion, but also at the half-remembered comfort of her old nanny who she now recalled saying the familiar words when she cut her knee or fell off the hay cart. 'Surely to goodness, Miss Harriet,' she would exclaim as she dealt with the subsequent cut or bruise, 'you shouldn't never have been doing such a thing!'

Nanny Rogers was now staring down at the pale, wizened face of the hungry baby and, tut-tut-tutting at its wet clothing, recognized the cry from forty years of experience with tiny infants. She looked questioningly at Harriet. 'Are you not able to feed your child?' she asked. 'That's a hunger cry if ever I heard one.'

Attempting to stem her tears, Harriet shook her head. She was on the point of replying that she could not do so because the infant was not hers, but her old nanny was already barking instructions to the footman. He must send the nursery maid upstairs as quickly as possible, she told him, with hot milk, and the tweeny must go, too, with jugs of hot water for the south-facing spare room together with the tin bath, soap and towels. One of the maids must light the fire in the bedroom nearest to the nursery, make the bed and put a stone water bottle in, and

he must ask Cook to warm some of her broth and have that sent
upstairs in twenty minutes time.

Noticing that Harriet had no luggage large enough to contain
clothes, she turned to Una's personal maid who was staring at
the curious visitor from the foot of the stairs. She must find one
of Her Ladyship's night dresses and put it to warm by the fire
in the spare room, she ordered.

Turning back to Harriet, she said gently, 'Whatever mishap
has befallen you and your baby, Miss Harriet, you're safe now.
Nanny will take care of you and your little one.' Her tone was
once more one which Harriet instantly recalled from her nursery
days.

'No more talking!' Nanny Rogers was instructing her. 'Up we
go and you shall have a nice hot bath and go straight to bed.
Then I want you to have some of Cook's chicken broth and
afterwards, you're to have a good sleep. I never in my life saw
you look so poorly!'

As they walked upstairs, she informed Harriet that Miss Una
and Sir Patrick weren't expected home until the next day, as they
were away visiting Sir Patrick's parents, so Harriet should sleep
for as long as she wanted.

'I'll see to your baby,' Nanny added as if there wasn't any
doubt that Harriet would wish her to do so. 'Goodness me, Miss
Harriet, she's that small she can't be more than three weeks old!
You should be resting after the birth, not travelling. No wonder
you're in such a state!'

Harriet was too exhausted to explain that the baby was not
hers and that it was a little boy, not a girl, and that he had been
given to her by his mother to take care of. Still less was she able
to explain how she had been given no real option but to do so.
Now that her old nanny had relieved her temporarily of all
responsibility for the baby's – as well as her own – welfare, she
wanted nothing more than to enjoy the cleansing bath, and sleep.
She would explain everything later, she told herself, and then
make up her mind what she must do.

It was tea-time when she awoke from a deep, dreamless
refreshing sleep of utter exhaustion. It was a moment or two
before she realized that she was not in the narrow iron bedstead
at the convent, but in a soft feather bed in Una's house. A fire

was burning brightly in the grate and soft chintz curtains were keeping out the bitter November wind now rattling the panes of glass. For a moment, she was conscious of nothing more than the feeling of comfort and safety which encompassed her. Only then did she remember her arrival. At that moment Siobhan, the nursery maid, came into the room and put a tea tray on her lap.

'Nanny is in the nursery, madam,' the girl said as she crossed the room to put some more coal on the fire. 'She told me to tell you that Violet, Her Ladyship's maid, will be in presently with some clothes for you, and when you are dressed, will you go up to the nursery where the children are having their tea.'

A quarter of an hour later, Harriet made her way upstairs to where Siobhan had said she would find the nursery. For the first time in months she felt more like her old self. Una's maid had found drawers and petticoat trimmed with lace and with broderie anglaise insertions. Over them was a lovely emerald green, moiré silk gown which, surprisingly, fitted her perfectly, and the maid had washed and dressed her hair in a fashionable style.

Long before she reached the landing, she heard the shouts and laughter of the children. The noise stopped abruptly as she entered the room. All the little girls curtsied and the boys bowed as Nanny introduced them. The formalities over, they all started to talk at once without shyness but with avid curiosity. Was she really their aunt as Nanny had said? What was her baby called? Why was it so small? The questions poured from them, their small faces alight with curiosity and friendliness.

Answering them as best she could, Harriet crossed the room to where Nanny was sitting, the baby sleeping peacefully on her starched white aproned lap.

'Don't look so worried, Miss Harriet,' she said comfortingly. 'Your little boy, bless him, is going to be just fine. He's keeping his food down and hasn't cried once.' Smiling, she pointed to one of the little girls. 'Constance wants to know if you will allow them to keep him. She says we haven't had a new baby since Colin and she likes babies better than dolls. Cedric wants to know how long you can stay and will the baby grow quicker than Colin who he is still waiting to be old enough to join in the ball games he enjoys. At present he only has Clifford and his sisters to play boys' games with.'

Harriet sat down at the nursery table beside the three little girls who had been finishing their tea before her arrival. They began plying her with questions: where was her baby's father? Was it pretty where she lived? Had she any older children? Finally, they asked her if she would like to see them dance.

'Not one of them knows the meaning of shyness,' Nanny said, then insisted they tidied their books and toys away before going down to the drawing room where the pianoforte was. 'Their parents have quite different rules from the ones you children had when you were little. They like to see them running all over the house, hearing them laughing and singing and such. Running wild, I call it, but I have to say, they are never impolite, and they do what is told them.'

Constance, the eldest girl, came to stand beside Harriet. 'Would you like to come downstairs now? I can't dance for you as I will have to play Mama's pianoforte since she isn't here to play for us. I don't play as well as she does but I learned to play a jolly Irish jig. Some of the boys and the smaller ones aren't very good dancers, but Papa says we will all be splendid performers when we grow up. The pianoforte is in the drawing room so we have to go downstairs.'

'I would love to watch you!' Harriet replied. 'That is, if Nanny says it is permitted.'

The elderly nanny returned her smile. 'I'll be happy to have a few minutes' peace and quiet before bedtime!' she said. 'I'll just sit quiet here with the little one.'

Harriet looked down at the sleeping baby, thinking how he had been transformed from a pale, wizened, wailing scrap of humanity into this angelic-looking infant now cradled in the old woman's arms. As she stood there, the children waiting patiently for her by the nursery door, the baby opened his large blue eyes and, so it seemed to Harriet, focussed upon her. Seeing the expression on Harriet's face, Nanny said gently, 'Do you want to hold him awhile, Miss Harriet? Seeing the way you used to be with your dolls, I don't wonder you love this little one: you was born to be a mother. Miss Una – I mean, Her Ladyship – and I have wondered from time to time why you haven't had babies before and . . .'

Seeing the look of distress on Harriet's face, she quickly changed the subject, telling the waiting children not to make their parents' drawing room untidy, and not to stay for more than half an hour as it would soon be the youngest two children's bedtime.

The next half hour was one of unbelievable happiness for Harriet. Although not very practised, the older children performed the dance remarkably well, and very sweetly offered to teach her the steps next day if she wished. The younger two cuddled up to her, putting their arms round her shoulders and telling her how pretty she was, and vying with one another to think of a name for her baby. The eldest of the boys informed her that all of them had the letter 'C' to start their names. Nanny had told them he was a cousin, which made him a part of the family, so could she give her baby a boy's name also beginning with 'C'.

How, Harriet wondered, was she going to confess that the baby was not hers: not their cousin, and almost certainly must be going to an orphanage? Would she ever be able to find the courage to do so? *Must* she do so?

The children were still discussing possible names for the baby as they made their way up the wide staircase to the nursery quarters at the top of the house. They were now adding to Harriet's discomfort by begging her to invite them all to the baby's christening. They had never yet been to England, they informed her, and their papa had promised them they would go there soon. Mama, too, had often talked about her family in England.

When finally they had all bidden her goodnight and disappeared off to bed with the nursery maid, Harriet found herself alone in the nursery whilst Nanny was downstairs discussing supper with the cook. The baby was now sleeping peacefully in the outgrown wooden cradle one of the maids had brought down from the attic. Somehow, she told herself, she must tell Nanny and these friendly, happy children that the baby was not hers: that it was unwanted, and must go to an orphanage. They would not understand how his mother could bring herself to part with him; still less how she, Harriet, could now give him to an orphanage where he would have no father or mother of his own. Nanny, she reflected, would not only be incredulous, but deeply shocked by her deceit in allowing so much time to pass before admitting that the baby was not hers.

Why was she finding it so difficult to do so? she asked herself. She had known all along that she could not keep him however much she might want to do so. If she had not been so certain of Brook's reaction, she might well have taken him with her when she returned home. Charles, the children had decided he could be called – after the former king of Ireland who had also been a king of England. They would shorten the name to Charlie. Not only did it begin with a 'C' as they wanted, but Charles was their grandfather's Christian name: her father's, too, Harriet thought, imagining how pleased he would have been, had he not died the previous year, to have a grandson named after him.

Harriet caught her breath as for the first time she found herself questioning whether there might be a way she could keep the baby with Brook's approval. The mother was well born, his father not an aristocrat but from a respectable family, so his parentage was no stumbling block which an unknown orphan's might have been. *Could she keep the baby?* She and Brook had so longed for the children as yet denied them. Here in this house with Una's large brood of delightful sons and daughters – the sound of their laughter, their affection, their bright little faces – had made her even more aware of her losses, her deprivation.

When later that evening, Nanny handed the baby to her to nurse after his feed, her heart contracted. So many times in the past had she longed excitedly to be able to hold her coming baby in her arms, only to suffer yet another miscarriage! Suppose she was never able to have a child, as the doctor had warned might be a possibility? Her own mother had died at her birth: could she have passed on to her a physical defect unknown to the medical profession? Why should she, Harriet, not be able to carry a baby full term when Una had six healthy children and, according to Nanny, was possibly carrying another? Could she bear to remain childless all her life? How would Brook feel if he knew there was never going to be a son?

It was only after she was in bed, the glow of the fire softly lighting her room, that Harriet allowed herself to consider whether this baby, thrust unasked upon her, could possibly compensate for the son he might never otherwise have: the son who, when he was older, Brook could teach to share all the manly pursuits he so enjoyed . . .

Try as she did, Harriet could not find freedom from such thoughts in sleep. Wide-eyed, she began to think of some of the kindly Sister Brigitte's beliefs – not least that 'God sometimes worked in mysterious ways'; that the way He chose to compensate the distressed was not always obvious. Was it conceivable, she now asked herself, that after her most recent miscarriage, God had decided to send this baby to her, not just to improve matters for the stricken mother but for her sake as well?

Realizing unhappily that this was simply wishful thinking, Harriet tried once more to make a solemn promise to herself that she would confess the truth to Nanny the following morning before Una returned and was allowed to believe the lie that the baby was hers. Another long hour passed before Harriet realized that no lies were necessary: that simply by saying nothing to anyone, Una, too, would assume the infant was hers just as Nanny and the children had done. Had she not miscarried at the convent, her own baby would be almost the same age as this one. *Nor need she tell Brook the truth.* If she kept silent, she would be the only person to know. His real mother, the widowed Mrs Lawson, knew only her Christian name, Harriet, and that she was English. The very last thing the woman would want, with all her problems, would be to have her unwanted baby returned to her. She had said that if Harriet did not want him, he must be left in the care of an orphanage. Therefore, *there was no need for her to lie to anyone, Brook least of all,* she told herself, her heart beating furiously. *She had only to remain silent to be able to keep the baby she had been given: the baby who she had started to love as if he had been her own. She need not ever tell another soul.*

She was woken next morning by soft voices whispering, 'Nanny said we mustn't wake her . . .'

'She must be asleep, her eyes are shut!'

'I'm going to look. I think she's in there . . .'

Little fingers gently lifted one of her eyelids, which caused her to open both eyes and smile.

The three youngest instantly clambered up on top of the eider-
down vying with one another to sit next to her. The eldest girl,
Constance, was drawing back the curtains to reveal a brilliant,
sunny morning.

'Jack Frost came in the night,' Cedric informed her. 'Everything
is white like snow. Will you stay with us for Christmas?'

'Nanny said she only had to get up twice in the night to feed
your baby,' announced Caragh. 'She said he was very good for
such a young baby.'

'As I'm the oldest,' Constance said, 'please may I be the one
to show him to Mama?'

'And I'm the oldest boy,' announced red-haired Cedric, 'so
can I show him to Papa?'

These nephews and nieces of hers were delightful, Harriet
thought, wishing that Una and her family did not live so far away
in Ireland. Brook would enjoy their company, and by all accounts,
Una's husband, Patrick, was an even keener horseman than Brook
himself.

Una's maid helped her dress in one of Una's pretty day gowns,
after which she went downstairs. The postman had arrived, the
butler answered her query, but there was no letter from Brook
forwarded from Hunters Hall. She had half expected there might
have been one waiting for her. He had promised to write as often
as possible, but it was now sixteen weeks since she had received
his unhappy letter informing her he must remain much longer in
Jamaica than expected.

There being no further word from him, when Una and her
husband returned home, at her sister's request, Harriet agreed to
stay on in Ireland much longer than she had originally intended.
Not only did she have no wish to return to an empty house, even
though she would have the baby with her but, here in Dublin,
her much-loved childhood nanny was giving him the very best
care he could receive.

Una, having heard Harriet's account of Bessie's disappearance,
now promised she would ask her housekeeper to recommend a
capable Irish girl to return home with Harriet when she left, to
act as her maid and nanny to the baby. Irish girls were not only
hard working, she assured her, but of cheerful character, loving
to sing as they went about their work, and especially good with

children, most of them having been raised in very large families where the eldest took care of the younger ones.

Una made a big fuss both of Harriet and the baby. Acting as if she were Harriet's mother, she insisted that she had plenty of rest and good food. Her husband, Sir Patrick Morton, was a delightful man in his forties, devoted to his wife and always joking with his large brood of children. It was small wonder, Harriet thought, that the children were so happy and loving towards one another. She would miss them all dreadfully when the time came for her to leave.

Last thing at night, when she said her prayers, she thanked God for sending her the baby now called Charlie by all the family. He had begun very occasionally to smile and the children insisted that he was really listening when they sang songs to him or when Nanny brought him downstairs to listen to Una playing the pianoforte.

'He is going to be musically inclined like our mother was,' Una said, leaving Harriet momentarily guilty that she had deceived this loving sister who knew nothing of the baby's musically talented father and was doing everything she could to make her visit a happy one. By now, she was totally enraptured with him – as much as if he had been her own child, Harriet thought.

Christmas was a particularly jolly time. Carols were sung and a fir tree brought indoors – a custom initiated by the late Prince Albert. It was lit with tiny white wax candles in little tin holders. Presents were made, wrapped, and then unwrapped on Christmas morning on their return from a jubilant service in the nearby beautifully decorated church. On Boxing Day, the local hunt gathered in the driveway, stirrup cup was passed up to the huntsmen, and Harriet stood with Una and the children cheering as the huntmaster set off down the drive with the hounds barking and jostling one another around him.

The following day the staff were given a whole day off after breakfast, having left an elaborate cold luncheon ready in the dining room for the family. Only Nanny opted to remain at home, partly on account of her age and rheumatism, but also because she did not want to leave the baby in Harriet's inexperienced care. The most time she was prepared to concede was in the afternoons when Harriet took the baby from her, leaving the old woman free to go to her room for what she called 'forty winks', which usually took two hours. On such occasions, by the time Una and the children had taken it in turns to nurse the baby, Harriet had to plead to have him for a little time herself.

On New Year's Eve there was a huge reception for their friends and neighbours. A banquet was prepared by Cook and her minions, and the outdoor staff decorated the house with yew and fir tree branches to which the children attached brightly coloured ribbons. Una lent Harriet one of her ball gowns and, Harriet's health now fully restored, she looked so pretty that Sir Patrick remarked teasingly that if Brook did not come home soon, his wife would be stolen by one of her many admirers at the party.

Wonderful although this Christmas had been, however, it had only made Harriet long more deeply for Brook's return, and as if in answer to her prayers, on the first day of the new year, she finally received a letter from him. He could not give her a date, he wrote, but he was now confident he would be able to leave Jamaica within a matter of weeks.

'I must go home at once, Una, dearest,' Harriet told her sister. 'Much as I have loved every moment of my stay here with you and your lovely family, I must be at home to welcome Brook.'

Una put her arm around her and kissed her. 'My darling sister,' she said, 'by the look on your face, I don't doubt that you would be every bit as disappointed as Brook were you not home to greet him!'

Three weeks later, the children with Nanny all waving from the nursery windows, and Una and her husband waving from the front doorway, the flurries of snow covering the house and grounds, Harriet climbed into the family coach. Beside her sat her new maid, Maire, while the baby was in her arms. Both were well wrapped up against the cold, on the start of the journey home. Only two thoughts were in Harriet's mind as they drove through the gates out on to the road – seeing Brook again, and how he might react when he saw little Charlie.

As the horses trotted smartly though the streets towards the port, she prayed the day would never come when he would doubt that the baby she had grown to love as her own was not after all his son.

EIGHT

1866

B rook had endured a difficult six months trying to settle
the smooth running of his family's estates in Jamaica.
The freedom of the slaves was supposed to bring peace
on the island, but instead it seemed to ferment discontent. The
unrest amongst the native Jamaican population throughout
the island had culminated in a riot in Morant Bay last October.
Thankfully Brook's workers were not involved in the rebellion,
as the Edgerton family were considered fair employers.

However, the political repercussions were unforeseen. The
Jamaican Assembly voted away its independence and constitution
and the island was declared a Crown Colony. Brook was called
as a witness to the Royal Commission when Eyre, the Jamaican
governor, was recalled to England for incompetence, and Brook
and Hastings returned to England in the same ship.

Although thankful to be home at last and free of the cramped
life on board ship, he was bitterly disappointed not to find his
beloved wife there to welcome him home. Following Hastings
upstairs to his dressing room, he was now regretting that he had
not sent advice ahead of him from Kingston that he would be
home within two weeks. Not only had he discovered that Harriet
was in Ireland with her sister, but the house was unprepared for
his return, the furniture still covered in dust sheets and the fires
in the bedrooms and living rooms unlit.

It now became a hive of activity, but although Hastings was
doing his best to encourage the fire one of the maids had lit in
Brook's dressing room it was bitterly cold, particularly, Brook
remarked, after Jamaica where the temperature was seldom below
seventy degrees.

He did not, however, wish himself back on that troubled island.
He appreciated the fact that it had proved very necessary for him
to go there, but not for so long a time. As his valet went to his

wardrobe to find fresh clothes for him to wear, he said, 'You know, Hastings, I had dreamt of this reunion with my wife every night of the voyage home. Of course I cannot blame her for not being here, but I do very much hope it will not be long now before she is back. I expect you are waiting to see young Bessie, too.'

He knew that Hastings and Bessie had an understanding – that when Hastings returned from abroad they would become officially engaged. Before he'd accompanied Brook to Jamaica they had spent all their time together whenever their half days off coincided.

He took his watch out of his waistcoat pocket. Had it not already been dark on this cold February day, in Harriet's absence he might have ridden over to see his father who he knew would be agog to hear all the news of the plantations and their new manager; or Paul Denning and his sister, who would have been delighted to see him whatever the hour, they being less conventional than their neighbouring families who would have expected him to announce his intention of calling beforehand.

Paul Denning was a generous host with a cellar of excellent wines, and a French chef who produced exceptionally good food. When Paul was not in London, where he spent a great deal of his time, Brook found him jolly company – refreshingly outspoken and forthright, with a fund of slightly risqué jokes which he kept strictly from the ladies' ears.

Perhaps he would visit Paul and his sister tomorrow, he told himself as Hastings helped him out of the large tin bath in which he had been soaking himself in the deliciously hot water – something that had been denied him throughout the two-week journey home. Denning's sister, the widowed Mrs Felicity Goodall, was as good company as her brother. She was quick with her laughter and repartee, and openly flirtatious with men of whatever age. That particular trait was criticised by the wives, who amongst themselves considered her fast. He and Harriet, however, liked both her and her brother, finding their friendliness and lack of formality enjoyable after the strict adherence to convention of their other neighbours.

That Felicity Goodall was openly flirtatious with Brook had never annoyed or disturbed Harriet, who delighted in the older

woman's comments about her good fortune in having such a
devastatingly handsome husband; nor had it worried her when
they joked that if Harriet hadn't 'snapped him up', the young
widow, Mrs Goodall, would not have hesitated to do so. Instead,
Felicity had become one of Harriet's few close friends, frequently
riding out with her in the environs of their homes, or calling on
a rainy afternoon to play whist or backgammon whilst he, Brook,
worked on his estate papers or visited his father to discuss the
troubles with the plantations.

Brook also had reason to be grateful to Felicity for being particularly sympathetic each time his darling Harriet had miscarried,
jollying her out of her inevitable depression with amusing descriptions – not always kindly – about her straight-laced neighbours'
activities. Widowed and childless as Felicity was, she always had
time on her hands and, an excellent horsewoman, she never missed
a day's hunting. She was taller than the average woman and full
figured, and when mounted, Brook had once laughingly told Harriet,
she tended to look like the carved figurehead on a Viking ship as
she sailed ahead of him over even the highest hedges despite her
more precarious side-saddle.

On one such occasion, one of Brook's male friends had
remarked confidentially that were he not married, he would have
been tempted to see if the iconic widow would respond to a
discreet 'little flutter', as he put it.

Now, however, Brook gave Paul Denning and his sister no
more than a passing thought. First thing next morning, he told
Hastings, he would ride over to see his father, hoping that perhaps
Harriet had written to him to say when she planned to return
home.

The following morning, after a hearty breakfast such as he
had never been able to enjoy abroad, he rode over to Firlbury to
see Sir Walter. The old man was sitting in his favourite armchair
in front of a blazing fire, his leg propped up on a footstool. The
doctor had told him that in future he should drink less wine,
whisky and brandy if he wanted to stay clear of these painful
attacks of gout, but despite the warning, he had a decanter of
sherry on the table beside him.

Disappointingly for Brook, neither had his father any word
from Harriet, so having brought Sir Walter up to date with the

situation in Jamaica, and eaten a delicious game pie for luncheon, Brook returned to Hunters Hall. It was growing dark as he rode up the drive. The trees on either side, their branches bare of leaves, looked ghostly in the darkening twilight as he hastened towards the house. Lights were shining from nearly all the windows, including those in the top-floor nursery wing, and the lovely old house looked wonderfully welcoming. As he drew nearer, Brook's heart jolted, the thought striking him suddenly that, just possibly, so many lights were lit because Harriet had arrived home.

Spurring his horse up to the front steps, he dismounted, and Fletcher, his usual formal countenance wreathed in smiles, opened the big oak door.

Brook handed his horse's reins to the groom who had appeared from the stables, and his heart pounded with excitement as Fletcher informed him: 'The mistress is home, sir! I told madam you'd said you would be back before nightfall, and she is waiting in the drawing room for you.'

Harriet was home! In a few minutes, he would see her, hold her in his arms, feel her soft body melting against his! His hunger for her was such that his legs were trembling as he bounded up the stone steps, threw his hat, gloves and whip on to the hall chest and divested himself of his coat, which he thrust at Fletcher. Pushing past the footman who was opening the drawing room door, he hurried into the room.

Harriet had arrived home early that afternoon. It had been quite late when the ferry from Dublin had docked and she had spent the previous night with Maire and the baby in the Adelphi Hotel in Liverpool, and had boarded the first train to Leicester knowing that it would be so much quicker by rail than by coach. On reaching home soon after luncheon, she was told by Fletcher that Brook had already returned from Jamaica and had ridden over to see his father. This had given her time to see Maire settled in the nursery quarters with one of the maids to assist her before Brook's return. She had then enjoyed a welcome bath and change of clothes. Mrs Fraser, the housekeeper, on learning of Bessie's disappearance after the attack upon them, was to act as her personal maid until a suitable replacement could be found.

Harriet was hardly able to contain her excitement as she was helped into the beautiful coral and green glacé silk gown she had last worn on her honeymoon. Round her neck she wore the gold and coral heart-shaped locket which Brook had given her on her nineteenth birthday, and Mrs Fraser fastened a coral brooch on to the velvet ribbon tying back her hair.

Finally, satisfied that she looked her best, Harriet went up to the nursery to ascertain that Maire and Charlie were happily settled before going down to the drawing room to await Brook's return. She welcomed the fact that, during the ensuing hour before he came home, she had time to consider how best she could break the news to him that they now had a baby son. She would inform him that he was upstairs with his nurse, probably asleep by now, and that Brook could see him in the morning.

Her excitement at the thought of being reunited with him after so long was tempered by fear of his reaction. Just for this evening, she told herself, nothing must cast a shadow on their reunion. Although Brook might rejoice that he was now a father, she dreaded the many questions he would be sure to ask; and which would necessitate her telling him a whole sequence of lies.

Her resolve to tell those lies gave way momentarily to a desire to tell him the truth in the hope that he would agree to raise Charlie as his son, or even as a foundling like Hastings, but she knew in her heart that he would not do so. He had spoken so often of 'heritage' and his ancestry, family traits when they had discussed the children they would have. He'd even confessed he longed for a daughter as well as a son, who would remind him of the little sisters who had died in his youth.

She had been wrong, she told herself, ever to have pretended Mrs Lawson's baby was her own. Now it was too late – she had come to love him as if he was indeed hers and she could not contemplate parting with him.

To tell Brook the truth was to risk never seeing or holding Charlie in her arms again. If Brook insisted she part with him, to lose the two-month-old baby boy would break her heart. Her thoughts went to the little boy in the muslin-draped bassinet she had prepared for her own babies, his eyelashes lying like two tiny fans over his cheeks, which were rosy with health after Nanny's weeks-long care, and knew that she now loved the infant

every bit as if he was indeed her own. It was then that she knew
without a doubt that she dared not risk Brook's refusal to keep
him. Nothing – but nothing – must mar their reunion. She would
this very minute give all the staff strict instructions that there
was to be no mention under any circumstances of Maire and
Charlie, that she wished to be the one to surprise the master,
who knew nothing of the baby's birth. This evening, she told
herself, she wanted Brook and his attention all to herself. If he
had missed her even half as much as she had missed him, their
reunion was going to be more wonderful than any moment as
yet in their married life.

Thinking now of the night of love which was to come, Harriet
wondered if it would result in her conceiving another baby such
as the one she had miscarried in Liverpool. The thought reminded
her of what she must later tell Brook, another lie: that Charlie
must have been conceived just before he had gone to Jamaica,
and that had she and Bessie not been beset by the fire and then
attacked by robbers, she might not have given birth so soon. If
questioned further she could tell him that, thankfully, the prema-
ture baby had progressed under her old Nanny's expert care, and
was now a healthy, happy infant of whom they could both be
proud.

All such thoughts and anxieties vanished instantly as Brook
came into the room. Disregarding the presence of the footman
and Fletcher who was hovering to see whether his master required
refreshment, Harriet abandoned decorum and ran into his open
arms. For once, Fletcher, too, abandoned decorum and allowed
himself to exchange smiles with the footman as they backed
quietly into the hall and quietly closed the door.

Brook paused only briefly between his hungry kisses to
murmur: 'You cannot know, my darling, how terribly I have
missed you!' He did not even allow her a chance to tell him how
unhappy she had been lying night after night alone in her bed
missing him. It was almost as if they were back on their honeymoon and so much in love that they were unwilling to be beyond
touching distance of each other.

Brook's arms moving to her waist, he led her to one of the
big sofas where, still kissing, they lay entwined. Smiling happily,
Brook confessed that were it not for the imminent arrival of one

of the servants to announce the readiness of their evening meal, he would undress her and make love to her then and there.

Looking at his flushed, handsome face, his dark eyes seeming to caress her, Harriet knew that nothing and no one in the whole world mattered to her more than her husband. They were home together at last, and even now he was vowing huskily that he would never go anywhere without her again.

Fletcher knocked discreetly on the door and came in to announce that Cook had planned to prepare a cheese soufflé – Brook's favourite dish – to precede the roast pheasant for dinner that evening, and wanted to know what time he and the mistress wished to dine. Brook rose to his feet, his eyes dancing as he told Harriet he would make haste changing out of his riding clothes and hopefully manage to match her elegance at the dinner table in half an hour's time.

When he returned looking immaculate in his black dress coat and trousers, white waistcoat and bow tie, he took her arm in his and led Harriet into the dining room, where Cook's perfect soufflé followed by roast pheasant was served to them. As they ate, Brook wanted an account of Harriet's activities whilst he had been away. Sadly, he said, he had had no news since her letter, which he had received soon after his arrival in which she mentioned her intention to visit her sister.

She told him truthfully about the journey by coach to Liverpool, the fire, how Bessie and she had been attacked and robbed, and that, horrifyingly, Bessie was missing, at which point in the story, she stopped, saying, 'Please don't ask me to talk anymore about it now, Brook. I will tell you the whole story tomorrow . . .'

Brook's face became a mask of concern. 'My darling, I had forgotten selfishly that you have only today reached home and that you must be quite exhausted. Let us finish this delicious Charlotte Rousse and then we will retire.' He regarded her anxiously. 'Who is attending to you, my love, now that Bessie is not here to do so? We must find you a likeable lady's maid as quickly as possible.' His brow cleared. 'I know just the person to find a suitable replacement quickly,' he added. 'Do you recall when we last dined at Melton Court last year, Mrs Goodall kept talking about the success of their new cook who she and her brother had obtained from a London domestic agency – I think

she called it – which had started a business in Leicester. That
quail pie the woman cooked was quite memorable, so perhaps
you might find a replacement for Bessie there quite quickly.'

Although Harriet was grateful for Brook's possible solution
to the problem, she knew she would have difficulty in choosing
anyone who could take her dear Bessie's place. Often she would
think of her faithful maid, wonder if she was still alive or a
prisoner, perhaps, of the evil men who had robbed them. Perhaps
it would be a good idea if she let the capable Mrs Felicity
Goodall engage a new maid for her if she offered to do so
because, of a certainty, she would not be able to do so herself
impartially.

But even Bessie slipped to the back of her mind when, their
meal finished, Brook declined his usual glass of port and drew
back his chair, telling Fletcher he would not be needing him any
more as they were now about to retire.

It was not long before Harriet had completed her night-time
toilette with Mrs Fraser's assistance, and climbed eagerly between
the linen bed sheets, which had been warmed by the stone water
bottles the maid had put there earlier. Comfortable as Harriet
had been in the large feather bed in Una's house, she thought
that there was nowhere on earth she would rather be than back
in her own bed, waiting for Brook to appear from his dressing
room.

The maid left the room, the fire burning brightly and the candles
glowing and, unbidden, Harriet's fears returned. How could she
be risking the loss of Brook's love? No matter how much she had
grown to love Charlie, he was not her baby, or Brook's baby. Was
she wicked to be lying to him on so vital an issue?

Guilty as she was feeling at the deception she had planned,
she knew without doubt she must go ahead with her plan. Her
thoughts took another, optimistic turn: surely, even if Brook were
to discover the truth, he would understand her need to keep the
baby and allow her to do so? Harriet lay there in turmoil, her
head spinning.

Then Brook came into the room and she forgot everything but
the joy of knowing she would be back in his arms again.

Tired though Harriet was after her journey – the first she had
ever undertaken on a steam train – when the moment came to

do so, she responded to Brook's love-making as eagerly and ardently as he could have wished. They had been without one another far too long, he said, his arms tightly around her, his body pressed to hers; he would never leave her side again. Nothing, short of death, he vowed, would part them.

'I love you – love you with all my heart and soul!' he told her. Then added: 'If no further good fortune should ever come my way again, I would still feel God had blessed me well enough the day he sent you into my life. You *are* my life . . .' This time, he made tender love to her until they both fell into an exhausted sleep.

They slept late next morning. Harriet was the first to awake. A pale February sun was slanting in between the heavy damask curtains. Seeing Brook's eyes still closed, she lifted her head gently from his shoulder and lay looking at him, her heart filled with tenderness and passion lingering from the night before. She had dreamt so often at Una's house of the joy of their eventual reunion, but had never imagined it could be so idyllic. Her love for him was so intense that the emotion she felt brought tears to her eyes.

Then, she remembered the baby . . . wondered how well he had passed the night after their long journey home from Ireland. She desperately wanted for him to look well, to smile when Brook first saw him. She must no longer delay telling him that he had a son the first moment he awoke.

Fear returned and filled her whole being. Suppose Brook refused to believe Charlie was his child? She had no proof to support the lie. Suppose if she confessed the truth he were to demand that she took the baby to the nearest orphanage as his mother had suggested? Could she bear to be childless once again after these past two months of holding him, feeding him, falling in love with him? It had seemed the most natural thing in the world to allow Una's delightful children to believe he was their cousin; to take turns rocking his cradle or helping Nanny bath him as the older girls had once bathed Cedric, Clifford and Colin. She had never felt so fulfilled. *The love she shared with Brook was a different kind of love*, she realized. He made her feel complete as a woman, whereas the baby who she now called hers made her feel complete as a mother.

Somehow . . . somehow, when Brook awoke, she must find the strength to tell him the lie that she prayed would make their marriage complete.

She slipped quietly out of bed and, pulling her warm Paisley shawl round her shoulders, went to sit by the fireside. The embers were still glowing, allowing a little warmth to come into the room. Nevertheless, she shivered with apprehension knowing that at any moment Brook would wake.

Almost at once she saw him stir, open his eyes and turn to look for her. Seeing the space beside him was empty, he sat up quickly, looking round the room in alarm.

'My darling, what ails you? Are you unwell?' he demanded anxiously when he saw her by the fireside.

Harriet attempted a smile before saying, 'No, Brook, I have been waiting for you to awake. I have a surprise for you; one I believe will give you great pleasure.'

Brook held out his arms. 'Come back to bed, dearest. No surprise could afford me greater happiness than to have you in my arms!'

Harriet made no move and forced a smile to her face. 'I think what I am about to tell you will please you even more than I could,' she said. Taking her courage in hand, she added softly: 'We have a son, Brook, a little boy. He is upstairs with his nurse. As soon as we are dressed, I will take you to see him and . . .'

She got no further before Brook was at her side. There was a look of utter amazement on his face as he said incredulously, 'A son? A baby? You have had a child? But how so, Harriet? Why did you not write and tell me? When . . .? How old . . .? I cannot believe this. Have my ears deceived me? You said *we have a son*?'

Harriet's hesitation was so slight as to be imperceptible, but she could not voice the lie a second time, so she nodded, saying quickly, 'I must have conceived the baby before you departed to Jamaica. I had not fully realized it when I decided to visit my sister. Unlike those occasions when I miscarried the other babies, I felt so well this time I supposed I had simply put on a little weight when I made the decision to travel to Ireland. Were it not for the attack upon Bessie and myself, I think I may have carried

Charlie . . .' she used the name unconsciously, '. . . for the full
nine months. As it was . . .' She paused, and Brook, wide-eyed,
urged her to continue.

'I was hit . . . rendered unconscious by the villains I told you
about who attacked Bessie and me,' she said, her voice firmer
now that she was telling the truth. 'When I regained my senses,
Bessie had vanished and I was in a convent being cared for by
nuns. It was there the baby was born . . . far sooner than he
should have been.'

Seeing the look of amazement on Brook's face, she added
quickly: 'The nuns took the greatest care of us both, and when
I finally reached my sister's house, we were so spoilt by Una
and my old nanny that it was not long before both the baby and
I were in the best of health. I . . . Una and the children . . . all
of us, that is . . . called him Charles after my father, but if you
do not care for the name . . .'

She got no further before Brook was lifting her from her chair
and covering her face with kisses. 'You suffered all that without
me by your side!' he exclaimed huskily. 'Oh, my darling, if I
had known . . .'

This time it was Harriet who interrupted. 'There was nothing
you could have done to protect or assist me from so far away,
which was why I did not write and tell you this in a letter,' she
whispered. 'But now that is all behind us, Brook. I know that
you will have to tell Hastings that Bessie is missing, but otherwise
I really would prefer not to talk or think about it. Charlie is
thriving, as you will see for yourself as soon as we are dressed.'

Brook's expression changed from one of anxiety to one of
pure joy. He kissed her again and again, his eyes shining with
excitement and happiness. 'You are the bravest, kindest, most
wonderful wife a man could have!' he told her, his voice choked
with emotion. 'A son, Harriet – the child I longed for! When we
lost the others, I knew you were as saddened and disappointed
as I was, but I did not want to add to your distress by telling
you that I felt my life would never be complete if I did not have
a least one boy to carry my name.'

He kissed her yet again, and continued joyfully: 'Now . . . now
I shall not mind even if we never have more children . . . although,
as you have now proved the doctor's fears were unfounded

you might well give me a daughter next time who will look like you.' He laughed delightedly, then looked down at Harriet as a thought struck him. 'Why did you not tell me this last evening, my darling? How could you have kept such a wonderful surprise a secret from me?'

Harriet caught her breath, dismayed by the fact that she must tell yet another lie – or at least not confess the true reason, that she had been afraid he might question the lie she had told him.

'I instructed the staff to remain silent, Brook, because I wanted to be the one to tell you; and as it was quite late and Charlie would be asleep, I decided to wait until now when you could go straight to the nursery to see him.'

The questioning expression on Brook's face gave way to one of adoration. 'Only you, dearest, could have such consideration for my happiness. I shall go at once and impart the wonderful news to Hastings whilst he dresses me, but before I do I will have to tell him the very distressing news of Bessie's disappearance. I shall give him as much time as is needed for him to travel to Sussex and see her family.'

With a last loving look at Harriet, he turned and flung his brocade dressing gown around his shoulders and left the room. Harriet remained seated, staring into the fire, and wondered which of the emotions she felt was uppermost – relief that Brook had not doubted her, or shame that she had so successfully deceived the husband she loved.

NINE

1867

Harriet sat facing Felicity Goodall on the opposite side of the fireplace in the drawing room of Hunters Hall. The February afternoon was chilly, and a cold draught was managing to find a way through the mullion windows – a problem which always occurred when the wind was in the east. Their chairs were therefore pulled close to the cheerful blaze.

Brook had gone out after a quick luncheon to see to a problem on the estate, and the two women were on their own.

Harriet, of course, had no idea of the ugly thoughts going through her friend's mind. This past year Felicity had been devastated that Harriet had given birth to a live child. She had been living in ever-increasing hope that Harriet's marriage would collapse if Brook did not get the heir he wanted.

It was now twenty years since one rainy afternoon when she had sat on a footstool at her paternal grandmother's feet and listened to the former chorus girl's advice for ensuring that she only accepted a marriage proposal from the right man.

'Who is the right man?' she had asked.

'One who knows when to be strong and when to be weak; when to be kind and when to be severe; when to be inflexible and when to be yielding and when to disregard both your "no's" and your "yes's".'

Felicity had not really understood at the time, but even at a young age she used her grandmother's maxim for judging her would-be suitors, and so it was not until she met the eighteen-year-old Brook Edgerton at her brother's twenty-first birthday party that she'd known what her grandmother meant. Throughout her girlhood she had scorned all the eligible young men her father and brother had introduced her to and had refused several proposals of marriage. But she had known then, when she had first met Brook, that she should be married to him. But her father had persuaded her to marry his friend, the wealthy George Goodall, and she had been totally distraught when, as a widow, she had discovered Brook was marrying pretty, young Harriet Drake. As soon as was possible, Felicity had befriended the girl, thus ensuring she was able to remain close to Brook. The fact that he clearly doted upon his young bride was almost as distressing as was the euphoria she always felt when she was near him. And the more intense her feelings grew, the greater was her determination to be both friend, confidant and counsellor to the younger girl. Brook's lengthy absence in Jamaica had furthered her encroachment into Harriet's life and thus Brook's.

Hiding her disappointment, she said, 'You know, Harriet, that husband of yours is going to spoil your child. I have never in my life seen so many toys as there are in the nursery. I wonder he can ever make up his mind which one to play with!'

Harriet laughed. 'I know his birthday was in December but we decided to delay it for a couple of months, mostly because the weather was too bad for Brook's father to leave the house. Charlie is far too young to know it was not his real birthday yesterday. As for that beautiful big rocking horse you remarked upon, Sir Walter gave it to him, although he knows it will be several years before Charlie is big enough to ride on it. He dotes on him almost as much as Brook does.'

Felicity gave Harriet a speculative glance, her eyes turning imperceptibly to the younger women's figure as she repeated, 'It sounds as if Master Charles is going to be very spoilt indeed! Which I suppose is inevitable, he being the only child, or are you perhaps soon to add to your family?'

Harriet reminded herself quickly that Felicity could not possibly know that such an event was highly improbable, and in any case, it was not very conventional to discuss such a subject. Ever since her return from Ireland the attractive young widow had been a regular caller, and as Harriet was missing Una's company, their easy friendship had grown much deeper. Felicity had established herself as Harriet's closest friend, fulfilling her need for female companionship. For there was not even Bessie now with whom she could discuss the virtues of a new gown, a new way to dress her hair or the success or otherwise of a dinner party.

She had become accustomed to Felicity's outspokenness and the way she often disregarded social conventions some time ago. She addressed Brook and herself as if they were a brother or sister, and thought nothing of kissing both of them when arriving on one of her frequent visits.

When Brook saw her seated side saddle on her large black mare with only a groom accompanying her, he had once described her as looking like a beautiful Boadicea charging into battle, needing only a chariot with knives on the wheels to complete the picture. Harriet might have felt a trifle jealous of his praise had he not told her that no one was more elegant or more beautiful than she, herself, when wearing her midnight-blue riding habit. It had a tight-fitting jacket finished with a velvet collar and cuffs, and he particularly admired her black silk hat with its gauze veil worn at such a jaunty angle.

More often than not, Felicity rode with the hunt, but Harriet had ceased doing so of late, suspecting as she did that she might once more be with child. Were this to be so, she thought, and she managed not to lose the baby as before, she could not imagine that she would love it more than she adored Charlie. He had grown into the most attractive, cherub-faced little boy, his blue eyes always crinkling in a smile when he saw her or Brook. His high, piping voice was heard wherever he went in the house, singing without words the Irish songs Maire often sang to him.

Every member of staff loved Charlie, but none as much as his father did. Brook's interest in the child had deepened even further when he discovered how much the boy loved him. Whenever he was home of an evening, he would call Maire to bring the child down to the drawing room when he was bathed, fed and ready for bed. As soon as Charlie saw Brook, he struggled to get down from his nurse's arms, stretching his own not towards Harriet but towards Brook.

Harriet loved watching them both, Brook often holding his hunter watch to Charlie's ear and smiling at the child's delight at the sound. Sometimes when he heard Charlie attempting to sing the melody of one of the nursery rhymes Maire had taught him, Brook would add a verse or two in his rich baritone, and laugh when Charlie stopped, wide-eyed, in order to listen to him.

'He's my most appreciative audience, aren't you, you young scallywag!' Brook would say, and insist Harriet should instruct the boy to sing to his grandfather, Sir Walter, when next he visited. Brook's father was now almost as frequent a visitor as Felicity Goodall. He openly admitted that he came to see his grandson, not Brook or Harriet. He doted on the child almost as deeply as Brook. Once, hearing the little boy's piping voice perfectly in tune and noticing how he took instantly to any form of melody, Harriet was reminded of a fact she would far prefer to forget – that his real father had been a musician.

'Did you never wish for children before your husband died?' she asked Felicity now.

Felicity shook her head. 'I hope this will not shock you, Harriet,

dear, but to be truthful, I prefer dogs! Although I only have two
of them, a deer hound and a King Charles spaniel, Paul complains
he is always falling over one or other of them, and forbids me
to have more. He is allowing me another horse though as, being
stabled, he doesn't often see them.'

She laughed at Harriet's expression and added: 'Brook was
quite upset the other day at luncheon when Paul remarked that
horses would soon become redundant now that we had steam
engines. Of course, he, like our late father, is entirely besotted
with train engines, and he tells me that one day there will be
railway lines all over the country, and people will be able to
travel very quickly to any town or village they choose. It is hard
to believe, is it not, that there will be lots more railways travelling underground like the ones they have built in London. I have
asked Paul to take me on one when he invites me to the house
he has bought in London. I shall stay there with him whenever
I fancy. Just imagine, Harriet, riding in a railway carriage under
the ground!'

Brook had long since told Harriet that Paul Denning and his
sister were probably among the richest people in the country;
that it was new money made from the father's involvement in
the railways, and they could therefore afford to buy a palace – if
such were vacant and it was wanted. He had added that if the
plantations in Jamaica continued to be doing so poorly, far from
buying property he might have to sell the London office and
think twice about renting the house in Wilton Crescent for the
season.

The previous year they had removed to London for three
months and Harriet had enjoyed riding in Hyde Park where all
the fashionable people rode or promenaded. They had enjoyed
an exciting day trip to Epsom with a party of Brook's friends
and their wives to watch the Derby, gone to St James's Theatre
where the famous Henry Irving was appearing in a play called
The Two Lives of Mary Leigh in the part of Rawdon Scudamore
and, one wonderful night, they had listened to Madame Patti
singing 'Violetta' in the opera *La Traviata*.

Harriet had liked all Brook's friends, mostly former Oxford
graduates like himself, nearly all of whom she remembered
slightly from Brook's and her wedding day. Their wives were

charming and only too pleased to escort Harriet on shopping
expeditions where she could replenish her wardrobe with more
fashionable attire than that Una had bought for her after she had
lost her belongings in Liverpool.

Felicity, needless to say, was always quite up to date with the
latest fashions, employing a dressmaker in Leicester who had
been working in Paris with an up-and-coming young designer
called Charles Frederick Worth. The woman was adept at copying
any dress pictured in the *London and Paris Ladies' Magazine*
and, since cost was irrelevant, was sent to London for all the
latest and best materials.

Miss Felicity Goodall was very far from being a conventional,
somewhat helpless female, Brook commented when Harriet spoke
of her. He'd seen her lift her horse's leg and remove an offending
stone from its hoof as fearlessly as if she were the groom! In
other ways, too, she was a resourceful, self-assured woman.

As Felicity had promised on Harriet's return from Ireland, she
found a very efficient replacement for Bessie, a fully trained
woman from London called Ellen Reed who had, so far, proved
to be faultless. Harriet, however, found it impossible to feel any
great liking for her. Whilst not actually disliking her, she felt as
if there was a transparent wall between them, other than the
normal conventional one between servant and mistress. Ellen
seldom talked about herself other than to say that her family had
always been extremely poor; that all but her sister, Susan, had
passed away. The girl was handicapped and dependent upon
Ellen, the only wage earner, for financial assistance.

She told Harriet in a rare moment of discussion about her past
employment that the nuns at her school had found her a position
as a tweeny in a big London house, and by dint of uncomplaining,
exhaustingly long hours of work, she had managed to gain promotion to housemaid, then parlourmaid. Finally, having studiously
learned from her mistresses the requirements of a lady's maid,
she had reached her present position, and learning that a Mrs
Goodall was looking for a lady's maid, she quickly applied for
the position. So far, Harriet had been unable to find fault with
her which, she confessed to Brook, had not always been the case
with her dear Bessie.

Once a month, on Maire's half day off, Harriet took little

Charlie to the Norman church in the village. There, she would kneel in one of the pews and pray for Bessie's return whilst Charlie played in the aisle. She did not expect ever to see her again, but she had had a surprisingly optimistic letter from Bessie's father. On her return from Ireland she had travelled down to Sussex and given Bessie's parents an account of the attack upon them in Liverpool. His daughter, her father insisted, was no weakling, and as nobody had ever been found and identified as her, he was convinced she must be kept prisoner, and that one day she would find her way home.

Subsequently, Harriet had written to the Liverpool police asking them to continue their search for Bessie, but they had failed to find a single trace of her. She had been missing for over a year now, but Harriet still prayed for her return.

It was after such a visit to the village church that she came home to find Felicity awaiting her return in the drawing room. Harriet rang for tea to be sent up and joined her on the sofa, saying, 'So much seems to have happened this past year, Felicity, and yet when I think about it, Brook and I have not been very sociable with our neighbours – other than with you, Felicity, dear. You and your brother have been so generous with your hospitality. We both so love your beautiful house. Were you to remarry and move elsewhere to a new home, we would miss you so much.'

Felicity was regarding her strangely. 'I have not the slightest intention of remarrying, my dear friend. I am not saying anything disrespectful about my late husband, who was a kind, generous and thoughtful man, but he was thirty years older than me – a friend of my father's, and it was to please Papa that I agreed to marry him. I never loved him. When I marry again, it will be to someone as charming and handsome as your Brook – someone I could love as much as you love him.'

Harriet smiled and turned to regard Brook, who had just come into the room and was also smiling as she replied to Felicity, 'Then I can only wish that he had a twin brother! Living alone as you do, it must be quite lonely at times when your brother is not visiting. He told me he had many business commitments in London.'

Felicity sighed. 'It is only to be expected. I think Paul loves his railway empire even more than Papa did!' She smiled at Harriet, adding: 'However, I am a great deal less lonely since you and Brook moved into Hunters Hall. You always make me feel so welcome when I come here, and I think it is vastly kind of you, Brook, to waive protocol and permit me to ride over to see you both without prior invitation. You make me feel almost like one of the family.'

For a moment, a picture of Felicity and Brook playing backgammon in front of the drawing-room fire one wet winter's day with much laughter came to Harriet's mind. She had been spending an hour in the nursery watching Charlie as he tried doggedly to walk over to her, frequently sitting down with a bump and laughing as he struggled back on to his feet and made yet another attempt.

The slight, unexplained feeling of unease at seeing the two by the fire like a happily married couple quickly vanished when Brook had immediately stood up when she'd entered the room and come straight to her side. He had kissed her on the cheek and told her to come and sit down on the sofa beside him. Their game was almost finished, he said, and he would concede defeat.

Harriet knew he liked Felicity and admired her repartee, her spirit and her horsemanship. She agreed with Brook when he said that her repartee was so amusing that her occasional lapses from conventional ladylike behaviour were of little consequence; it was not her fault. Her father, despite his relatively humble origins, had given his children an excellent schooling, Felicity being finished at a very costly and genteel establishment for training daughters of the growing number of newly rich men who were buying their way into acceptance by the upper classes.

There was no doubt, Harriet agreed, that Felicity was always most beautifully attired whether it be on the hunting fields, at a ball or a simple dinner party. Shyness was unknown to her, and she was a faultless hostess.

'I do believe you are a little jealous of her, my love!' Brook had once teased Harriet. 'You talk as if you were not admired every bit as much as our flamboyant Mrs Goodall. You are intelligent to converse with, utterly charming and far more lovely than Felicity could ever be.' He had kissed her, held her close to him, and added: 'You would not believe how many of my men friends have slapped me on the back and told me what a devil of a lucky fellow I am to have you for my wife.'

It was silly of her to have felt inferior in some way to Felicity, Harriet had told herself. Were it possible, she and Brook were even more deeply in love than ever before. Brook was unable to forget the lonely months when he had been living so far away without her, and often, when he had made love to her, he would renew his vow never to leave her again. He was never far from her side, except on occasions when he joined Felicity and her groom on a morning ride, or once when he had driven her into Leicester when she wanted his advice about a horse she was thinking of buying. It pleased him to be asked for his opinion on the making of a marble fountain for the garden on a visit with Felicity to the stone mason in the village near Ramsbury.

Once or twice Harriet had accompanied them on such outings, but she felt the winter cold quite badly, and often preferred to spend an hour or two in the nursery with Charlie.

On this cold February afternoon, Harriet was enjoying Felicity's amusing account of the week she had just spent in London with her brother.

'You and Brook should come up to town more often,' Felicity told her. 'Paul would love to have you to stay at his house.' She glanced out of the window and rose to her feet.

'It will be dark in an hour or so,' she said, 'so it is time I made my way home. If you will be kind enough to ask your footman to tell my groom to bring the curricle round to the front, I will pay a quick visit to your water closet and be on my way.'

Harriet smiled as she pulled the bell rope to summon Albert. There were few women who would mention the words 'water closet' in their hostesses' drawing room!

Felicity Goodall was not smiling as she made her way upstairs. She had arranged on her arrival that Harriet's maid, Ellen, would wait for her in Harriet's dressing room where she could speak with her privately. Ellen was now standing with her back to the large wardrobe containing her mistress' gowns. She dropped a quick curtsy as Felicity hastily closed the door behind her. From the pocket in her dove-grey foulard skirt, Felicity drew out a half crown and placed it in the maid's open hand, saying sharply, 'You have a fortnight's report to make to me. What have you to tell me?'

Pausing a minute before replying, Ellen's thoughts winged back – as they often did – to the day she had been selected by Mrs Felicity Goodall as the most promising candidate for the position of the lady's maid to her friend, Mrs Edgerton. There were several other candidates – some with far more promising backgrounds and experience than herself, yet she had been the only one to be interviewed by Mrs Goodall.

She had not realized until later why she had been chosen. It was for no other reason than that she had admitted her financial circumstances, and her determination to improve her sister's life. She had declared that she did not mind how many hours she would be required to work, or what tasks she might be asked to do, provided she was suitably rewarded.

It was at that juncture Mrs Goodall had fed her a fictitious story about the need to keep a close eye on her friend, Mrs Brook Edgerton: how she had once tried to kill herself following a series of miscarriages. It was imperative, she told Ellen, to ensure at all times that the young mother remained on loving terms with her husband. She, Ellen, must keep secret watch upon the couple, and report the facts personally to her. She would be rewarded for the additional time this might incur.

It had been less than six months before she, Ellen, had realized the real reason why the woman who was secretly doubling her pay wanted such information: she had fallen passionately in love with the husband and was waiting only for some discord or other in order to be able to step into the wife's shoes.

Ellen herself did not dislike Harriet, and the husband, Mr Brook Edgerton, was always polite and pleasant on the few times she saw him, so she was quite pleased to see that they remained devoted to one another. On the other hand, she realized that she could extort a great deal more money from Mrs Goodall if things started to go wrong between them, and she needed more. Her sister had been unwell and required a doctor's attention on several occasions, which had made inroads into Ellen's precious savings.

'I am awaiting your answer, Ellen!' Felicity was saying sharply, hoping that for once the woman had something to tell her. But Ellen's face remained impassive.

'I'm afraid I have little to tell you, madam,' she said in level tones, wondering at the same time why she had not long since given up hope of her, Ellen, discovering any discord between husband and wife. No couple could be more devoted, and both were totally besotted with their little boy.

Ellen herself was not fond of children, and had never wished to marry and have a family. All she had ever wanted since the day her younger sister had been run over by a carriage and so badly injured that she had been physically handicapped was to make Susan's life as bearable as possible. Nearly all of the money Ellen earned went to pay the rent for the two cold, damp basement rooms in London where her sister lived out her purposeless life. One day, Ellen had vowed, she would have saved enough money to buy a little bungalow by the seaside, where they both could live; take in a lodger, perhaps, to help make ends meet.

'The master is still sharing madam's bed each night,' she reported. 'As you asked me to do, I always take note of the bed after I have dressed madam and she has gone downstairs and it is always in its usual state of disarray. Jenny tells me that when she comes up in the morning with madam's hot chocolate she quite often finds them with their arms about one another if they haven't heard her knock on the door.'

Felicity frowned. 'So there is still no marital discord!' she muttered. 'As you know, Ellen, I expect you to tell me immediately if they disagree with one another or quarrel in your hearing. Are you taking note of any gossip in the kitchen about them?'

Ellen's face remained expressionless as she replied in level tone, 'Yes, madam! I am obeying your instructions precisely.' She paused, looking down at her hands before adding in a quiet tone. 'It is not my place to comment, madam, but I think I should say that it seems to me as if they are still very much in love.'

It was a moment or two before Felicity, her forehead creased in a frown, said sharply, 'Perhaps you are not present when they have disagreements, Ellen. You should keep better watch upon them. I will pay extra if this requires more of your time.'

Ellen's face remained impassive. 'Do you wish me to enquire if any of the staff have seen . . .'

'Certainly not!' Felicity interrupted sharply. 'I do not wish anyone but you to know I am concerned. Your position here is important to me for reasons I have no intention of explaining to you. All I require of you is that you will continue to do your best to observe any discord between the couple, and report it to me. Now give me my cloak and hurry yourself. I have been here quite long enough.'

Without bothering to say goodbye, she opened the door and made her way back downstairs. She did not, therefore, see the look of scorn on the Ellen's face as she muttered to herself, 'She wants him, wants the master, and the only way she can hope to get him is if he turns against the mistress – but why should he? She dotes on him every bit as much as he dotes on her. Not that I care if Her Ladyship chooses to waste her money in the hope they will start quarrelling or lose their interest in their marital pleasures. So long as she continues to pay me, I'll do what she asks and keep my mouth shut.'

She would, she told herself, do anything within reason to be able to move her crippled sister to the seaside. Ellen went down the backstairs to the kitchen in the hope that the delicious-smelling game pie Cook had baked for luncheon had not all been eaten, and that Mr Fletcher would permit her to sit down belatedly at the servants table and eat what remained. Mr Fletcher was the undisputed head of the Edgerton household staff and a man not to be argued with. His rule over all the servants prevailed; he was only unable to control Ellen's movements when her mistress required her services.

One thought always uppermost in Ellen's mind was that she would do anything required of her that would not put her job in jeopardy – anything that the lovesick Mrs Felicity Goodall required in return for the much-needed addition to her present pay.

Returning downstairs to the drawing room, Felicity put her arms round Harriet's shoulders and, thanking her for an enjoyable afternoon, kissed her warmly goodbye. She would have liked to have kissed Brook, too, but knew she could not do this casually as if she were no more than a close friend. For the time being, no one in the world, last of all Harriet, must know that she had fallen hopelessly in love. It was the first time in her life that

Felicity had ever been in love. Despite being the daughter of one of the richest men in the country, the fortune her father had left her and Paul could not buy Brook for her. As she rode home with her groom, Felicity contemplated the fact that it had almost ceased to be a pleasurable excitement standing close to Brook, feeling his lips on her hand when he greeted her, being in his arms for the duration of an old-fashioned waltz on one memorable evening at a New Year's Eve ball. Her marriage had been virtually barren. Her late husband, a heavy drinker, was almost incapable of enjoying a normal husband's pleasure in his wife's body. When he had done so, there had been no enjoyment in it for her, nor any desire for it, but even standing close to Brook Edgerton was enough to set her heart racing and her knees to tremble. It was only with enormous self-control that she had been able to appear no more than a good-natured, amusing friend and neighbour.

There had been moments, Felicity thought as Melton Court came into sight, when she'd felt a sudden frisson of fear that Harriet might see or sense the effect Brook had upon her: but she circumvented any such suspicion by flirting very obviously not only with him, but with any other man in her vicinity. She played the part of a merry widow, as her brother called her, and was unfailingly welcomed as a friend, not least by Brook. It was, however, never less than painfully obvious to her that, even at the end of a happy afternoon riding side by side, he was always in a hurry to get back to his wife.

TEN

1867

Paul Denning was a cheerful, likeable fellow and Brook, who was much the same age, enjoyed his company. From time to time when Brook was in London on business, he would dine with Paul at his London house in Cadogan Square. He was, too, impressed by the way Denning had made himself responsible in many ways for his widowed sister.

On the last occasion, after Brook had left the house to return to his club for the night, Paul found himself harping back over the past. He poured himself another glass of port and carried it slowly up to his bedroom. He had, with some difficulty, refrained from confiding in Brook the reason for his exceptional mindfulness of his sister.

In the days of their childhood they had lived with their parents in Stockton, a seaport over two hundred miles from London. Their father, Matthew Denning, had started work as a boy in the ship-building industry and became more and more interested in the development of the Stockton-and-Darlington Railway where they had produced the first train to carry passengers as well as goods to the capital.

With single-minded purpose, Matthew Denning had over the years worked himself up to a senior position. Convinced that it would be only a matter of time before railways were constructed all over the country, he saved as much money as he could and invested it in rail transport shares. By the time he was fifty, he was a very wealthy man.

It was then that Matthew Denning had married a woman twenty years younger than himself, and a year later, fathered Paul. The following year his wife died following the birth of a baby girl.

From stories Paul's father had told him, Paul knew how perilous the life of his little sister, Felicity, had been. Only the constant care of an experienced wet nurse had saved the baby's life although, at first, they feared she would be mentally handicapped. Two more years passed before she suddenly started speaking and taking note of what went on around her. By the time she was five years old, she was not unlike other children of her age, although considerably more active than they were. 'Hyperactive' was the phrase their doctor had used to describe her behaviour.

Matthew Denning was by then rich enough to move himself and his family south, where he bought the imposing Melton Court, a large, red-brick mansion set in established grounds, sent Paul to one of the best public schools and hired a governess – an impoverished gentleman's widow – to tutor his daughter and teach her the manners pertaining to the class of society which he intended to infiltrate.

Away as often as not at school, Paul only learned much later

of some of his young sister's transgressions. Hopelessly spoilt
by her indulgent father, she expected all her likes and dislikes
to be met without delay. At the age of twelve she was so resentful
of her governess's discipline that she began putting tiny
amounts of juice, from the poisonous berries she had squeezed
from deadly nightshade berries she had found in the hedgerows,
into the unfortunate woman's food. It was her unlucky victim
who had warned her about the dangerous effects they produced.
Felicity had made no excuse when confronted with the failed
attempt to kill her governess. As she was still quite young, their
father had shrugged off the matter, saying Felicity would have had
no idea that her childish 'prank', as he called it, could have such
very serious consequences – might even have killed her. The
governess was dismissed with a handsome remuneration for the
shock she had received, and Felicity was cautioned never again
to ignore grown-ups' warnings about dangerous substances.

With Felicity being so young, it was not long before the whole
episode was forgotten. Seeing no further need for his pretty
daughter to have an extensive education, Matthew Denning did
not replace the governess but arranged for her to be tutored three
hours a day by the local curate – he was unaware that Felicity
ran rings around the young fellow and seldom completed the
homework he set for her. When she reached the age of fifteen
he finally sent her to a select finishing school.

Other incidents of a less serious nature than that of the
governess had followed when Felicity reached her teens. She was
a highly strung, vivacious, energetic girl, always laughing and
singing if she were not having one of her tantrums, which occurred
when she could not get her own way. She was popular with the
various girls of her own age at the finishing school and had many
friends. Paul, by then up at Oxford, was proud of the compli-
ments his university friends paid his sister, and their father boasted
his daughter would have no problem finding a husband when she
came of age.

Only Paul, when home for the holidays, was aware of Felicity's
dark moods: days when for some reason or other she could not
achieve what she happened to want, and would fly into an ungovernable temper. On one occasion she had even threatened to kill
him because he would not agree to include her when he went

with a group of friends to ski in the French Alps. At the time he was hard put to shrug off the episode, having been quite frightened by the look on his sister's face as she threatened him, brandishing one of their father's ornamental swords as she did so.

On another occasion, Felicity had run over one of the dogs in the governess cart to whom she had taken a dislike. She claimed it was an accident, but having seen the incident from a window, Paul knew it had been quite deliberate. Deeply concerned about these incidents, he had consulted with his father as to whether the unfortunate start to his sister's life could have affected her brain in some way. Matthew Denning, now a very sick man on the verge of death, refused even to consider such a thing, telling Paul that females were known to have what he called 'funny turns' at certain times of the month, as Paul would discover for himself when eventually he was married, and he should be more tolerant.

The result of his sister's erratic behaviour thus explained as customary for females, Paul had elected to remain a bachelor, amusing himself when he felt like it with chorus girls who were always available to wealthy young men like himself. Their jolly behaviour never reminded him of the worrying side of his sister's dark moods.

It had been a relief when Felicity agreed to marry the man her father had chosen for her before he died. George Goodall was almost the same age as her father, and was every bit as indulgent. For a year or two all had been well with the marriage, Felicity lacking for nothing that her wealthy husband could buy for her. Then, without known reason, he had suddenly died. The doctors were unable to discover the cause of death. His heart and other vital organs all seemed to have been in excellent condition for someone his age, and it was only after his body had been released by the authorities for burial that Felicity had said quite casually to Paul, 'Now at last I can go on a steam ship to America. George would not even consider it no matter how hard I pleaded, silly man, saying he would be ill on board ship.' She had gone on to say that although her husband had bought her anything she asked for without question, and paid all the bills she ran up, he would never give her money of her own. Now that he was dead, she told Paul, she was free to do as she pleased without having to ask for money or permission to do so.

'Did you not love him?' Paul had asked, shocked by her indifference to her husband's death. 'When you agreed to marry him, despite my warning that he was too old for you, you insisted upon accepting George's proposal.'

Felicity's reply had shocked him still more. 'I didn't dislike George. For one thing, I knew that, being an old man, he would almost certainly spoil me the way Papa always did. If I had married one of the silly young men who proposed to me, I would have had to lead the kind of life expected of a wife, catering to their husband's wishes, their demands. Had I been born a boy like you, Paul, I could have done as I wished when I grew up. I made up my mind a long time ago that I was not going to waste my life having to obey a husband's wishes. George so doted upon me, he almost always agreed to whatever I wanted – that is, until I asked him to take me to America.'

Surely, Paul had thought at the time of her marriage, his sister was not devoid of the usual feminine wish to fall in love and be loved? All the poets, writers, dramatists had love as their main topic, yet since her husband's death his sister had seemed quite shockingly pleased with her widowhood.

For one distressing week, Paul was unable to get out of his mind the suspicion that somehow Felicity had contrived the untimely death of her elderly spouse. The thought was all the more distressing because, much as he wished it to be so, the suspicion did not seem utterly ridiculous: in the past, his sister had quietly disposed of anything she disliked or did not want. Least of all did he wish to remember the episode of the unfortunate governess who, as a child, Felicity had so disliked.

It was with a sense of relief when, at first, after the funeral, Felicity had retired to the country for the necessary period of mourning. Visiting her there as often as he could, Paul managed to persuade himself that he must have been out of his mind ever to have considered such a shocking thing as his sister contriving her husband's demise. He recalled how she had always been a bright, carefree, amusing companion, popular wherever she went in society and with her neighbours. It was no less than shocking of him, he told himself, ever to have had such unlikely suspicions of someone with Felicity's vivacious, outgoing personality contriving her indulgent husband's death.

Paul had expected Felicity to fulfil her desire to go to America when she came out of mourning, but by then she had made new friends in the neighbourhood and become exceptionally close to the newly married Edgertons, who she saw several times a week.

Paul liked Brook Edgerton, who never failed to invite him to his shoots, and was charmed by his lovely young wife, Harriet, who had become Felicity's best friend. He well understood his sister's laughing comment that if Harriet had not married Brook Edgerton first, she would most certainly have tried to 'nab him as a husband!' as she put it. Sharing the joke, Harriet promised that if anything ever happened to her, she would bequeath Brook to Felicity in her will. She had no cause to be jealous as Brook treated Felicity much as he might treat a sister or a male friend, and shrugged off what he termed her childish teasing.

As time passed, Paul did find himself questioning whether this banter might have a more serious side, at least where Felicity was concerned. For the first time ever, she was behaving in a far more feminine way – as if she was intent upon winning Edgerton's admiration. In her conversations alone with Paul at mealtimes, she seemed to mention Edgerton's name particularly often. Edgerton, however, had eyes only for his wife, who he so clearly adored.

Not altogether easily, Paul managed to put his disquiet to the back of his mind, helped by the fact that he had fallen in love with a charming young French girl who had been sent to live in London with her aunt in order to learn English. He had neither the time nor the inclination to delve further into his sister's life, and spent less time with her at Melton Court.

It was only at night, after an evening carousing with his friends, that he found himself waking in the early hours unable to prevent the dark thoughts surfacing from deep inside his throbbing head. If Felicity really did want Edgerton for herself, she was certainly not going to be able to break up such a devoted couple, he told himself, nor was Edgerton the type of philanderer who might be tempted to take her as his mistress.

What, he asked himself, would his sister do when she finally realized the desires he suspected her of having were thwarted?

How serious was her mental state, which had been so determinedly ignored by their father?

Tossing uneasily in his bed, Paul's thoughts went round in circles. He had always shied away from the suspicion that his sister's mind was at times undoubtedly deranged, still less that she might have caused her husband's unexplained death. The memory returned of her driving deliberately over a young dog she had disliked, surfacing with other such thoughts: the day when she had screamed at him, her face distorted with fury, when he'd told her he would not take her to France with his friends. He had never quite forgotten the look on her face that day.

When Paul awoke next morning, it was to the awareness of a very unpleasant hangover which he must overcome before he met his French *demoiselle* for luncheon at her aunt's house. Then, as so often in the past, he pushed all thoughts of his sister to the back of his mind – the only place where his fears could be forgotten.

ELEVEN

1867

Harriet sat on the flagstone terrace in the autumn sunshine embroidering a new, prettily-frilled collar for the blue-and-white-striped frock her little boy was wearing. It was one of several Felicity had bought for him, and Harriet sighed as she recalled how upset Maire had been at the time. As a rule she made Charlie's clothes, and she had been quite put out when Felicity had ordered three fashionable outfits to be made for him by her own dressmaker. Pretty as they were, they were not nearly as practical as his usual workaday attire.

On the lawn below the terrace, Harriet could now see Brook with the little boy. It was warm enough for him to have removed Charlie's woollen jacket, which now lay discarded on the lawn along with his sailor hat. Harriet smiled happily, thinking how it had now become habitual for Charlie, whenever he espied his father, to run as fast as his little legs could carry him, calling, 'Papa! Papa! See horsey!' As now, Brook would stop whatever he was doing and take Charlie down to the stables to see the horses. She should, she supposed, smiling, be jealous of the fact that Charlie's speech, which had developed so remarkably quickly, was nearly all words he needed to converse with his father.

Felicity had remarked that Brook was without doubt in danger of spoiling him, an observation with which Harriet could not disagree. In truth, it was a matter of great joy to her, tempered with relief, that Brook doted on Charlie, sometimes almost excessively. Whenever he had been away from the house, his first enquiry was for Charlie's well-being even before hers! Seeing the two most precious people in her life so united, she told herself, had finally removed the last vestige of fear that she might have done a terrible thing allowing Brook to believe he had fathered the little boy.

Father and son now disappeared round the side of the house in the direction of the stables and Harriet told Maire there was no need for her to wait for them to return; she would bring Charlie indoors in due course for his tea. As Maire disappeared, it struck Harriet not for the first time that Una's recommendation of the young Irish girl was in no way misplaced. When they had first arrived back at Hunters Hall, Maire had been no more than a nursery nurse but she had proved so capable in every respect, and Charlie seemed so contented and thrived so well in her care, that she, Harriet, had promoted her to the superior position of Nanny. Harriet's thoughts now turned to Felicity. In the past six months, she and Felicity had become even closer friends than before, despite the almost ten-year difference in their ages. She never objected when the older woman offered her advice, and Felicity had become like an older sister to her. That was not to say they always agreed. One difference between them was Brook's habit of putting Charlie's demands on his time before their own.

It was simply not normal, Felicity would reiterate, frowning, for a gentleman to behave in such a way, putting a baby's interests before that of his guests, even such a frequent one as herself.

Still less that a man should bother himself with children as young
as Charlie. She had been hard put to conceal her irritation when
she and her brother had invited Brook to attend an important
horse sale they knew would be of interest to him, and he'd
declined the invitation for no good reason. He had arranged to
see his father's carpenter, he told her, who was making a Noah's
Ark and miniature carved animals to go inside it for Charlie's
birthday. As she remarked to Paul, Brook could perfectly well
have seen how the man was progressing on a different day!

She had sounded so vexed, Harriet had laughed. Felicity could
not understand it.

'I would have thought, Harriet,' she remarked, 'that knowing
how you adore your husband, you would resent his preference
for the boy's company to yours! I most certainly would be
jealous!' Which *she* already was, Felicity had told herself, even
though she was not Brook's wife but merely a friend.

All too often of late, she had lain awake at night imagining
that one day . . . one day in the future, if she could find a way
to make Brook fall out of love with Harriet, he would turn to
her for consolation. She had only to bide her time before an
opportunity arose for her to find or fabricate a reason for him to
turn against his wife.

For the time being, Felicity lived in hope that sooner or later
the maid, Ellen, would report some discord between husband
and wife – one she would quickly magnify until such time as it
became a serious rift in their relationship.

It was usually after a day spent in Brook's and Harriet's
company that Felicity was beset by such thoughts. There had
been men in her past to whom she had been attracted. After
her marriage to a husband the same age as her father and
partially impotent, she had taken the occasional lover, but more
for entertainment than because she enjoyed their physical attentions. Ever since she'd first seen Brook's tall, handsome figure
across the room, watched the habitual, slightly quizzical smile
light up his face, she had realized that this was a man she
instantly desired.

For a while, Felicity had tried ineffectually to ignore such
hopeless yearnings, but it soon proved impossible to subdue her
longings, which now seemed to intensify every time she saw

him. The desire he had woken in her had become an obsession, dominating her thoughts as well as her actions.

Assured of her welcome, Felicity went more and more frequently to Hunters Hall, compelled by her need to be in close proximity to Brook. Whenever she was near him her heart would double its beat, her legs tremble and her whole body ache with the desire to be in his arms, to be a part of him. She wanted his kisses, his touch, to be naked in his embrace. Most of all she wanted to feel him deep inside her – for him to belong absolutely to her and her alone. She ceased making any effort to subdue such feelings. The need to be near him was, she sometimes thought, as compelling as opium – a drug in which she sometimes indulged.

Over a year ago, Felicity had told herself that provided she could force herself to be patient, in time she could achieve her desire. Adoring as Brook found his charming, pretty wife, she had learned that men could tire of a willing consort when the delights of those first early years of marriage had worn off; and that they would go looking for fresh conquests. When that happened with Brook, she reassured herself, she, Felicity, would be there.

Felicity was fully aware of Harriet's past miscarriages, and how disappointed Brook had been not to have the son he wanted: to not be able to enjoy the start of the large family he and Harriet had planned. It had not then escaped her mind that if Harriet remained childless Brook might well decide his marriage had been a mistake. Although realistic enough to appreciate that even if Brook did divorce his wife, he might not consider marriage to someone of her lower origins, she would be willing to accept second best, she admitted, simply to be his mistress. Her frustration had grown as time passed with no sign of Brook's discontent.

When Harriet had returned from Ireland with the baby which no one had known she was carrying, Brook had become even more what she, Felicity, chose to describe as besotted with his wife. At first his interest in the child did not much differ from the ordinary behaviour of a father, but gradually, as the baby had become a little boy, Brook had become captivated by him.

Felicity was forced to consider that not only was Charlie a

very pretty child, he was always cheerful, happy and positively adoring of his father, and Brook spent more and more time with him. Consumed with jealousy, Felicity determined to find a way to put a stop, by some means or another, to this increasingly idyllic marriage.

She had pinned her hopes of finding those means when she found the new maid who would act as a spy for her, but now, over eight months later, she was losing patience. She started to wonder whether there was some other way to achieve what she wanted. Somehow, she kept telling herself, Harriet must go, and make way for her in Brook's arms and in his bed.

Blissfully unaware of the intentions of the woman she looked upon as her dearest friend, Harriet was enjoying the sunny afternoon in the garden, watching happily as Brook disappeared with Charlie towards the stables. She was also unaware of the significance of what was about to occur and the effect it would have upon her life as she laid down her sewing and went with Maire into the house to fetch a length of embroidery silk with which to edge the collar she was making. Maire disappeared up to the nursery and Harriet, having found what she wanted, was on her way back out into the garden when she was approached by Albert.

'Excuse me, madam,' he said, 'but a lady has come to the house asking to see you. I told her I was not sure if you were at home and she said the matter she wished to discuss with you was of the greatest importance. Begging your pardon, madam, but I took the liberty of showing her into the morning room as she sounded quite respectable although she declined to give her name.'

Harriet sighed. It was probably one of the ladies from the village dame school committee to ask for her patronage, or her assistance with a forthcoming fund-raising function, she thought, but as Albert had reported the matter to be discussed was of singular importance, she followed him across the hall to the morning-room door.

When she went in, the visitor was standing by the window with her back to the room. She was staring out at the beautiful flowerbeds bordering the lawn and the huge copper beech tree glowing red in the sunlight. Hearing the door open, she swung round and lifted her clasped hands to her face as if in surprise. She appeared to be speechless.

Harriet took a step towards her. As she did so, she had the strangest feeling that the stranger was known to her. Her features looked oddly familiar but she could not recall her name, or where they might have met.

The woman held out her hand. 'Mrs Edgerton, I hope you will pardon me for calling on you without invitation, but I knew if I did not do so today I might never have the courage again.' She paused for the fraction of a second before adding to Harriet's bewilderment. 'Please, don't be afraid. I am not here to make trouble for you. On the contrary, I have come to offer my help should you require it. My husband insisted I should do so. He said . . .'

She got no further before Harriet turned so white she looked about to faint. She stared unbelievingly at her visitor who she had suddenly recognized – it was the widow with all the children on the ferry to Dublin – Mrs Lawson, *the woman who had given Charlie to her.* Her fear of what the woman was about to say was so intense she felt physically sick. She even remembered her Christian name – she was Mrs Joan Lawson, Charlie's real mother, who must have come to ask for her son back!

The woman took a step forward and put a hand gently on Harriet's arm. 'Please!' she said. 'Please do not look so distressed. There is no need. I am not here to cause any difficulties for you.'

With an effort, Harriet pulled herself together as yet another wave of fear gripped her. At any moment, Brook might return to the house with Charlie and demand to know who the stranger was and why she was here.

'We cannot talk here,' she said quickly. 'Will you be so good as to accompany me to the conservatory. It is the one room in the house where we are unlikely to be overheard and . . .'

'Do not be concerned, Mrs Edgerton. I do assure you I am not here to cause any problems for you; rather, I am here to solve a problem for myself.'

Too worried about the possible appearance of Brook and Charlie to register what her visitor was saying, Harriet led her quickly through the hall and out into the conservatory. She pointed to one of the cushioned basket chairs and, seating herself opposite, said, 'Do sit down, Mrs Lawson,' adding as she did so, 'I cannot believe that I am talking to you of all people in the world. When we last met I did not give you my name, nor did I give you my address, so how did you find me?' That day . . .' her voice faltered for a moment '. . . that day when you left your baby with me . . . . I never expected to see you again . . .' Her voice broke. 'I cannot bear it if you have come to take Charlie from me. I will not let you do so! He is . . .'

'Please, Mrs Edgerton,' the woman interrupted again, 'there is no need for you to distress yourself. I have not come to take him from you. Will you permit me to explain how and why I am here?'

Still fearful as well as incredulous, Harriet nodded. She was finding it difficult to reconcile this respectably attired gentlewoman, looking in excellent health, with the thin, exhausted, bedraggled woman who she had befriended on the ferry; the widow with so many children and who had been unable to feed her new-born baby, to whom she herself had given money for food and milk.

As if mirroring her thoughts, the woman said, 'That day we met, Mrs Edgerton, you looked so ill, so lonely! You told me how the nuns had befriended you, nursed you through your miscarriage; how they had provided you with clothes and the means for you to reach your sister in Dublin, but you made no mention of this – this beautiful home you have and, if I may say so, your affluence. However, it was clear to me that you loved children, that you were a natural mother, and that having recently lost your own baby, you might find comfort with the one I could not keep.'

She paused briefly to draw a photograph from her small bag, and before handing it to Harriet, continued, 'After I had abandoned you in the waiting room, the good Lord had mercy on me, my father allowed me to return home on the condition I had my children christened in the Catholic faith. In due course, I came to know our next-door neighbour, a Mr Peter Bates, a widower with two young children. His wife had died in childbirth and Mr Bates asked me to marry him a year later.'

She then held out the photograph for Harriet to see. 'My husband is fifteen years older than I am,' she continued yet again, 'but he is a very kind, good Catholic man who found it in his heart to forgive me when I confessed I had left my fifth child with a stranger. However, he insisted that I should make such amends as was possible: that I must try and discover who you were . . . find you, and find out whether you kept my baby or placed him in an orphanage.'

Momentarily, her expression became one of anxiety. 'He made a further demand – that I should relieve you of the baby if all was not well with you or the child. He insisted I discover which orphanage you placed him in if you had not kept him, and that I take him to live with us.'

She looked anxiously at Harriet as if for understanding as she said, 'I used to cry out in my dreams: confess that I had committed so great a sin in the eyes of God that He might never forgive me. Only this way, he maintained, could I right the wrong I did when I gave my child away.'

She finally stopped talking and, seeing that Harriet looked on the point of tears, she continued quickly, 'You will not believe how difficult it was for me to find you. You had told me only your Christian name, Harriet, and that you were visiting your sister who lived in Ballsbridge Street. There were several large houses in that street and I enquired in every one of them if the lady of the house had a sister called "Harriet".'

She gave a brief smile as she said, 'I was losing all hope when, at the very last house, the butler who opened the door to me asked me did I mean Mrs Brook Edgerton whose Christian name was Harriet. I thought it almost certain this was you and I asked to see you, but he told me you did not live there and had long since returned to your own home in England. He then, at my request, gave me your address so that I might write to you.'

'I had no letter!' Harriet said huskily.

'Because I did not write. My husband said I must call and see you in person, or else you might reply to a letter saying you did not wish to see me and I would not then know whether you had kept the baby or if he was in an orphanage.'

With great difficulty, Harriet forced herself to speak. 'Are you trying to tell me, Mrs Bates, that now you are happily married you are able to take care of your child? That you want me to give him back to you?' Her voice broke and immediately the woman rose to her feet and went to put an arm round Harriet's shoulders. 'Since meeting you today, hearing you speak, seeing the look in your eyes when you first recognized me, I do not need to be told you have kept the baby, that you love him very much and . . .' she smiled, '. . . might even fight to keep him had I asked for his return. Please believe me! *You have no need to be afraid.*'

'My husband!' Harriet whispered. 'He believes Charlie is his son. I, too, am guilty of sinning. I lied to him, told him I had had the baby when I was in the convent after being attacked, not that I had had yet another miscarriage. He loves Charlie . . . dotes upon him, as does his grandfather, his nanny, the staff and I . . .' She broke off, too emotional to continue.

'Then please, dear Mrs Edgerton, forget I ever came to see you. Your mind, like mine, can now be at peace. I want nothing from you, not even to see for myself if he is well and happy. I know that he must be so.' She paused and, in a quieter tone, said, 'I do have one request – a request my husband thought I should make lest in future I started worrying about my . . . my cruelty in giving my baby away. That is . . . could you . . . would you consider writing to me once a year? To let me know that all is well with him and all your family? I know it is a great deal to ask and you must refuse if you think it so . . .'

Such was Harriet's huge feeling of relief that she quickly interrupted, saying that of course she would write. She needed only to know Mrs Bates' address. And that if Mrs Bates wished, she would send a photograph of Charlie . . .

At that point, it was her visitor's turn to interrupt. 'I know you must think me cruel and uncaring to have left my baby to someone almost a stranger,' she said, 'but such were my dire circumstances when we met, I could not keep him. I loved all my other children dearly, but . . . well, I could not have left him with you that day had I felt any love for him. Perhaps now, if I saw any likeness to my first husband, I might have some maternal feeling, but I do not wish for such a thing. My four children are thriving and give me great joy, and I also care for my husband's two motherless children. No, I want nothing more than a letter every year – and I confess that this is at my husband's request rather than my own.'

Harriet drew a long, trembling sigh of relief. She reached forward, took the other woman's hands in both of hers and

reassured her again. '*Of course* I will write, every year. You have
my word . . . on his birthday, the date of which I could only
guess. I had to invent one when my sister took me to register
his birth in Dublin.'

'As you pretended, so did I,' Mrs Bates admitted. 'Before my
marriage to Peter, I pretended I had never had that baby. I only
confessed my guilt to my husband later. I would never have
come here but for his persuasion. He is a good man – a very
staunch Catholic, and when I cried out in my dreams he insisted
I should search for you and come here today. I can now reassure
myself a hundred times over, and he can, too, knowing that,
after all, I did the right thing in giving my child to you. It is
very clear to me how much you and, you tell me, your husband
both love him, so from now on I shall only remember him as
yours.'

Harriet's eyes filled with tears. She tried to express her gratitude, and then said, 'May I ask where you left your carriage,
Mrs Bates? I did not see it by the front door.'

Mrs Bates smiled. 'I thought it better to have my groom to
drive me to the tradesman's entrance,' she said. 'I wasn't sure,
you see, if my presence would be an embarrassment to you – as
I now see that it would have been so.'

She walked beside Harriet to the conservatory door, saying,
'I hope the child continues to be a joy to you both and never,
ever a disgrace. Now I shall return by way of the garden door
through which I came – much to your footman's surprise! I assure
you that I do not wish you to accompany me to my coach. One
of the servants can show me the way.'

When her visitor had departed, Harriet remained where she
was for several minutes, thinking how, after her initial shock, a
huge burden had been lifted from her shoulders. She need never
fear that one day Charlie might be taken from her, or that Brook
might somehow discover the truth. She had no doubt whatever
that Mrs Bates meant every word she had said, had meant the
promise she had made to never attempt to see her or Charlie in
the future. The kindly woman had gone to great lengths to find
her, and whilst her visit may have given herself relief, it had
given Harriet even more so.

As she returned to the garden Brook came across the lawn

towards her, Charlie riding on his shoulders. Brook inclined his head and kissed her lightly on the forehead, saying, 'When Charlie and I did not see you in your seat by the beech tree, we wondered where you had disappeared to. Did you have a caller? I thought I heard a carriage disappear down the drive.'

Harriet steadied her voice. 'Yes, it was a lady I met on the ferry on which we both travelled to Ireland,' she said. 'She called because she was passing this way but I am unlikely to see her again. She lives in Ireland, you see, and is returning there.' Brook was barely listening. He lifted Charlie down on to the lawn where he scampered off to see the goldfish in the ornamental lake. Tucking his arm through hers, Brook's face glowed with excitement as they walked towards the house.

'I have decided to buy Charlie a Shetland pony!' he told her. 'Do you know, dearest, he let me lift him on to Shamrock's back and protested quite strongly when I went to lift him off. I think if I hadn't promised to take him for a ride with me tomorrow when I am in the saddle he would have howled his eyes out! I know he's only young, Harriet, but it will be good for him to get accustomed to riding, and I can tell him the pony will be his very own – far better than that rocking horse in the nursery he loves so much!'

Harriet laughed. 'I think you are the one who wants to see him mounted, my darling. When you buy this Shetland pony, I do hope Charlie won't disappoint you by preferring to be up on Shamrock's back.'

Brook grimaced. 'I know, I know! I am far too impatient for him to grow up and be old enough to go hunting with me! I shall have to content myself with you and the stately Felicity at my side.'

Harriet laughed. 'Honestly, Brook,' she chided him, 'I do not think that is quite the way Felicity would wish to be described. "Fearless" would be a better adjective.'

Brook laughed. 'One of these days that good lady is going to take a very nasty fall,' he declared. 'All the same, I have to admit Felicity is a very fine horsewoman, even if she does sometimes shout too loudly as she sails over the gates!'

As Brook now took Harriet's hand in his, it crossed her mind that her friend, Felicity, who she knew to be a great admirer of

Brook, would be very unhappy indeed were she to hear his criticism of her.

TWELVE

December, 1867

B rook had gone up to London to the firm's offices for an important meeting concerning the future expansion to the family's estates in Jamaica. His father had invested in the first rail road currently being built out there. It extended the existing line from the capital Kingston to Spanish Town and Brook felt the time had come to purchase some neighbouring land and start growing a crop of bananas and citrus fruit to supplement the income from the sugar cane.

With the new rail road planned the Jamaican hinterland was opening up and produce could be moved down to the port more easily, but first he needed to try and persuade the cautious company directors of the advisability of this plan. He would stay two or three nights at his club, he had told Harriet, and would take the opportunity to buy Christmas presents for Charlie, his father and her. He would also look for something suitable for Una's large brood as she and her family would be enjoying the festive season on holiday with them at Hunters Hall.

The house was a hive of activity, the bedrooms aired, beds made up and fires lit to ward off any dampness. Cook was busy preparing all the food for such a large number of visitors – Una and Patrick now had seven children – batches of mince pies, four large Christmas puddings, a Christmas fruit cake for the adults and pastry gingerbread men, marzipan angels and an iced chocolate cake for the children.

Although Cook was hot, flustered and spent a lot of time giving endless orders to the overworked kitchen maids, Harriet knew she was actually enjoying the challenge. As a rule, she had only to prepare food for Brook and herself, the staff and an occasional visitor or two. She made clucking noises about all the extra work she had to do but, in reality, she was looking forward to having a house full of children.

'Mrs Kent has a soft spot for the little ones,' Harriet remarked, smiling at Brook. 'In particular Charlie who, when he can escape his nanny, makes his way to the kitchen where she gives him a toffee apple or a cinnamon biscuit or other such treats. The other day, I found her with him on her lap, regaling him with his favourite nursery rhymes, his favourite, needless to say, being *"Diddle-diddle dumpling, my son John, Went to Bed with his trousers on . . ."* She substitutes "Charlie" for "John". Now it sends him into peals of laughter. When she hears Maire searching for him, she hides him behind her chair and swears she hasn't seen him – a useless fib as the seat of his trousers is usually white with flour after sitting on Cook's lap.'

Brook, too, spoiled the little boy. Both Harriet and Maire, his nanny, would have liked to have done so but they tried to be less indulgent – not that he seemed in any way spoilt. He simply took it for granted that everyone loved him as he did them. Another of his special friends was the head groom. If Brook was not there to do so, Harriet would walk Charlie down to the stables on a sunny morning to be led round the field on the back of the old farm horse.

His other great friend was his doting grandfather, Sir Walter. The elderly man had always professed in the past that children should be 'seen and not heard', yet when Brook or Harriet visited with the boy he gave far more of his attention to Charlie than he did to them.

On this particular cold but sunny December day, Harriet drove over in the governess cart with Charlie and his nanny to visit Sir Walter. They found him once more laid up with gout, his leg heavily bandaged and propped up on a footstool. His favourite armchair was drawn up close to a vast log fire burning cheerfully in the drawing room. He had given strict orders that he was not at home to visitors, but when the footman enquired if he would see Harriet and Charlie, he told the servant not to be "so damned silly!" That of course he was at home to his daughter-in-law and grandson. As the footman showed them in, a look of delight spread over the old man's bewhiskered face. 'Come in! Come in, my dears!' he said. 'Harriet, sit here by the fire, and you, you rascal, you can sit on my lap *provided* you don't jolt my leg!'

'Poor Grandfather!' Charlie said as he climbed carefully on to Sir Walter's lap. He gazed, frowning, at the bandaged leg and shook his head doubtfully. 'Shall I ask Mama to kiss it better?' he asked.

Sir Walter shook his head and chuckled. 'You've grown as tall as a Christmas tree since I saw you two weeks ago, young man!' he said.

The small boy frowned and then replied thoughtfully, 'I don't think I am nearly as tall as our Christmas tree, Grandfather. Ours has candles on it and an angel on the top and I think it's much bigger than me.'

Sir Walter winked at Harriet. 'Maybe you're right, young man. Now tell me what Santa Claus is going to bring you on Christmas Eve – *if* you are a good boy, that is, and *if* he hasn't eaten too many mince pies and is so fat he can't get down the chimney.'

His own growth forgotten, Charlie launched excitedly into details. He was hoping for a pony his father had promised him, and some soldiers, and did his grandfather know his Aunt Felicity had sort of promised she might give him a clockwork train that would go around all by itself and even pull two carriages.

Sir Walter looked questioningly at Harriet, who nodded. 'Had you forgotten the Dennings' involvement with the railways, Sir Walter? Paul Denning has managed to acquire a model of a miniature engine and carriages which was made for his company by a German toy manufacturing firm.'

'Papa has gone to London in a real train,' Charlie prattled on. 'He has promised to take Mama and me to London to see a pantomime. Have you ever seen a pantomime, Grandfather?'

'My parents took me every Christmas when I was a boy!' Sir Walter informed him. 'Now down you get and fetch the playing cards from the drawer by the window. You can try and build a card house the way I showed you last time you were here.'

As soon as Charlie had removed himself, Sir Walter turned back to Harriet. 'Never had much time for children – not even my own: left them to their nannies and m'wife!' he said. 'Always preferred animals – well, horses and dogs. Can't be doing with cats!' He chuckled. 'Prefer 'em to a lot of people I know!'

Aware suddenly that he was rambling, he said to Harriet, 'Ring the bell rope, m'dear, and I'll ask Jennings to bring up some tea and maybe Cook can find one of those coconut thingamajigs for young Charlie. Good little chap! Very fond of him . . . Charlie, not Jennings!' he chuckled. 'You and Brook must be very pleased with yourselves. Had to wait a long while for him, though, didn't you? Well, you've more than made up for it: this one's worth a dozen others. Very clever little chap. Don't you go spoiling him, m'dear!'

Harriet laughed. 'It is not I who is likely to spoil him but you, Sir Walter. I wager you couldn't bring yourself to deny him anything he asked for. Brook told me about the Shetland pony he'd planned to give him but that you insisted upon doing so as you wished to let Charlie know it was your present, not his father's!'

Sir Walter harrumphed, 'Dare say his father spoils him quite often enough.' He changed the subject. 'If I can't get rid of this confounded gout by Christmas, I won't be able to get over to you on Christmas Day for lunch. Haven't met that sister of yours and her husband since your wedding; I seem to remember the husband was quite a decent sort of fellow for an Irishman!'

'Really, Sir Walter!' Harriet reproached him with a smile. 'I do declare there isn't another country in the whole world you think can match up to ours.'

'And nor can they!' Sir Walter replied, shifting his leg an inch or two with a groan. 'We are an empire, for goodness' sake! The rest of the world looks up to us, copies our way of life!'

Harriet sighed. 'Well, we have actually made the Irish part of the British Empire, haven't we? Brook told me the other day that Queen Victoria rules a quarter of all the countries in the world.'

Sir Walter decided to ignore Harriet's remark. 'What the devil's Jennings doing with our tea?' he said. 'Ring the bell again, m'dear!'

But before Harriet could do so, the parlourmaid came in with the refreshments and Charlie quickly left his playing cards and came hurrying over to his grandfather.

'Cat's tongues,' he exclaimed excitedly. 'Did you order them 'specially for me, Grandfather?'

Sir Walter shook his head. ''Course not, old chap! Had them sent down from Fortnum's especially for m'self.'

Charlie's eyes widened. 'But last time I came to tea with you, Grandfather, you said you didn't like them.'

'Did I now? Must have forgotten! Well, you'd better eat them all or they'll be wasted, won't they? A lot of poor children in the world would give their eyes for one of those.'

Charlie paused in the process of helping himself. 'I can't eat ALL of them, Grandfather. Can you send some to the poor children? Why are they so poor they have to give their eyes?'

'Enough!' Harriet broke in. 'You will tire your grandfather out with your questions. Ask Papa to explain such things to you when he gets home. That's where we will be going as soon as we have finished our tea. It will be dark in little over an hour and I'd prefer to be home by daylight.'

'Quite right, too!' said Sir Walter. 'Will you be so good as to pass me that tobacco box on the sideboard, m'dear?'

Harriet put down her teacup and went to fetch the pretty brass eighteen-inch-high box, and brought it over to Sir Walter. She already knew that it was not tobacco he kept in it – he only smoked cigars imported from Havana. She sighed as she handed the box to him.

'Please!' she said as he beckoned Charlie to come closer. 'Not too much!'

She knew perfectly well from this ritual what was about to happen – it always did when it was time to leave. Sir Walter would take a silver threepenny piece out of the box and conceal it in one of his hands. Holding out both closed fists to the small boy, he'd say, 'Well, which one has the money in it? Find the right one and it's yours.'

Sometimes Charlie did find the right one by chance. When he failed to do so, Sir Walter would say, 'Best guess out of three: so two more guesses, m'boy.' This time, the silver coin was not quite completely concealed, and the child could spy it.

'As you are now on your way to becoming a rich man,' Sir Walter remarked, 'you will soon be able to buy a palace to live in just like our Queen Victoria.'

Not, as he'd said on an earlier occasion to Brook, that Her Majesty ever lived in Buckingham Palace these days. She seemed to have made up her mind to spend the rest of her life mourning the death of Albert, her beloved Prince Consort, down in Osborne House on the Isle of Wight. 'Isn't quite the right thing to be doing.' He'd echoed the thoughts of a great many other people. She had a duty to her subjects and it would be far better for the country if she made an effort and got on with life . . . did her duty to those who looked up to her for guidance.

Harriet bent and kissed Sir Walter's cheek, and Charlie would have climbed back on to his lap to say his thank-you's and goodbye had not his grandfather reminded him quickly about his painful foot.

'You will come to see us on Christmas Day, won't you, Grandfather? Mama says all my cousins will be there so we can play lots of games.'

'I'll do my best!' Sir Walter told him, and as he watched the two of them leave the room, he gave a long sigh followed by another groan as he moved his bad leg by mistake. His glance caught the picture of his wife with her beloved King Charles spaniel on her lap which was hanging on the wall facing him. The portrait had been painted by the artist Edwin Landseer, who had come principally to paint Sir Walter's favourite Labrador. It struck him suddenly that Brook's youngster had just the same eye colouring and pretty brown curls. The boy was more like his grandmother than Brook or Harriet, he thought – bloodline skipping a generation the way it often does with dogs and horses.

The thought reminded him that he'd not seen, since luncheon, his new Labrador, Napier, named after the admiral, Sir Charles, who he happened to admire. One of the footmen was to have taken the dog for a walk. The poor chap was missing his days out shooting, Sir Walter thought, once more cursing his 'confounded gout'.

He would have a whiskey and soda, he decided, despite the doctor's stupid orders not to drink alcohol. Young Harriet and the child's visit had tired him. Pretty girl! He could see why Brook had married her! He himself preferred females a bit more meretricious, like that neighbour of theirs, Mrs Felicity Whatsit! Made one wish that one was a good deal younger . . . able to enjoy a bit of a fling with her. He'd gathered there wasn't much class there, but a great deal of money. She'd make a useful wife for someone. Brook could have done with a rich wife – not that he ever thought badly of Brook's choice. Harriet was a sweet girl – a good mother, too, even if she wasn't much of a breeder. But he wasn't going to complain about that – not now she and Brook had produced the grandson he doted on.

The parlourmaid interrupted his reverie, and he told her she could remove the tea things and, gout be damned, she must tell Jennings to hurry up and bring him a whiskey and soda.

The old man had fallen asleep before the butler returned with his drink, and with a fond look at his master, the servant put the decanter down on the table by his chair and left him to his dreams.

Charlie chattered all the way home, and Harriet was happy to leave him to Maire's loving care as they went indoors. Fletcher was in the hall waiting for them, as was Charlie's nanny, who took him upstairs to have his hot milk and biscuits before putting him to bed. Fletcher bid Harriet a good evening and took her cloak, bonnet and gloves, before telling her that she had a visitor who was downstairs in the kitchen awaiting her return.

'Who is it, Fletcher?' Harriet broke in, a cold fear invading her body as it crossed her mind that, despite her promises, Mrs Bates had come uninvited yet again.

Seeing the dubious expression on his mistress's face, Fletcher said quickly, 'It is someone I think you will be very pleased to see, madam. She has asked me not to tell you her name as she wishes to surprise you. Have I your permission to tell her you will see her in the morning room?'

Still uneasy, Harriet nevertheless made her way to the empty room. Felicity would not be in the kitchen of all places, she thought, but no one else came to mind who would pay her a call unexpectedly at this time of the evening and refuse to give her name to Fletcher. Had one of her sisters arrived unexpectedly from their distant homes wanting to surprise her? But they would surely have written to announce their intentions.

Her thoughts came to an abrupt halt as the door opened and her 'visitor' came into the room. One glance was enough to set her heart thundering in her chest. Tears of joy sprang to her eyes as she held out her arms . . . *It was Bessie!* Bessie, who she had feared never to see again – looking a little older, perhaps, but rosy-cheeked and nicely dressed.

Smiling happily, Bessie clasped Harriet's hands. 'I came as soon as I could, Miss Harriet. I wanted to write but they wouldn't let me. I was their prisoner, you see . . .'

She broke off as Harriet pulled her down beside her on the sofa. Harriet felt as if she must be dreaming. It was two long years since she had last seen her dear, dear maid; two years during which she had feared she might be dead. Now Bessie was here . . . here in Hunters Hall beside her! Harriet was too full of emotion to speak.

Bessie continued to hold her hands. 'I understand what you's feeling, Miss Harriet!' she said gently. 'I only discovered that *you* were alive and well when I reached home yesterday and Ma told me. It was quite late and I was that tired after my journey, I thought it best to wait until today to travel up here to the hall to see you. I got here an hour since but you'd left to go to Sir Walter's house. I would have let you know I wasn't dead after we were attacked that night, but I couldn't, me being in another country and helpless.'

Harriet was bewildered. 'Bessie, dear! Start at the beginning,' she begged. 'What happened to you that terrible night in Liverpool?'

Bessie drew a deep breath and said, 'I was took to a real hovel of a place where the men what had attacked us was living. They locked me in one of the rooms, and I could hear them next door in what turned out to be a filthy kitchen. They were discussing whether they should keep me for their own pleasuring or . . .'

She broke off, shuddering. Harriet caught her breath realizing that Bessie – her faithful Bessie – had been alone and unable to defend herself.

Seeing the look of horror on Harriet's face, Bessie said quickly, 'After a bit, they decided not to despoil me: their greed for money was more important to them than I was. They were in the pay of an oriental gentleman, you see, who paid them to get hold of young females. He didn't want them for his pleasuring, but because he could get very large sums of money for them in his own country and, if the girls had not been despoiled, his reward would be even greater, as would the pay of them who found us.'

Harriet's face was a mask of horror as Bessie paused for breath before continuing her story.

'So's them two rogues realized there'd be far more money for them if they left me alone. They took me to the oriental gentleman's house and he kept me prisoner there for several weeks. He wasn't unkind to me – fed me and bought new expensive clothing for me to wear and a clean bed to sleep in. I had everything I asked for except to be allowed to go free. Nor would he let me write to you as I hoped by then you'd be safe back at Hunters Hall. I wanted to say I wasn't dead.'

She paused momentarily for breath and then continued, 'A foreign woman who couldn't speak no English watched me all the time like a hawk so as I couldn't escape through a window or else; but otherwise she waited on me as if I was a lady like yourself, Miss Harriet.'

'Oh, Bessie, I cannot believe this!' Harriet whispered. 'You must have been so frightened!'

Bessie nodded. 'Yes, I was, but mostly I was worried for you, Miss Harriet. I'd seen you lying on the ground with your eyes shut, and I didn't know whether you was alive or dead. One of the men what attacked us had said how you was bleeding ever so much – not just from that gash on your head, but down your legs. Then, three days later, the oriental man who had bought me from the robbers came to see me, and when I begged him to tell me if he knew what had happened to you, he said a constable had taken you to a convent for the nuns to look after you as the hospitals were full, and that you was having a miscarriage.'

There were tears in her eyes as she added: 'If I'd knowed you was carrying, Miss Harriet, I'd never have let you travel to Ireland to see your sister, not after all them other mishaps.'

'Don't cry, Bessie dear!' Harriet broke in. 'I kept such suspicions as I had from you; I even pretended to myself that nothing unusual was happening as I so wanted to go to Una's. I wouldn't allow any doubts. I hated being in my house without my husband,

and when he wrote and said how much longer it was going to be before he came home, well . . .'

Bessie put her arms round Harriet and rocked her, the way she had last done when they were young girls. Harriet had been bitten by one of the ferrets and had to be stitched by the doctor whilst she lay on the kitchen table.

Afraid now that Bessie was going to ask her more about her miscarriage, Harriet turned the conversation quickly back to Bessie's shocking adventure. Listening as Bessie talked, she almost wished she need not learn the terrible facts.

Her captor, Bessie now told Harriet, had taken her in a boat from Liverpool to his own country; Bessie was not sure whether it was China or Japan. There she had been put in a strange house with a number of other young women, and forced to allow strange men to do what she called 'intimate things' to them – things only a husband should do with his wife, she explained.

Harriet's dismay intensified as Bessie continued her story. One of the girls who befriended her, she said, who could speak a very little English, explained that the men who owned them were paid very big sums of money by other men wanting to do as they wished with pretty white girls like themselves. They did not receive any of this money, she said, but were kept in luxury as if they were ladies in their own countries: given beautiful clothes to wear, good food, comfortable single rooms, and even a maid to clean and wait on them.

Bessie drew a long, trembling sigh. 'I was never beaten nor hurt,' she said. 'I wanted for only two things – my freedom and that I might never again be obliged to have strange men doing dreadful things to me.'

Harriet was horrified. She had often in her thoughts imagined Bessie being beaten, starved and ill-treated, but never that she would have been spirited to the Far East and made to become a 'fille de joie' – a profession Felicity had once explained to her when she'd queried a comment she had heard one woman make to another at a garden party.

'I was fortunate, Miss Harriet!' Bessie was saying as if to ameliorate Harriet's distress. 'One of the men who came regularly to see me was a much-travelled government official who spoke good English. He took pity on me when he heard my story and that I was there against my will. He was a very rich man, and as I was no longer untainted, he was able to pay the price my owner demanded for my release.'

She paused briefly for breath and before Harriet could comment, she said in the same level tone of voice as before, 'He brought me back to England on the first occasion his business required him to make the journey. He was a good man, Miss Harriet! He wanted me to stay with him when we reached Liverpool, but when I told him all I wanted was to be allowed to go home he gave me sufficient money to do so.'

Harriet was having difficulty in believing this extraordinary adventure of Bessie's, whose appearance gave no inkling of the ordeal she had suffered so bravely – none of which would have occurred but for her own selfish wish to get away from Hunters Hall for a holiday with her sister.

She put her arms round Bessie and hugged her. 'I am so very, very glad you are safely home!' she whispered. 'I have missed you so much, Bessie, not only as my maid but as a friend.'

'You will have had to replace me, I know,' Bessie said sadly, 'but my ma said I was to tell you that you will be welcome any time in our house, so we shall still see each other if you want. It's perhaps as well I won't be living here – Hastings, you see. I can never marry him now, and I couldn't stand for him to know that other men have . . . despoiled me. I realized that as soon as I knew I would be coming home.'

'Oh, Bessie!' Harriet whispered sadly, 'surely Hastings would understand that none of this was your fault, that . . .'

'No, Miss Harriet, I couldn't tell him. I wouldn't want him to think badly about me even if he didn't blame me. Any road, I dare say as how he may have found himself another girl, thinking I was killed or summat. No, it's to be a secret 'tween you and me, Miss Harriet. I dursn't even tell my family.'

A secret! The word hit Harriet with as much force as if it had been a flash of lightening. *She* was the one with a secret! She was the one who dared not tell a single soul ever that Charlie was not Brook's child. Not even Bessie must know.

No matter how devoted she and Bessie were to one another, not even to her trusted servant dare she tell the truth.

For some reason, Harriet thought unhappily, she was finding it harder to voice the lie to Bessie than it had been for her to allow Brook to assume Charlie was his child. Barely above a whisper, she said shakily, 'Bessie, I have news to tell you: unlike yours, it is good news which will surprise you. That night in Liverpool I wasn't having a miscarriage as the policeman who found me thought – I was having a child, a little boy. He is upstairs now in the nursery, and his name is Charlie . . .'

Close to tears, she broke off, unmanned by Bessie's look of astonishment and joy, and her own mixed feelings of guilt and relief.

THIRTEEN

1868

As was customary, Brook and Harriet repaired to the morning room, after they had finished their breakfast, to discuss the plans for the day.

'Felicity is calling for me at ten o'clock,' Harriet said. 'She is taking me to her dressmaker in Leicester to have a new gown made for Viscount and Lady Harrogate's ball.'

Brook smiled. 'I could hardly have forgotten, my love, with you and Felicity talking of nothing else every time she lunches with us or we go to Melton Court to dine with her and Paul.'

Harriet laughed. 'I know you enjoy their company as much as I do, Brook.'

Brook smiled. 'We are lucky to have such good neighbours, are we not? Denning is a clever chap – takes after his father, I suppose; he seems to be managing their finances just as successfully. He has given me some excellent tips which have done well for me on the Stock Exchange.'

'I admire the way he cares for Felicity,' Harriet said. Then, adding with a smile: 'Even if he wasn't so kind, you would like him, dearest, simply because he is the best shot you have encountered or so you told me!'

They both laughed, and then Harriet continued, 'Felicity told me yesterday that her second footman, Robert, asked her permission to court Maire. Now don't laugh, Brook: I understand the two of them have got to know one another quite well when Maire comes with me to visit Felicity.'

Brook laughed once more.

'It isn't funny, dearest,' Harriet protested. 'Maire is quite taken with him. Felicity has told her she would employ her as a maid if I was agreeable to let her go.'

Brook frowned. 'Are you agreeable to lose the nanny Charlie is so fond of?'

'It is the perfect solution!' Harriet answered him. 'As now Bessie is back, and if I can persuade her to return, I would dearly love to employ her again. I did not feel it fair to dismiss Maire, who could not have been a more satisfactory nanny. Charlie does love her, but Bessie has immense experience with young children, and I would have no anxieties were she to become Charlie's nanny in Maire's place. I thought it hugely kind of Felicity to suggest this solution.'

Brook sighed. 'Well, I'm sure you know what you are doing,' he said. 'Now, remind me, my love, when exactly in August is this ball taking place? Actually, I'm surprised the Harrogates are holding it here in the country rather than in London. I am also surprised that they have invited Denning and his sister, conscious of their rank as they are. Still, money seems to be quite an entrée into society these days, beside which I happen to know Denning made a great many titled friends at Oxford.'

He drew a long sigh. 'Frankly, Harriet, I've come to the conclusion that society pays far too much attention to breeding. Personally, I don't see how anybody could find fault with Paul Denning, or indeed our jolly widow, Mrs Felicity Goodall! If one did not know of their background, one would have no idea that they were not our social equals.'

Harriet smiled as she reminded him that only the other day he had remarked that Felicity's laugh was sometimes a little too loud for comfort. 'I agree they are a very likeable couple,' she

said, 'and as you know, Felicity and I have become the very best
of friends. She is one of the kindest, most thoughtful people I
know.'

Pretending concern, Brook frowned. 'Are you implying that I
am not always kind or thoughtful?'

Seeing the twinkle in his eyes, Harriet laughed. 'Indeed, you
are not!' she exclaimed. 'You have not kissed me since we awoke
this morning.'

Getting swiftly to his feet, Brook chuckled as, ignoring the
footman, he crossed the room and said, 'Only one kiss, my love,
and then regrettably I shall have to leave you. Hollingsworth has
asked me to look at the new coups and runs he has made for the
pheasant chicks he is rearing for the shoot. He says we shall
have an excellent year's sport. What with the ducks on the lake
being so prolific this early in the year, and the ducklings likely
to survive now he has got rid of the pike which took most of
them last year.'

As they walked arm in arm from the room, Harriet said, 'I do
hate the thought that the birds have to be killed, Brook. I know
there would be insufficient sport for you all were you not to raise
the chicks but . . .'

Brook sighed before he interrupted her, saying, 'Can't change
our national sporting heritage, Harriet, and when Charlie is older
I'll be teaching him how to shoot. Won't do to have him soft-
hearted. I think his grandfather has already bought him a 410; I
had to remind him Charlie was still only two-and-a-half years
old!'

'Your father spoils him quite dreadfully,' Harriet replied,
laughing.

Brook nodded. 'Bound to happen, the boy being the only one.
It will rectify itself when younger ones come along.'

Seeing the expression on Harriet's face, he added quickly, 'I
shouldn't be impatient, I know. Doctor Tremlett assured me that
although you haven't managed it again yet, there is no reason
why you cannot have more babies now you've produced this one.
Meanwhile, I for one am more than content with that rascal of
ours.' He crossed the room to ring the bell for his valet.

A terrible stab of guilt, almost unbearable, pierced Harriet's
heart, and she longed desperately to be able to confess her

deception whilst knowing it was far too late to do so. Instead, she forced a smile to her face as she followed Brook into the hall.

Hastings was waiting to give Brook his linen coat and felt hat. Brook dropped another kiss on Harriet's head and disappeared through the front door with his valet.

Upstairs, Ellen was laying out a chip hat trimmed with a posy of violets for Harriet to wear with the new paletot mantle trimmed with lace that she would be wearing that morning.

When Harriet was dressing with Ellen's help ten minutes later she was delighted to hear the sound of carriage wheels in the driveway below her window and see Felicity alight.

It had now become habitual for Felicity to visit Hunters Hall no less than three times a week. Very occasionally, Harriet wished she and Brook were able to enjoy those afternoons alone together if he was at home, but at other times she thoroughly enjoyed the older woman's company. Brook, too, enjoyed her slightly risqué conversation, and remarked very favourably on the attention she devoted to young Charlie if the little boy was in their company. Children in other households spent most of their time with their nannies in the nursery, but now that Charlie had progressed from babyhood to that of a child with whom he, Brook, could converse, and who wanted nothing more than to be with his papa, Brook loved to have his company.

Whilst such occasions gave Harriet great pleasure, there were others when she was reminded painfully of the little boy's real parentage. He had discovered the pianoforte in the drawing room, and whenever he was permitted, would kneel on the piano stool and try to find the right keys to produce the sound of one of Maire's songs. Fortunately, Brook's mother had been very accomplished at the pianoforte and had always been asked to play or sing at soirées, so Brook never queried the child's unusual talent.

As for Bessie, she was radiant with happiness at being once again a member of Harriet's household. She had resolutely decided to put all thoughts of eventual marriage to Hastings out of her mind. He had been overjoyed to see her, as she was to see him, but she cared too much for him to let him think she was the innocent girl she'd been before her abduction. She was also too proud to confess the real reason why she had changed her mind about renewing their courtship.

Albeit slowly, she was beginning to forget her ordeal. Although she did not see as much of Harriet as before when she had been her maid, Harriet was a frequent visitor to the nursery and they would sit watching Charlie playing quietly by himself, chatting as if they had not lived apart for over two years.

Hastings was both hurt and demoralized by Bessie's unexplained rejection and kept his distance. His very obvious avoidance of her was a matter for gossip amongst the maids as to the possible cause of so serious a quarrel between the two of them.

Easy-going and good-natured as Bessie was, she had no difficulty renewing friendships with the rest of the staff with one exception, Ellen. It was not that she resented the woman who had replaced her as Harriet's lady's maid. She, too, would have felt it unfair to be dismissed simply because the previous maid had suddenly reappeared. No, it was the way Ellen remained apart from all the staff, never rude or impolite, meticulous where her duties were concerned, but never willing to relinquish the wall of reserve she kept tightly around her.

From the way Harriet spoke, Bessie was in no doubt that she still held first place in Harriet's affection. Moreover, she loved her somewhat unconventional position as nanny to Charlie. The little boy had quickly taken to her despite the loss of his much-loved Irish nanny.

Bessie was not alone in her dislike of Ellen. Felicity was becoming more and more irritated with her, accusing her of failing to report quarrels or tiffs between husband and wife and threatening that she would withdraw the money she paid her if she did not come up with some results soon. She refused to believe that any married couple, albeit as devoted as were Brook and Harriet, did not on occasions have misunderstandings.

Felicity's wish to see a rift in the marriage had now become part of her obsession. Her attempt to assuage her desire for Brook by taking a lover only served to do the opposite. Now a regular visitor to her brother in London, she sometimes accompanied him to social gatherings. At one of these, she had met a Frenchman who promptly set about trying to seduce her. Her flamboyant behaviour, and her somewhat masculine liking for alcohol, had led him to believe there was no need to prolong his seduction, which he set about with daily bouquets of flowers and invitations to the theatre, the opera, and dinner. He was encouraged by the fact that Felicity made only half-hearted attempts to keep him at bay.

The resulting affair lasted for two weeks, during which time Felicity strove to assuage the physical desire which tormented her whenever she was in Brook's vicinity. She failed to do so, and when the Frenchman informed her that he must return to Paris, they parted quite amicably. Her short-lived lover left behind him the present of a beautiful and costly pair of drop earrings, studded with emeralds and pearls. The following day, Felicity returned to Melton Court and renewed her tormented visits to Harriet and Brook.

Felicity's jealousy of Harriet was becoming harder and harder to conceal. She even pondered during long, wakeful nights, whether there might be some way she could get rid of Harriet since any hope of instigating a rift between husband and wife was looking even less likely. If anything, she thought bitterly, they had become even more united in their shared devotion to their child. The boy was growing older, and with every day was becoming a greater source of pride to Brook.

Felicity now found her need to be physically close to Brook increasingly hard to control. Even though in one way it distressed her to have such desires thwarted, she could not bring herself to stay away, and Harriet provided her with the excuse she needed to be such a constant visitor to Hunters Hall. She had thus succeeded in maintaining a firm, seemingly harmless friendship with the very person who stood between her and the man she wanted for herself.

However unlikely it began to seem, Felicity never doubted that one day Brook would turn to her and desire her the same way she desired him. She had long ago decided that if she could only entice him to one act of unfaithfulness, she would make it so special he would want her again and again . . .

With this vain hope always in the front of her mind, Felicity dressed for the Harrogates' ball with the greatest care. Her new white-and-blue-striped satin dress was off the shoulder, the tightly fitting bodice revealing the curves of her ample breasts. The hem of the full skirt was embroidered with beautiful blue and black birds, the little black bows covering the folds fastened with tiny sparkling diamonds.

She had had the dress made in London deliberately for this occasion. Because she was certain that it would appeal to Brook, she disregarded the exceptionally huge sum it had cost her. It came with a spray of blue-black bird-of-paradise feathers to adorn her hair. Her maid had now drawn it back from her forehead and pinned it into elaborate curls. The spray of feathers had then been fastened to her head with a diamond clip. Regarding her reflection with satisfaction, Felicity selected from her jewel case a diamond and jet double-stranded necklace which she fastened round her throat. This done, the maid helped her to pull on her elbow-length, white silk gloves. To complete this ornate ensemble, Felicity clipped a silver and pearl bracelet around one wrist.

The maid regarded her mistress with approval. 'You look quite magnificent, madam,' she said. 'If I may say so, I think you will outshine all the other ladies at the ball.'

Felicity felt a momentary thrill of pleasure at the comment. She certainly intended to be the most noticeable female; for Brook to take note of her voluptuous attributes, so cleverly exhibited by her contours, and which had been so much admired by her French lover.

Harriet, she knew, would be adequately but not outstandingly attired. She had stood beside her at the little dressmaker in Leicester and helped her select a pleasing, if commonplace yellow silk moiré for her gown. It was to have looped sides to the billowing skirt and be decorated with rosebuds and rosettes, these to be draped over her underskirt crinoline.

As Felicity had intended, the effect was quite charming but in no respect as striking as her own attire. Her only concern was that Brook might prefer Harriet's less conspicuous appearance to her own slightly daring one.

She now waited impatiently for the hour to leave for the ball. There had been many other lesser gatherings in the county but none were of such illustrious note as that of Lord Harrogate and his wife. Felicity had feared that she and Paul might not be invited, but had been thrilled when the invitation for her and her brother had arrived. Paul, more cynical than she was, had not been surprised.

'All very well for the High and Mighty to look down their noses before Father's money opened all the doors for us. I found it quite amusing,' he added, 'when last month one of the viscount's grandchildren approached me in my London office enquiring if by chance I had suitable employment for him now he had come down from Oxford. Her Ladyship could hardly have left us off her guest list, could she?'

Felicity had been agreeably surprised. Although the growth of the railways could not be termed 'trade', neither was it a gentlemanly profession. To have been excluded would not have particularly bothered her, except that she knew Brook and Harriet had received invitations.

Now she could not wait for the evening to commence, knowing that Brook would have at least one dance with her. She planned to ask the orchestra leader to play the popular new waltz once she knew what number Brook would put his name to on her dance card. She wanted to be close in his arms, not in a quadrille or whirling round the floor in a polka.

It was her intention to slip away during an interval and bribe the orchestra leader to do as she wished, and she was reasonably certain this would not be difficult, having long since learned that there were very few people in employment who were not prepared to fulfil a request if the reward was a generous one.

Harriet, too, was looking forward to the ball, although she had not long since suffered an early miscarriage which had left her with less energy than usual. She'd said nothing of it to Brook, and refused to notify the family doctor. Now, dressing for the occasion, she felt obliged to use rouge on her cheeks, fearing that in her pale yellow ball gown she would look like a faded primrose.

Paul Denning had suggested that as their house passed Hunters Hall on the route to the viscount's mansion, they should stop by and conduct Brook and Harriet to the ball in their coach. Brook had happily agreed to the suggestion, saying that their accompanying servants could also travel together, in their family Brougham.

It was, therefore, a jolly foursome who presented themselves to their host and hostess on the warm, balmy night of the ball, and although Felicity was tense with anticipation, her plan for the evening had been carefully worked out. It held only one element of risk, which depended upon others rather than herself. First and foremost, she had to ensure that Brook marked her dance card after rather than before the supper dance. For her plan to succeed, their dance must be the popular new waltz which would require her to be in Brook's arms. She needed to know exactly when it would be played in order to give her time beforehand to ensure this happened when she wished.

The first dance, a polka, was claimed by her brother, Paul, and Brook partnered Harriet. They had agreed to exchange partners for the next dance, but as the music started Felicity told Brook that she had trouble with one of her shoe straps and would have to leave the room. Before doing so, she invited him to put his name down for a later dance after the interval for supper. Unsuspecting of her motives, Brook readily obliged.

As soon as Brook was safely on the floor with another partner, Felicity went in search of a footman. There was no shortage of attendants and wrapping a piece of paper round a half sovereign, she instructed the servant to give it to the orchestra leader, asking that he play a waltz at the time she now knew she would be dancing with Brook.

Returning to the ballroom, Felicity, although not as youthful as some of the girls, did not lack for partners. She glimpsed Brook from time to time and later, as she had expected, he was joined by Harriet for the supper dance. From where Felicity stood at one end of the long buffet table, she could see him talking to his wife who like himself was holding a glass of champagne. Catching Felicity's eye, he raised his glass to her in a friendly gesture which was enough to start her heart leaping in anticipation.

Dancing was resumed at the end of the lavish banquet, and the floor was once more crowded. The room became very hot and some of the men dabbed at their foreheads with their white silk handkerchiefs as they escorted their partners back to their chairs at the end of the dance. Several couples who had exerted themselves on the dance floor went out through the open French windows on to the terrace.

Felicity declined her partner's suggestion that they should do likewise and quickly returned to her chair, where she waited, her heart beating furiously, for the orchestra to strike up the opening bars of the waltz. After what felt like eternity, Brook approached her from across the room and led her on to the dance floor.

As he put his arms around her, Felicity realized that in all the eight years she had known him she had never been as close to him as she was now, her hand clasped in his, her body moving in unison with his. She could feel his breath on her cheeks, even the warmth of his arm where it rested on her waist. Through the open French windows, she could see a harvest moon lighting up the statues on the stone terrace surrounding the house.

Before the dance ended, her heart leapt at the sight of two couples, clearly overcome by the heat, walk out on to the terrace and she knew her opportunity had come. The dance was nearing an end, and in as casual a tone as she could manage she remarked to Brook that she was feeling a little faint: perhaps they could go out on to the terrace for a few minutes, where the night air would be cooler.

Brook was at once solicitous and, taking her arm, guided her through the throng of other dancers out into the night. For a minute or two Felicity stood breathing quickly and fanning her cheeks with her dance card.

'Can I get you a glass of water, Felicity?' Brook asked anxiously. 'Are you certain you are all right? It was very hot indoors.'

Felicity shook her head. 'I think I am a little less giddy now,' she said in a faint tone of voice. 'Could we walk a little way? I need to test my balance before I return to the dance floor.'

'Why, of course!' Brook replied, linking his arm in hers. 'I, too, am finding the cooler air very welcome.' He led her slowly away from the house and asked, 'Have you ever seen so many stars? I do declare there is nothing more beautiful anywhere in the world than a summer night in England.'

He turned his head to hear Felicity's reply. Her eyes closed and she swayed towards him. He heard her whisper that she was afraid that she was about to faint. Instantly solicitous, he put his arm around her. Keeping her eyes closed, Felicity arched her body backwards so that her white voluptuous breasts spread up from beneath her corsage. Her arms lifted to the back of Brook's neck as if to support herself from falling.

'I am so giddy!' she whispered. 'Please hold me, Brook, I think I am going to fall . . .'

She now fell forward against his chest. Tightening his arms around her, Brook said urgently, 'Let me help you indoors, Felicity. There will be a rest room where you can lie down and recover, and there is certain to be a maid on hand to wipe your forehead with cologne. Do you think you can walk?'

Felicity shook her head, surreptitiously moving her body closer to his as she did so. The sound of the music from the terrace, of laughter, made Brook realize suddenly what a compromising position the two of them must appear to be in. He should take her back to the house without delay, he thought uneasily, conscious as he was of the fact that she was a very alluring, seductive woman. He was reminded suddenly that several of his friends had remarked somewhat crudely on her desirability. Brook always told them to cease their banter: that Felicity was a very close friend of his wife's, and should be shown suitable respect.

Nevertheless, he could now see very clearly why they thought as they did. Not only was Felicity's figure entirely womanly, but her movements, her laughter, her readiness to banter with them – or indeed with him – made her an amusing companion. He, of course, had no wish to bed her. He was still very much in love with his wife and entirely satisfied with their love-making. Holding Felicity now in his arms, seeing her breasts full and enticing in the moonlight, he could not avoid the thought that were he not happily married, and she not a friend of his wife's, he could well be tempted to take what she was offering, albeit, he was certain, unconsciously.

The moment passed, and he gently pushed Felicity away from him. 'I insist upon taking you back indoors where you can receive proper attention,' he said firmly. 'Come now, Felicity, I will put my arm around your waist and support you as we walk.'

Allowing no argument, he did so and, despite the brilliance of the moonlight, he failed to see the look of fury and frustration on Felicity's face.

FOURTEEN

1868

Brook and Harriet rose quickly to their feet as Doctor Tremlett, the family physician, came into the morning room. He was smiling.

'I am very pleased to be able to tell you that you have no need for further worries: young Charles has turned the corner. His temperature is back to normal, and when I left the room his nanny was giving him some chicken broth.'

Tears of relief filled Harriet's eyes and Brook's voice was husky as he thanked the doctor, who had called religiously every day since he had diagnosed Charlie's illness as measles. The childhood disease could quite often be fatal, he had warned Brook, and the utmost care must be taken of him.

'I have instructed Nanny that now he is on the mend he is to be fed small quantities of nourishing foods in increasing amounts as he gets better,' he continued. 'He may also have small quantities of port wine, and I have here a prescription for the action on the skin and kidneys which the apothecary will make up for you, half a teaspoonful of which he is to have every two to three hours.'

'How are the children in the village who were similarly afflicted?' Harriet enquired after thanking him again. 'I was informed that the epidemic of measles amongst the village children was severe.'

The doctor shook his head. 'I'm afraid two of the babies and one little girl have died,' he said. 'The saddler's wife's twins and one of the carpenter's little girls. The rest are recovering, some quicker than others. The speed of their recovery, I believe, has much to do with how well they have been fed in the past. As I dare say you know, Mrs Edgerton, one or two of the villagers cannot always afford the kind of nourishment growing children need.'

When the physician had been duly thanked once more and had departed, Brook looked at the piece of paper in his hand. '"*Acetate of Ammonia*", "*Impecacuanha*", "*Mucilage*" . . . never heard of 'em,' he said. 'Still, if that is what the man recommends, Albert shall go straight down to the village to the apothecary to have it made up.'

'I would like Albert to wait a few minutes,' Harriet said, 'whilst I write instructions for him to go to the baker, greengrocer and dairy. I wish them to make up baskets of food for Albert to give the families of every child who has been similarly afflicted as Charlie. Oh, Brook, how great is the relief of knowing he is on the way to recovery! I dare not think if . . .'

Brook went over to her and put a comforting arm around her shoulders. 'It is better to forget such dreadful fears as we have endured this past week, my darling. Now we must do what we can, as you have so kindly suggested, to help the village children recover as our Charlie is doing. Let it be known in your note to the shopkeepers that I expect them to make their deliveries generous ones as I shall not complain about their subsequent charges.'

He dropped a kiss on top of Harriet's head before adding: 'I will pay a quick visit to the sickroom and then I must go down to the stables to see Jenkins. He sent word this morning that Snowball was lame and he thought he might have laminitis. The veterinarian may be needed . . . and will probably say he must not be ridden. Ah, well, Charlie won't be riding on his precious Shetland pony for a while!' He gave a sudden smile. 'I shall tell him that the veterinarian says Snowball has had the measles too! That will make more sense to him than laminitis!'

Harriet laughed and departed to write her notes for Albert to give the various shopkeepers. Sitting at her escritoire in her bedroom she was suddenly reminded that in two weeks' time it would be Charlie's third birthday, and that as a consequence of his being so ill this past week she had delayed writing the promised letter to Mrs Joan Bates. She would do so as soon as she had completed the orders for Albert, after which she would pay her morning visit to the invalid.

At lunchtime the previous day, Felicity had arrived, unexpectedly bearing a delightful clockwork toy for Charlie – a box which when wound up played the noise of a drum which the little wooden bear on top was beating. She had stayed to have lunch with them, after which she had managed to persuade Brook to ride home with her, knowing as she did that his morning exercise routine had been interrupted by his wish not to miss the doctor's daily visit. As she had expected, Harriet had still been too concerned about Charlie to go with them.

It had been quite dark when Brook returned, having stayed to take tea with Felicity and her brother, Paul, who was on one of his rare visits home.

Brook had laughed off her fears for his safety, pointing out that no harm could have come to him with his groom accompanying him back from Melton Court.

'I suppose I was being silly to fret!' Harriet had admitted as he put his arm round her. 'I start imagining all the perils that might occur, and how I would not be able to bear it if you came to serious harm and I lost you.'

Brook's arm had tightened around her. 'Nothing short of death can ever do that, my darling,' he had said, 'and I can assure you that I was never in danger of that happening this afternoon.' He had stopped to kiss the top of her head, his eyes suddenly alight with laughter. 'Mind you, my darling, I might have been tempted to have a little flirtation with your friend, Felicity. I swear, if Paul had not been present this afternoon, she would have been quite agreeable to a little coddling. I don't think she is aware of it, but sometimes she can be overly flirtatious.'

Harriet had smiled. 'It's just her way, Brook. She told me once that she enjoys men's attentions, which is why she dresses so beguilingly. She calls herself a merry widow, but one thing I am sure of is that she would never in a hundred years try to come between you and me.'

'Nor could she if she did try!' Brook had replied. 'Now, my love, I shall go upstairs to enjoy that hot bath Hastings is supposed to be preparing for me, and I will see you at dinner.'

'And I shall go and change into my most seductive gown to see if I can rival my dear Felicity in your eyes!' Harriet had smiled, confident as she was that she had nothing in the world to fear.

The following morning, when finally they had risen from the
marital bed after a night of love-making, Brook departed to his
study to write some overdue replies to the letters on his desk.
Harriet had decided that she, too, had a seriously overdue letter
to write to Felicity on Charlie's behalf, thanking her for all the
gifts she never failed to bring him each time she visited.

After looking in on Charlie as she'd intended, Harriet thought
once more about her letter to Mrs Bates. It would not be a
difficult one to write, she thought as she went to her escritoire,
as there was so much to tell her: not least, of Charlie's ability
to pick out with one finger the first six notes of the National
Anthem with only an occasional mistake. She might also like
to know of the Shetland pony his doting grandfather had given
him and, most importantly of all, Charlie's complete recovery
from an onset of measles which had laid him very low for
several weeks. The first paragraph of her letter would be the
easiest to write as the words would come so readily from her
heart.

Ten minutes later she was seated at the desk, her pen in hand.

> *It is not possible, dear Mrs Bates, for my husband and
> I to love the little boy you gave me that day in Ireland three
> years ago more than we do. He is the happiest, most affec-
> tionate little boy and . . .*

She broke off as there was a knock on the door and Ellen
came into the room.

'Excuse me, madam,' she said in her customary toneless voice,
'but Cook has sent up to say that young Doris has cut her finger
so badly it might come off, and shall she send Jenkins to ride
down to the village and fetch Doctor Tremlett to come up and
stitch it on?'

Harriet rose quickly to her feet, saying, 'Thank you, Ellen.
I'll go straight downstairs and see Doris. The poor girl! I suppose
she was disobeying orders and using one of Cook's carving knives
again!'

She hurried down the big staircase and through the green baize
door leading to the kitchen. Sixteen-year-old Doris, the kitchen
maid, was sitting with her arm on the scrubbed table top, her

hand bandaged in a blood-soaked teacloth. She was white as a
sheet, and even the implacable cook was looking shocked.

'Her finger's hanging near right off!' she said to Harriet. 'I
don't know how many times I've told that girl not to use the big
knives for cutting up carrots but . . .'

'I know, Cook!' Harriet said firmly. 'This is not your fault.
We shall get Doctor Tremlett up here as quickly as possible. I'll
ask Hastings to hurry down to the stables and tell Jenkins it's
very urgent.'

Keeping her voice as calm as possible, she turned back to
Doris, saying, 'I know it must hurt, Doris, but try to be a brave
girl, which I'm sure you can be. Cook shall make you a nice hot
cup of cocoa while we wait for the doctor.'

'Will he cut my finger right off, ma'am?' Doris enquired in a
shaky voice.

Unwilling to lie, Harriet said gently, 'I don't think that is
likely, Doris, but even if the very worst happened and he did
have to do so, it wouldn't hurt any more than it does now.' She
had a sudden inspiration. Upstairs in one of her wardrobes she
had already packed in tissue paper and tied with red ribbon
Christmas presents for every member of staff. 'If you are very
brave, I shall have a little surprise for you!' she added.

Doris's tears ceased abruptly. Like all the staff, she was devoted
to both Brook and Harriet, and now she knew that if her mistress
was promising a surprise for her, it would surely be something
nice.

Cook made hot cocoa for Doris and Harriet, promising to
return when the doctor arrived, left them sitting round the big
kitchen table in a far calmer state than the one in which she had
found them.

On reaching her bedroom, she sat down once more at her
writing desk and picked up her pen. It was only then that she
saw the top sheet of notepaper on which she had been writing
the letter to Mrs Bates was missing. Had it slipped to the floor?
she wondered, stooping to see if it was there, but she could see
no sign of it.

Her heart pounding, she recalled the start of the letter she had
begun when Ellen had interrupted her with the message concerning
Doris. It told Mrs Bates how much she and Brook loved the little

boy Mrs Bates had given them three years ago. Realizing the
danger if those words were ever to be read by Brook, Harriet
began a desperate search around and behind the desk, but there
was still no sign of it.

White-faced, she rang for Ellen with one last hope – that her
maid had found it, blown on to the floor perhaps and, thinking
it rubbish, had thrown it away. No one else would have been in
the room as the bed had been made and the room tidied by the
housemaid whilst she had been having breakfast.

When Ellen arrived, her thin, expressionless face became one
of surprise as she heard Harriet's question. 'I'm sorry, madam,'
she said in her usual toneless voice, 'but I followed you out of
the room when you left to go downstairs to see about Doris.
Would you like me to ask if one of the maids . . .'

'No, no, it's not important!' Harriet interrupted quickly.
Although her heart was beating violently, she knew she must not
reveal her anxiety. The letter must be somewhere in the room,
and Ellen must not find it before she did, lest the woman's curiosity was aroused by her concern, and prompted her to read it.

Dismissing her, Harriet sat down heavily on the side of her
bed, her thoughts in turmoil. Why, she asked herself, should she
suddenly suspect that Ellen had been lying? Was it simply because
she knew for a fact that no one else would have gone into her
room in the brief half hour she had been absent? Or was it
because she was prejudiced by dislike of the woman?

Ever since Ellen had replaced Bessie as her personal maid,
Harriet had waged an ongoing battle with herself not to look for
ways to find fault with her. So far she had found it almost impossible to do so as Ellen was by far the most efficient servant she
had ever employed.

Unsure how next to proceed, Harriet considered the possibility
that a housemaid could have come to the room whilst she had
been downstairs, to refill the water jug, perhaps, or tend to the
fire which was kept burning these cold December days. A maid
might have thrown away what she'd assumed was a piece of
waste paper laying on the floor. Whenever she had closed the
door on her way downstairs, it caused a small draught which in
this instance could have wafted the letter off the blotter.

Perhaps it would be best to say nothing to anyone, Harriet

decided. Were a search to be made for it by anyone else but herself, the contents could be read. *How could she have been so careless as to leave it lying uncovered on her blotter?* She could but hope now – must hope – that it had already been found and thrown away as rubbish. Later today she must find time to write the letter again. For the time being she could not bring herself to do so.

Upstairs in her attic room, Ellen sat on the side of the bed reading and rereading the extraordinary but fascinating words – words that she had no doubt at all would compensate the scheming Mistress Goodall for the not inconsiderable amounts she had paid out to her, Ellen, since the start of her employment.

She gazed once more at the piece of paper she was holding.

'. . . *the little boy you gave me . . .*'

Master Charlie, the baby her mistress had brought back from her sister's house in Ireland – a baby she, Ellen, had been told by Cook was most particularly and surprisingly welcome after the mistress's many miscarriages. In the years since the start of her employment, Ellen had seen for herself how doted upon by both parents the boy was. '*My son,*' the master boasted whenever he had the chance, and his nanny, Cook and the other servants all sang his praises at meal times.

Quite suddenly, she recalled an occasion when she was finishing Harriet's evening toilette and her husband had come into the room. He'd fastened a new, beautiful emerald necklace round his wife's throat. After she had thanked him, he'd sat down on the chaise longue, watching her in her mirror whilst she, Ellen, had been searching for a pair of matching emerald ear drops. He'd then related his discovery of his son's musical ability. 'When I went up to wish Charlie goodnight,' he'd said to Harriet, 'he was in his little bed singing one of his nursery rhymes in a voice as pure as a choir boy's. He must have inherited that ability from you as I can't sing a note in tune.'

'Not in my family!' her mistress had replied. Hardly surprising, Ellen now thought with an uncustomary flash of excitement: not if young master Charlie *was not their child.*

Ellen drew a deep breath. This must be one of the astonishing facts which the devious Mrs Goodall wished her to unearth. The woman had never given a reason for paying her, Ellen, to spy upon the couple, although it had very quickly become apparent that she was hoping to break the marriage bond between the two and take Harriet's place as the master's wife. It had been quite a while now since Ellen had realized that Mrs Goodall's ever-more frequent visits to the house and her supposed friendship with Harriet were no more than a ruse to be in her husband's company.

Ellen's heart missed a beat as she considered the consequences were the master not to have known about the child's real parentage. She was holding the proof he was not here in her hand. She could now give her paymaster the very weapon she needed to break the marriage apart.

Ellen's next thought was that she must not simply hand the half-written letter over to Felicity. If she was to realize her dreams for her sister's future well-being, she needed a great deal more money than she was now receiving. This piece of notepaper would enable her to demand a very large sum of money indeed.

The lovesick woman, Mrs Goodall, could afford it, Ellen told herself, her heart beating furiously. She was the richest person Ellen had ever encountered. She herself had no experience of, or wished to have, human passions: their obsessive desires.

In her previous employment, Ellen had watched a happily married gentleman become helplessly enslaved by a chorus girl who bartered her favours for money. His wife had found out, taken him to the divorce court, and refused to allow him any further access to her very substantial dowry. The man was ruined, financially and socially, while his wife departed to America and quickly found another husband. She would have taken Ellen with her had she been willing to leave her invalid sister.

She may not have experienced obsession, Ellen now told herself, but she recognized it when she encountered it. Such thoughts were now momentarily diverted by a belated feeling of astonishment. It was difficult to believe that her God-fearing mistress had contrived such a far-reaching deception and, until now, done so successfully. She, Ellen, was in no doubt whatever that the master believed the child to be his.

She drew a deep breath. The longer she lived, she thought, the more surprised she became by the ways of the gentry. They claimed to stand for honesty, truth, fairness and all the other virtues, but when it suited them they did as they pleased regardless.

This evening, she now recalled, Mrs Goodall was coming to dinner with her brother, and she would almost certainly have an opportunity to inform her that at long last she had evidence which Her Ladyship could use very successfully to disrupt the relationship between husband and wife.

It was with difficulty she contained her impatience until Mr Denning and his sister arrived for dinner and Felicity came upstairs to leave her cloak in Harriet's dressing room.

'Well, why that strange look, Ellen?' Felicity greeted her sharply as Ellen closed the dressing room door behind her. 'Dare I hope you finally have something to relate to me?'

Her tone of voice was edging on sarcastic, but on this occasion Ellen was not disturbed by it. Any moment now, she told herself, madam would be begging – actually begging – because she, Ellen, had no intention of handing over the half-written letter until she had what she wanted – a promissory note for a large enough sum of money to enable her to ensure she could begin a new life with her sister.

'Yes, madam, I do!' she said quietly. 'I discovered a half-written letter from the mistress to a Mrs Bates . . .' She paused.

Frowning, Felicity said urgently, 'Well, go on! What about this Mrs Bates? I can't be away too long or your mistress will be up to see if all is not well with me!'

'I will come straight to the point,' Ellen replied. 'In the letter, madam thanks a Mrs Bates for giving her her baby. She refers to her doing so in Ireland three years ago; this was when the master was abroad and madam went to see her sister in Ireland. I wasn't employed here then but Bessie, who was her maid before me, told me no one knew madam was about to have a baby when she'd left here to go to her sister.'

Felicity was so overwhelmed by the importance of what Ellen was saying that she had not interrupted. Brook adored that child – spoke of him endlessly, proudly as *his son*. The letter seemed to prove he was not so, and that his beloved wife had deceived him: foisted another woman's child on him . . .

She stopped thinking and demanded fiercely, 'Give me the letter! Now! At once!'

'I'm afraid I do not have it on me, madam!' Ellen replied smoothly. 'I thought it best to keep it in my bedroom where it would not be found until I saw you.'

It struck Felicity suddenly that she had already been upstairs over-long and she should not remain talking to Ellen much longer. At the same time, she would not bring herself to leave without seeing the letter. She needed proof – proof that Ellen's extraordinary revelations were true.

'Then go and get the letter!' she ordered sharply. 'I may not have another opportunity this evening to come up here again without your mistress, so be quick about it!'

Ellen remained where she was.

'Did you hear me, woman?' Felicity said angrily. 'Don't just stand there! Go and fetch it at once.'

'Of course I will get the letter for you to see, madam,' Ellen said in a level tone, 'but I have had all day to think about it, and as I am the only person who could have gained possession of the letter, I realized that as a consequence of its discovery, I would almost certainly be dismissed and . . .'

'I'll give you an excellent reference,' Felicity interrupted. 'Get you a new job so . . .'

It was Ellen's turn to interrupt. 'Excuse me, madam,' she said quietly, but firmly, 'I do not want a new job. I wish to take my invalid sister down to live by the bracing air of the seaside. I shall need money to buy a bungalow; to remove her there and furnish it in a manner she – and indeed, I – would like. I have been able to save some of the money you have paid me to be your watchdog ever since you employed me but it is not nearly enough, so . . .'

'So you want more, is that it?' Felicity hissed, aware now that she was being held to ransom. 'Well, you will get it, my good woman – but only after I am assured the contents are as you say.' She paused to regain her breath before adding: 'and there is a further stipulation – *you* are going to be the one to show this incriminating letter to your master. I do not wish to be involved at all. If . . . and I do mean *if*, Ellen, it has the result I wish to achieve, I promise I will give you enough money to do as you wish without equivocation.'

Ellen's pale blue eyes narrowed, and her mouth tightened in

a thin line. Her voice now little above a whisper, she said, 'I do not wish to cause offence, madam, but before I carry out your wishes I need some kind of guarantee that . . . that you will fulfil your promise.'

Realizing that the woman doubted her honesty, Felicity's face flushed an angry red, but she managed to hold her tongue. If this letter really did prove that Charlie was not Brook's son, it would be no great loss to her if she now had to pay out a few hundred pounds for the evidence. In fact, she was willing to pay a very great deal more if it broke up the marriage, and as a consequence Brook turned his attentions to her . . . and she would make sure that he did.

Her heart pounding, she took a deep breath and said, 'When I come upstairs later for my cloak, I will leave this . . .' She pointed to the diamond and sapphire necklace at her throat. 'It is very old, and very valuable. It was given to me when my late husband was being honoured by Tzar Nicholas for services he had rendered him in Moscow. If I failed to give you the reward I promised, you would get a very large sum of money indeed for it. However, I have every intention of paying you the money you require if the letter is as incriminating as you say. When I do so, you will return the necklace to me, saying that you discovered it lying under this chair where I am now sitting. There will be trust, therefore, on both our sides.'

Her mind had been working furiously and she had reached the conclusion that Ellen would not have dared to blackmail her had the letter not been as she'd stated.

She rose to her feet, picked up her pretty embroidered purse from the dressing table, and in as level a tone of voice as she could achieve, said, 'I shall go downstairs now so there is no need for you to get the letter. Tomorrow I will ride over here to report the supposed loss of my necklace. You are to present the letter after breakfast to your master, so by the time I arrive, Ellen, I will expect to discover what result it has achieved. Should the letter not be as incriminating as you say, you will not only receive no money but I will ensure you are imprisoned for the theft of my necklace. Is that understood?'

When Ellen nodded, it was with the greatest difficulty that Felicity was able to control her excitement. Throughout the rest of the evening her thoughts alternated between moments of hope that her patience was at last being rewarded, and doubt as to whether Ellen had read the letter correctly. Harriet had been thanking a Mrs Bates for giving her her baby. Even if Brook were to forgive Harriet for such a mammoth deception, he would know that there was not, after all, a likelihood that she would eventually give birth to his child. His deep attachment to Charlie proved how important it was for him to have a son.

That evening, sitting by the fire in the drawing room with Harriet, Brook and her brother, Felicity attempted to join in the discussion about the coming Christmas festivities, but all she could think about was the letter and, despite what she had decided earlier, the need to read its contents herself so she could be certain that the possibility really did exist for her to achieve her heart's desire. No, not just her heart, Felicity thought unashamedly, but her body's desire. She could no longer look at Brook for more than the briefest time, lest he read the desperate longing in her eyes. All too easily, her hands would tremble and her breath catch in her throat when he carried out such courtesies as lifting her down from the saddle of her horse or helping her up into her coach. She covered such moments of ungovernable desire with a loud laugh or meaningless chatter, but being close to Brook now was both a heaven and hell.

Harriet looked anxiously at her friend. 'Are you not feeling very well, dearest?' she asked solicitously. 'I'm quite worried about you. It is unlike you to be so quiet.'

'I was feeling a little faint,' Felicity improvised quickly, 'but I am feeling quite better now.'

Somehow, she thought, she must contain her euphoria until the following morning, by which time Ellen would have shown Brook the letter that she was praying would bring about Harriet's downfall.

FIFTEEN

1868

The following morning, as soon as Ellen was certain that Harriet had gone upstairs to the nursery, she went quickly down to Brook's study and knocked on the door. When he called to her to go in, she did so, closing the door behind her. Despite her determination to do what she must and show him the letter, she could not stop the trembling of her hands as she took it from her apron pocket. He regarded her with surprise and not a little irritation.

'Whatever it is, Ellen, you should not be bothering me. It is to your mistress you should take your concerns.'

'I thought it best to bring you this, sir!' she said quietly. 'It was on madam's dressing-room floor and . . .' She paused as she adopted what she hoped was a guilty expression before continuing, 'I know it was very wrong of me, sir, to read another person's letter, but I wasn't sure when I found it if it was to be thrown away. Madam had gone down to the kitchen to see about Doris so I thought I'd best read it and . . .'

'For goodness' sake, Ellen, stop pettifogging around and give the wretched thing to me,' Brook said impatiently. 'I happen to be extremely busy this morning.' He held out his hand and took the sheet of note paper from her.

Watching his reaction as he read it, Ellen saw his face go very white and then a dull red. His hands were trembling and he clasped them quickly together, saying violently, 'You had no right whatever to read this, *no right whatever,*' he repeated. 'Since you have done so and are aware of its contents, I am warning you that if you relate one single word of it to another human being, I will personally see to it that you never, ever receive employment again. Do you understand?'

Ellen nodded and, hoping that her expression looked suitably frightened, she apologised again and left the room.

The question crossed Brook's mind fleetingly: why had the maid brought the letter to him rather than to Harriet? But the question seemed irrelevant beside the enormity of its implications.

Brook lent forward, his elbows resting on his desk, his eyes closed, his hands either side of his face. Ridiculous though he knew it to be, he hoped that when he opened them the sheet of paper might no longer lie on his blotter, *'the little boy you gave me'*. The words jumped off the page as if they had been written in capital letters.

Much as he now tried to find a different meaning to the unbearable, incriminating truth – that Charlie, the little boy he loved so dearly, so proudly, *was not his son*, he was unable to do so.

Other heart-breaking thoughts now occurred to him one upon the other – Charlie's unexpected birth whilst he had been in Jamaica; Harriet's withholding the news from him until he returned home; her reluctance to tell him the name of the convent where the baby had been born when he wished to send them a grateful donation. Further facts came like knives into his mind, foremost of which was Charlie's unusual musical talent. This thought was followed by the memory of a discussion he and Harriet had had. It had been about her ignorance of the fact that she was already so far advanced in her pregnancy when she'd departed to Ireland.

It was then that he was suddenly overwhelmed by the realization that his beloved wife, Harriet, had lied to him . . . not a small fib but a terrible, unforgivable lie: one that would have its consequences all the rest of their lives . . . *Charlie was not his son.*

For one ghastly minute, Brook feared that his horror was about to give way to tears. Never again could he love the two people who had been nearest and dearest to him. How could he ever trust Harriet again? How could he hold Charlie – someone else's child – feeling so proud and happy to have produced such a delightful, intelligent offspring?

Such unhappy reflections were followed by a useless desire to convince himself that this past unbearable half hour had never taken place. That maid of Harriet's – the one Felicity had found for her but who Harriet had never really liked: could she have written the letter hoping to make trouble between him and his wife? What reason could she possibly have to do such a thing? Feverishly, he picked up the sheet of notepaper and saw at once that the handwriting was Harriet's. He started to read it again . . . *'the little boy you gave me'* . . . Unable to read further, he screwed the paper into a ball and threw it furiously away from him.

There was a knock on the door and Albert the footman opened it to announce Felicity's arrival. Brook would have refused to be interrupted but before he could do so she pushed past the footman and came towards the desk, smiling.

'Do forgive me for arriving so early, Brook,' she said. 'I shall not be staying, but I cannot find Harriet and I am a little worried. When I returned home, I discovered that my necklace was missing.' She touched the brooch at her throat. 'It is rather valuable – a present from the Tsar Nicholas to my husband and it matched with this brooch and earrings. I knew the clasp was a little weak, but the colour went particularly well with my dress, so . . .'

She became aware that Brook was not really listening to what she was saying but pretended not to notice as she continued: 'I think it must have fallen off when I went to Harriet's dressing room to put on my cloak and hat when I was leaving. I saw Ellen in the hall just now but she hadn't found it. She couldn't tell me where I might find Harriet so I thought I would pop my head round the door and ask you if, by some miracle, she had found my necklace and given it to you for safe-keeping.'

She broke off, and leaning towards Brook said in a different tone of voice, 'Oh, dear, Brook, you are looking quite ill! I should not be bothering you like this. Can I get you something? Or send your footman to fetch Harriet . . .'

'No!' Brook's voice was like a gun shot. 'Forgive me!' he said more quietly as he struggled to regain control of himself. 'It was most remiss of me to shout at you like that. It's just . . . well, just that I have had a rather nasty shock . . . a . . . a letter . . . news which has shaken me up a bit . . . I am sorry Felicity, I'm afraid I do not have your necklace.'

Felicity took a step forward, her face a mask of concern. 'Please don't trouble yourself about it, Brook!' she said. 'I feel awful coming in here when you have had bad news. Had I known, I would not have worried you with my trifling concern. Is there anything I can do? It worries me greatly to see you so distressed, my very dear friend.'

Brook drew a deep breath. He knew Felicity meant well, but she was one of the very last people who he would want to know of Harriet's treachery. Even thinking about the lies Harriet had told everyone – the servants, his father, their friends, and worst of all himself, made him feel sick. He stood up and held out his hand in appeal.

'I'd be most obliged, Felicity, my dear, if you would say nothing of this to my wife. I need some time to . . . to consider the . . . the problem which has just arisen before . . . before I decide upon the best way to . . . to deal with it.'

Felicity felt justified in reaching out to take his hand, which she clasped in hers. She held it as long as she dared, saying in a kindly tone, 'I promise not to say a word to any other person.' Her voice was soft and reassuring. 'I shall go home now, but if there is anything . . . anything at all you think I could do to help, I want you to know that you can call on me to do it.'

She released his hand and touched his cheek, saying, 'You and Harriet have become very dear to me and little Charlie, too, especially as I have no children of my own. It must be such a comfort to you, Brook, knowing that whatever disaster may befall, you will always have your dear little son and dearest Harriet to console you.'

Having rubbed salt into the wound she had inflicted on Brook, she decided to leave him and await with all the patience she could muster the outcome of the shattering information he had just received: information which, she was now convinced, would break the bond between husband and wife.

Deciding that she would speak to Ellen on another occasion, she now rode home with her groom, her hope soaring that it would not now be long before Brook turned to her for the comfort he would surely need.

Fletcher was in the hall as Harriet came downstairs from the nursery.

'How is Master Charlie this morning, madam?' he asked. 'When I showed the doctor out, he only said, "As well as can be expected!" I think he was in somewhat of a hurry!'

Harriet smiled. 'Doctor Tremlett is always in a hurry, Fletcher. He is a most conscientious practitioner and likes to see all his patients every day. Master Charlie, I am very pleased to tell you, is over the worst and now it is just a matter of getting him back on his feet again. Now, I must speak to the master. Is he in his study?'

Fletcher shook his head. 'He went out a half an hour ago, madam. He didn't say where he was going.'

'That's not like him, Fletcher! Did he say when he would be back?'

Fletcher shook his head. 'I'm afraid not, madam. I had the impression it was a matter of some urgency. Mrs Goodall was here a short while ago – I understood she had lost a necklace and had called to see if one of the servants had found it after she left last evening. The master went out not long after Mrs Goodall left, so perhaps his presence was required at Melton Court.'

'Thank you, Fletcher! Please let me know when he returns,' Harriet said. 'I shall now be in the morning room if I am wanted.'

She made her way there and settled herself beside the cheerful warmth of the fire to complete the list she had begun of all the tasks that needed to be fulfilled in time for the dinner party planned to follow Brook's Boxing Day shoot. Not only would the shooters and their wives be there, but also Sir Walter and a dozen or more neighbouring landowners to whom they owed hospitality.

She had yet to engage a small orchestra from Leicester to play music for dancing after the dinner, and as an amusing novelty she was hiring a conjurer from London recommended to her by Felicity. Paul was one of the guns and Felicity was arriving later with four house guests who she and Brook had yet to meet.

It was not a very large party, there being no more than sixty guests invited, but Harriet intended it to have a Christmas theme both decoratively and in choices of food. It should, of course, have been organized weeks ago when the invitations first went out, but Charlie's illness had brought all such matters to a halt, and until the doctor's visit this morning she had even suspected it might have to be cancelled. How could there be jollity if her poor, sick little boy lay at death's door?

The morning passed quickly and, occupied as she was, Brook's unexplained departure did not worry her unduly. When he did not return in time for luncheon, she began to feel anxious. Surely, she told herself, if he had gone over to Felicity's house to help with a problem there, he would have sent word back to say if he was staying for luncheon?

It was not unusual for Brook to go to Melton Court without her when Paul Denning was on one of his visits to his sister. Brook was now quite heavily involved financially in the Dennings' railway business affairs, and was himself immensely interested in the plans to extend the existing railway line further west. Nevertheless, it was unlike Brook not to advise her of a change of plan.

Harriet ate her lunch alone. It was five o'clock and darkness had fallen when Brook finally strode into the drawing room. He was followed by Fletcher, who removed the hat and cape he was still wearing. The fire was blazing warmly, and without approaching Harriet, Brook went to stand in front of it where he waited without speaking until Fletcher left the room.

Harriet was about to rise to go to him, but he raised his hand, saying, 'No, stay where you are. I have to talk to you.'

Harriet regarded him anxiously. 'What has happened, Brook?' she asked fearfully. 'I have been so worried. I kept thinking of all the awful things which might have sent you out of the house this morning without even stopping to say goodbye to me.' She made once more as she was going to rise, but again Brook held up his hand to stop her.

'I left without saying goodbye to you, Harriet,' he said in a cold, hard voice, 'because quite simply I couldn't bear to see you. Had this house not happened to be my home as well as yours, I would not have come back.'

Shocked almost to the point of fainting, Harriet was speechless as she was struck by a thought so shattering that instantly, she tried to thrust it from her mind. *The letter . . . the letter she had been writing to Mrs Bates . . . it had never been found . . . she'd presumed it must have been thrown away or put on the fire by a maid . . . but someone must have found it and given it to Brook . . .*

His voice was as chilling as his expression when he said, 'I see you have guessed why I could not bear to set eyes on you. You lied to me, Harriet! You let me live that lie with you – a lie so unforgivable that . . . you have wiped from my heart all the love I ever had for you. I cannot forgive you, Harriet, any more than I can now look at Charlie believing him to be my son . . . *my* son . . .'

Momentarily, his voice broke. Too shocked for words, Harriet was also beyond tears. She stood up, but Brook turned quickly and walked over to one of the windows where he stood with his back to her. He was telling the truth – he really could not bear the sight of her, Harriet thought. Her heart was beating fiercely in her breast; every nerve in her body was trembling as she held out her hands and cried out: 'Brook, I love you! It was for your happiness as well as mine that I lied. I had failed so often to give you the son you wanted, and when this woman asked me to take Charlie as she could not keep him herself, I was still in despair after my last miscarriage, and I thought . . .'

'Enough, I do not want to hear any more. Nothing, but *nothing* will excuse your deceit. For nearly three long years you have let me live a lie. Yes, I wanted a son . . . *my* son, not someone else's.'

He turned now to face Harriet as he said bitterly, 'I thought it would be impossible for me ever to stop loving you, but quite frankly, I now wish you out of my sight. And since you wanted a child so badly, you can keep Charlie – or send him away if you prefer. I want nothing more to do with him or you.'

He withdrew from his pocket the crumpled piece of notepaper Ellen had given him and which he had screwed up but not thrown away. He now threw it down on the floor between them, quoting furiously: '"*the little boy you gave me.*"' He walked past her, opened the door and, pushing the footman aside, slammed it behind him as he went out.

Harriet fell back dry-eyed into the armchair. She had wanted to ask him how he had come by that incriminating half-written letter, but now it did not seem to matter. Not only had it destroyed his love for her, but he no longer wanted anything to do with Charlie . . . Charlie, who adored him, who preferred his father's company even to her own.

Tears filled her eyes. How could they go on living in this house together? Was it possible Brook would retaliate by divorcing her? Even that dreadful disgrace would not be as terrible as the heart-breaking loss of Brook's love. Why could he not understand that she really had wanted to keep Charlie for him as well as for herself?

She drew a long, trembling sigh as she recalled how Brook had derived such happiness from the little boy these past three years. If she had been able to see into the future and known she would ultimately forfeit the love of her life, would she still have kept the baby Mrs Bates had left with her in the waiting room, or would she have placed him in an orphanage?

Her heart missed a beat as she faced the truth. She had known full well that Brook would not have permitted her to keep someone else's baby. Because she'd wanted so desperately to do so, she had accepted the need to deceive Brook. She had accepted the risk she was taking.

Was it too late now to win back Brook's trust? His love? If she were to send Charlie away – to Una perhaps, where one more child would make little difference . . .?

Her thoughts came to an abrupt halt. How could she bear to do such a thing when she had grown to love Charlie as deeply as any son she might herself have conceived? She loved him far too much to be able to part with him, yet to have lost Brook's love was every bit if not more unbearable. Might he not in time forgive her? Love both her and Charlie again?

She was weeping helplessly when Bessie came into the room to say that Charlie was asking if his father would come upstairs and read him a story. One look at the crumpled, tear-streaked face of her beloved mistress was sufficient for Bessie to guess that, on this occasion, the little invalid's wishes were not going to be fulfilled.

SIXTEEN

1868–1869

I t had been too late to cancel all of Cook's preparations for Christmas Day, but Sir Walter had not been well and Brook had used this as an excuse to depart immediately after lunch to visit his father. Fortunately Charlie had been preoccupied with his Christmas presents and for once had not wished to claim Brook's attention. Added to this Brook had invited Paul and Felicity to dinner that evening, which had provided the necessary distraction from the serious rift existing between himself and his wife.

It was now almost a month since Ellen had given Brook Harriet's letter to Mrs Bates: a month which had been the unhappiest of Harriet's life. Her only consolation was Charlie's steady recovery. Even that had partly added to her distress because Brook now ignored him. He no longer went to the nursery, and Bessie had been given instructions that he was no longer to be taken down to the drawing room to bid his father goodnight, no matter how much he pleaded.

'Papa is very busy,' Harriet kept telling Charlie. It was the same excuse she used when Charlie saw his father riding, or down by the lake fishing. 'We mustn't bother Papa just now because he has a lot of important things to think about.'

Heart-breaking though such explanations were to Harriet, Charlie accepted them, but whenever he happened to encounter Brook unexpectedly, he would pull away from Bessie's hand and run to his father, his face bright with pleasure, saying such things as, 'Are you a busy man today, Papa?' Or, 'Papa, can we ride horses today? I'll be a very good boy.'

Brook's replies were curt. 'I'm afraid not! I have other things I must do!' And he would walk away, not turning to see the disappointment on the child's face.

'I'm sure Papa will find time to take you riding again soon, Charlie,' Harriet would say, close to tears, knowing that Brook was no more likely to acknowledge Charlie than he acknowledged her. She only saw him now at mealtimes, which they would eat together as before but with the minimum, impersonal conversation – something Harriet knew only too well was to preserve some semblance of normality in front of the servants.

Bessie had told her that all the staff were aware there had been a rift between them but that, unlike herself, they did not know the cause. She had even heard gossip that their master was more often at Mrs Goodall's house than his own: gossip which was very quickly stopped by Hastings if it was within his hearing.

Bessie and the valet were once more walking out and, she had informed Harriet, he said the gossip about the master's visits to Melton Court was well founded. All too often now when Brook saddled his horse, he rode off there with instructions to Hastings that his presence was not required, and that Hastings need not wait up for him if he was late returning home. Nor did he always tell Hastings where he was going.

When Brook had first discovered the fateful truth, Harriet suspected that it could only have been Ellen who had found the letter, despite her many denials. If not Ellen, then she would give a very great deal to know who had done so, she told herself bitterly. Whoever it was had seen fit to show it to Brook.

Ellen was the obvious culprit, but her denials had seemed genuine, and it *was* possible that one of the maids had been into the room whilst she herself had been in the kitchen with Doris. A maid might have thought it wastepaper. She must try not to let her dislike of Ellen cloud her judgement. Harriet had made one attempt to ask Brook who had presented the letter to him, but he had only replied coldly, 'That is not something I intend to discuss with you.' And to her horror he had added: 'Or anything else of a personal nature. As far as I am concerned, our marriage is at an end.'

Aghast, she had drawn a deep breath and whispered, 'Brook, you don't mean . . . you *can't* mean you intend to . . . to divorce me?'

He had risen to his feet and in a hard and bitter tone of voice, said, 'I have not yet made up my mind. I will tell you when I have done so.' And without giving her a second glance, had walked past her out of the room.

Again and again since then, Harriet was on the point of going to him . . . begging him to forgive her for her deception, but pride forbade her doing so.

Brook now slept in his dressing room, and if he passed Harriet on the staircase or in the hall he would not even acknowledge her unless one of the servants was present, when he would do no more than inform her he was going out, or was about to engage in some other activity.

Least of all these acts of estrangement was the way he avoided touching her. It was as if any sign of physical intimacy was unbearable to him. He had announced that he did not wish the household to engage in any Christmas festivities this year – using Charlie's illness and his father's indisposition as an unlikely reasoning for this extraordinary ruling.

Nevertheless, Harriet had decided, Brook should not be allowed to spoil Charlie's Christmas. He had every right to punish her for the pain she had caused him, but no right to hurt Charlie – an innocent, loveable, trusting little boy even if he were not Brook's son. She would not stand by silently and do nothing to prevent him hurting Charlie, even if it meant she was alienating herself still further from Brook.

For a start, although Harriet would have liked, as was customary, to hang up Charlie's stocking from the drawing-room mantelpiece, she had hung it up in the nursery – not so far for Father Christmas to walk with his presents, she had said. Deeply depressed as well as anxious, Harriet was nevertheless still able to manage for a little while to find pleasure in her small son's happiness. She was also immensely relieved to discover that Brook had not seen fit to expose the truth about Charlie to Sir Walter.

It had become clear to Harriet that Brook had no intention of revealing the truth to anyone else. He had not tried to stop Charlie, now no longer infectious with the measles, from attending two children's parties at neighbouring houses. She herself had pleaded a migraine and allowed Bessie to escort him there.

Every day that now passed with no change in Brook's attitude towards her, her depression deepened. He avoided her whenever possible, passing her in a passage or on the stairs without speaking.

At night, she would lie in their big bed alone, longing for his body beside her, his kisses, his caresses, his protestations of love. How was it possible, she asked herself again and again, that he could withdraw his love so totally? That he could not find it in his heart to forgive her, to rediscover his love for Charlie, who was least of all at fault. She was tormented, too, by the suspicion that Brook's frequent visits to London were to see his lawyer to arrange a divorce.

It was not that she feared the loss of her home or even the disgrace if she were deemed the guilty party in a divorce and was barred from society. Nor was she afraid Brook would claim custody of Charlie, who he now addressed as infrequently as he did her. It was the loss of his love – not just for her but for the little boy who, despite Brook's neglect, continued to love him as much as she did.

It was almost nine years ago, Harriet reflected, when as a young girl of fifteen she had first set eyes on Brook at her father's shooting party, and told Bessie she had met the man to whom she wished one day to be married. There had not been a day in the whole of her life since then that she had stopped loving Brook, and never once had she wished herself anywhere but with him. To have to live apart from him now were he to divorce her would be unendurable pain, even if she still had Charlie to console her.

Bessie, her only confidant, did what little she could to bolster Harriet's growing despair. Hastings, Bessie said, was too loyal to his master to tell her what Brook did when he was in London, but he had admitted that Brook was very far from being a happy man; that he was drinking more than was good for him and, quite often, had to be helped to bed by Hastings when he returned from Melton Court.

Felicity continued to be her staunch friend. Seeing Harriet's depression, she had invited her to discuss the obvious rift between her and Brook.

When he came to Melton Court the other evening, she had told Harriet, he was by no means his normal self. He'd consumed far too much alcohol and had become loquacious. One of the maids, he'd told her, had brought him a letter which, as far as she could gather, suggested that Charlie was not his child.

Ignoring Harriet's gasp, she continued, 'Of course, I told Brook not to be so silly,' Felicity had related. 'I told him that of course Charlie was his son, but he insisted the letter contained positive proof that he was not so.'

Felicity had then assured Harriet that she had refused to take Brook's remarks seriously until finally he'd told her that the half-written letter had made it quite clear that some woman he did not know had given her own baby to Harriet.

Felicity had then put her arm comfortingly around Harriet's shoulders, saying, 'I told him a dozen times that I did not believe it for one minute, but that even if it were true, no one could love her husband more than you do, but Brook said he could never forgive you for deceiving him.'

Giving Harriet's hand a little squeeze, she'd said, 'I am so sorry, dearest, and I will continue to do whatever I can to make him see that you would never ever deceive him in such a manner. People say that time is a great healer, and I'm sure Brook will soon come to his senses. However, I do not think it would be advisable for you to plead with him for understanding, for forgiveness, for a sin you did not commit. It is for him to beg your forgiveness for thinking you capable of such deception.'

Her voice gained conviction as she added: 'Having lived with my brother for so many years, I do know a little about the way men's minds work – how they judge us women. My advice is to ignore Brook: turn the tables on him and behave as if he has wronged you by blaming you when you were only trying to make him happy. I can see that, however mistakenly, you meant well.'

'Thank you so much for being such a good friend, Felicity. Where would I have been without you?' Harriet had said quietly.

She took Felicity's advice. Brook did not leave the house after breakfast, as was his custom, and she would put on a warm cloak and seek the privacy of the summerhouse where she knew she would not be seen. It was there she gave way to the tears that inevitably followed her morning visit to Charlie. As often as not, she would find him kneeling on the nursery window seat staring down to the driveway below, and when she went to see what was interesting him, her heart would plunge. It was Brook, the man he called Papa, standing beside his favourite black stallion, Shamrock, who, saddled and harnessed, was pawing the gravel impatiently as Brook talked to Thomas, the head groom. Hoping to catch his father's attention, Charlie would wave both small hands, hoping Brook would look up and wave back to him as he had so often done in the past. His little face would look so crestfallen when Brook finally leapt into the saddle and rode off at a smart trot without so much as a glance at the nursery window.

'Papa gone!' he would say sadly. 'Papa's got busy work.'

She always tried to distract him by offering to read a story or allowing him to play with his toy castle which, being quite fragile, was usually kept out of harm's way. It was one of the very expensive presents Felicity had given him and never failed to divert him.

How could Brook be so cruel to the innocent child he had once loved so dearly? she asked herself tearfully. That he should wish to punish her for the lies she'd told him was understandable, but Charlie . . . Charlie who loved him almost as much as she did.

Harriet longed to go to Brook and beg him to tell her if he did intend to divorce her; and if not, would a time come when he would forgive her? When he could love her and Charlie again? Her pride which forbade such action might well have weakened were it not for Felicity's persuasions that he was far more likely to relent if he thought *she* was contemplating leaving *him* and would do so if he did not come to his senses.

Although her instinct was to follow her heart, Harriet was very conscious of the fact that Felicity was not only older but undoubtedly more experienced in the ways of men than she was, having grown up with a brother. Brook, Felicity said, knew better than anyone in the world how much Harriet loved him. He must know already that she had only ever wanted his happiness. If he had any compassion, any understanding, he would not go on treating her in such an unrelenting fashion.

January gave way to February, and Harriet could bear the situation no longer. For once, she did not consult Felicity about the action she was about to take. Tonight, St Valentine's Day, she resolved she would not allow Brook to sit at the opposite end of the dining table almost totally silent, answering her questions with no more than the minimum courtesy required of him. Tonight she would make him see that if he was not prepared for them to be reconciled and start to behave differently towards her, she might cease to care whether he divorced her or not.

Dry-eyed, she went to her dressing room and rang the bell impatiently for Ellen. When the maid came in, she instructed her to find in her wardrobe Brook's favourite evening gown – a lovely dark rose silk dress which she had worn on her honeymoon. It had a tight-fitting bodice, its décolletage trimmed with lace, and the billowing skirt was decorated with pink and lime-green flowers. Although it was by now somewhat dated, he always loved to see her in it.

'I shall want my gold and pearl locket, and the gold filigree earrings with the pearl drops,' she instructed Ellen. 'As for my hair, I will have it smooth on top, plaited, and folded into a chignon.'

Her final request was for plenty of hot water brought up by five o'clock so that she could take a bath before Ellen dressed her.

Looking at Ellen's expressionless face, she added: 'One more thing, please – my bracelet with the cameo and the eternity ring my husband gave me to celebrate Charlie's birth.'

Had she imagined it, she wondered as she went back downstairs to consult Cook about changes she wished her to make to the dinner menu, or had Ellen's customary expressionless face looked surprised? Disapproving? Uneasy?

Harriet had never quite made up her mind whether it had indeed been Ellen who had found her letter to Mrs Bates, and still less that having done so she would have shown it to Brook. Felicity, too, was adamant in her belief that it was the very last thing Ellen would have done; that, uncharismatic though the maid might be, she was at heart a very kind, selfless woman whose sole purpose was to improve her sister's life.

When Harriet pointed out that there would have been no one else in her room that morning but Ellen, Felicity had argued that the woman would have had nothing to gain and would have been certain of dismissal without a reference had Harriet found her guilty.

Since then, Harriet had tried even harder to overcome her antipathy to her maid, telling herself that the poor woman worked well and toiled long hours to support her disabled sister. It was unfair of her to compare Ellen with her dear Bessie. She still thanked God in her prayers every night for Bessie's survival and safe return home.

To her relief, Hastings had been surprisingly understanding about Bessie's situation in the Far East when he finally insisted upon her telling him all the facts about the months of her abduction. Now the pair were planning to marry when Charlie was seven years old and sent away to boarding school, at which point he would no longer need a nanny.

Sending Charlie away to school was a prospect Harriet dreaded but, she decided, need not be faced until the time came for him to follow in Brook's footsteps – if Brook still wished him to go to his old school. That evening, looking with unashamed satisfaction at her reflection in the cheval-glass mirror, Harriet's face lit up with a rare smile. Tonight she was just as she had hoped – at the loveliest she could be. She was going to seduce her husband: make him want her – want to kiss her, make love to her, come to her bed once again.

She had found out from Hastings that Brook was not – as happened so often – intending to absent himself from the house and, although he'd ridden off with his groom after breakfast, he had returned in time for luncheon and not left the house again.

Tonight she had instructed Cook to produce a cheese soufflé and eels *en-matelote*, followed by duckling roasted with chestnuts, Brook's favourite dishes. She had instructed Fletcher to bring up one of the mature clarets from the cellar, confident that he would not forget to remove the cork a half hour before the meal to let it breathe. It was a repast just right for Brook's discerning taste – one he would most definitely enjoy, and if her hopes and plans materialized, he would set aside his anger and take her to his heart again.

SEVENTEEN

1869

Brook opened his eyes and promptly raised his hand to shield them against the sunlight streaming through the curtains. He was instantly aware of a throbbing headache, and its cause. Last night he had done something he had sworn to himself he would not do: he had followed Harriet into the bedroom and . . .

At this point, Brook tried not to think further, but as his brain began partially to clear from the alcohol he imbibed the previous evening, he had all too clear a memory of what he had done. He had assaulted his wife.

Momentarily Brook's eyes closed, as if to blot out the vision of himself staggering upstairs behind Harriet aware of only one thing – he wanted her: he wanted to possess her. Starved of her beauty these past three months, and with her alluring appearance throughout the evening, her voice soft and enticing, his body craved release and the zenith of satisfaction he had only ever reached in her arms. Throughout the evening she had made it equally clear that she wanted him to desire her; that she was hoping he would return to her bed.

Brook was now painfully aware of Harriet's warm body as she slept beside him. He tried desperately to banish his recollections but they would not go away. He had drunk two bottles of claret, and afterwards made heavy inroads into the decanter of port left for him by Fletcher on the sofa table in the drawing room. Harriet, he recalled, had come to sit beside him and chattered about a party she and Felicity were planning. But then, after he had ordered Fletcher to bring him a brandy and leave the bottle on the table, he became aware that Harriet was no longer smiling. When she saw him refilling his glass a second time she'd stood up abruptly, saying she had a headache and was going to retire.

Brook now called to mind the hazy memory of enjoying the evening and Harriet's company hugely, so it angered him when she had, despite his protest, suddenly ceased to smile. She'd moved quickly away when he'd tried to touch her, and left him even more angry when she announced she was going to retire.

Brook's head was thrumming painfully and he wished he felt less giddy and could get up out of bed. Most of all, he wished his memories of the previous night would not keep surfacing. He must at some point have forgotten about Charlie; about Harriet's shocking deception and his resolve never to forgive her for it. He must, too, have forgotten that on several occasions he had contemplated – albeit without much conviction – taking Felicity's advice to put an end to what had become a sterile marriage: to divorce his wife. *He'd forgotten everything but his need to hold her in his arms, feel her kisses, her touch: his hungry need to possess her.*

Beside him, Harriet stirred. Almost immediately, and without speaking, she got out of bed, pulled on her négligée and disappeared into her dressing room.

Brook was momentarily overcome by a deep feeling of shame. He had forced himself on her. Drunk as he'd been, he'd ignored her protestations and taken her fiercely, hungrily, thrusting himself into her again and again until at last he had found release. Within minutes he had fallen asleep, only faintly aware that his face as well as hers was wet with the tears she had shed.

Hastily, Brook now rang for Hastings. He needed coffee to clear his head. He would have liked a drink but knew he must not have one.

There was a knock at the door and Hastings came into the room. He settled a large breakfast tray on Brook's lap and would have removed the silver covering the top of the breakfast dishes but before he could do so Brook pushed the heavy tray away.

Having seen his master drunk on many occasions since his rift with his wife, Hastings duly removed the tray and poured Brook a steaming cup of black coffee. When his master, considerably the worse for wear, had not come to his room last night, he had known that Brook had gone to his wife's bedroom for the first time in months. Now, seeing his condition, he wished he could have persuaded him to go to his own dressing room where he now usually slept.

Brook, too, was silently wishing the same thing. The coffee was helping to clear his thoughts, and he remembered with shocking clarity how Harriet had protested violently when he had ripped the clothes from her body, forced his kisses on her and used his own weight to push her backwards on the bed. All the time he had ignored her protests, her tears, her pleas to him not to take her in anger, only in love.

Brook now felt bitterly ashamed of himself, but it was only a matter of minutes before he began to find excuses for what he had done. Not only had Harriet been overtly seductive, it had been she who had destroyed their marriage: destroyed the trust they'd had in each other with her lies and deceit. Her perfidy left him with no alternative than to deny the loving, satisfying, intimate side of their marriage. It was Harriet who had virtually left him without a wife.

Telling Hastings to leave him alone, he lay back on the pillows and closed his eyes. How could he stoop so low as to rape his wife – because that was what he had done. Being drunk did not excuse him, nor did the fact that he'd had to lead a monastic existence ever since the day that wretched maid of Harriet's had shown him the letter.

Retrospectively, he asked himself now, would he rather not have known the truth about the boy? He had been so proud of him, so . . . yes, so devoted to him. Even now he found it hard when Charlie came running to him calling him 'Papa', a big smile on his little face. He'd been the child he believed to be a replica of himself, and his and Harriet's love for one another.

Men did not cry, he'd told himself on such occasions when he'd felt like weeping because he had lost not only the son he'd thought he had, but the unbelievably happy married life he'd once taken for granted. Not only was he now bereft of all he cared about, but he had totally debased himself. *Why had he done it?* It wasn't simply that he'd wanted a woman, any woman: he'd wanted Harriet. However much he might wish it otherwise, he still loved her. It was because he loved her so much that her deception had wounded him so irrevocably.

Once again, Brook now found himself questioning whether it might not be better for him to divorce Harriet. She was a constant reminder of what had once been and could never be again. As Felicity had said, he could provide Harriet and the child with a house, with money for her needs; he could provide for the child whose presence was invariably a painful reminder of what he had lost. As Felicity had pointed out, he was still a young man – handsome, according to her, financially well off and more than well able to find another wife who, this time, would be able to give him the family he wanted.

Felicity, Brook thought as he walked unsteadily back to his own dressing room, had been a tower of strength to him. What else were good friends for? she had replied when he had expressed his thanks for her welcome. She would continue to be a good friend to Harriet, she'd told him, despite her disapproval of the way Harriet had deceived him, because she was a very unhappy woman. Would he and Harriet not be happier living apart? Harriet most certainly would be so long as she had the child she doted on with her. He, too, would surely find life less stressful if they were not there as a constant reminder of the damage Harriet had done to him and their happy marriage.

It was clear to Brook that Felicity had a good knowledge of how men felt: that she appreciated the physical frustrations he must be suffering. As she pointed out to him, Harriet might not have betrayed him physically with another man, but she had cheated in a different way when she'd foisted another man's child on him. Brook should have no conscience, Felicity maintained, if he were to break his marriage vows to be faithful to Harriet for their lifetime. If he did not wish to divorce her, he might find contentment again if he took a mistress. If Harriet was not her friend, she herself would have done anything to see him happy again.

He'd been shocked but also intrigued by Felicity's outspoken implications. Yet, tempting as her voluptuous, inviting body was during the evenings they now often spent together in her private, comfortable sitting room, he had not pursued what he'd suspected was an unspoken invitation for further intimacies.

'Dammit!' Brook swore softly as he stepped into the bath Hastings had prepared for him. He'd altogether had enough of women, of worry, of shame for last night's disgraceful behaviour. He would go away for a bit – spend a day or two with his father, to whom he'd not told the painful fact that Charlie was not, after all, his grandson.

His father, he thought unhappily, was besotted with the child: he rode over to see him every week without fail unless his recurring attacks of gout prevented it. He spent hours playing 'soldiers' with him, monopolizing the dining-room table. Old and young sat at either end of it setting out their troops ready for battle. Brook, who in the past had watched one or two of these games, noted that more often than not his father's army were manipulated so as to lose the battle, the lead soldiers lying undignified in death with their feet and rifles pointing to the heavens. A group of Sir Walter's men, Charlie's 'prisoners', lay in neat rows in his camp.

Recently, Brook had pretended not to hear when the child turned to him for his advice on battle tactics. He had invented an excuse to leave the room.

There was no denying the fact that the little boy's presence was a constant and bitter reminder of his own deeply unhappy existence: of all the joy that, without warning, had been taken away.

On the other hand, he decided, finding a mistress would not help to divert him. He would go to London instead and enjoy its many entertainments.

He rang the bell for Hastings and ordered him to pack a valise for a possible week's stay in the capital. The coach was to be prepared for his departure in an hour's time, he instructed, and Cook made aware that he would not be requiring meals until further notice; nor would he need food for the journey. They would stop and eat at a coach house on the way down to London.

With an effort, he disregarded his throbbing head and allowed Hastings to shave and dress him. Hastings was the first to speak when Brook's dressing was completed.

'Do you wish anyone else to be notified that you will be in London, sir?' he asked.

Brook shot him a quick glance. 'And do you have anyone in mind, man?' he asked pointedly.

Unperturbed, Hastings said as matter-of-factly as he could, 'I wondered if Mrs Goodall should be told, sir, lest she were to ride here to see you and be wasting her time.'

Brook flushed and said angrily, 'I can do without impertinent remarks like that, Hastings. They are also ridiculous. Mrs Goodall's visits here are primarily to see the mistress, not me.'

'As you say, sir!' Hastings replied, his disbelief quite recognizable on his face.

Pretending not to notice, Brook said sharply, 'Find Bessie and tell her to inform her mistress that I will not be attending the Albermarles' dinner party with her this evening as I have been called away on urgent business. And for God's sake, Hastings, take that look off your face before I tell you to pack your bags and find a position elsewhere!'

Hiding a smile, Hastings only said, 'Yes, sir!' before turning to complete the finishing touches to Brook's attire.

Felicity received the news of Brook's absence from the groom when she dismounted from her horse in the cobbled yard in the Hunters Hall stables. Brook had arranged to ride into Melton

Mowbray with her to purchase a new saddle. She had been looking forward to spending the morning alone with him – a pleasantly warm and sunny one as it happened, and anger merged in equal parts with her disappointment. Harriet had told her she would be going down to the village, to distribute some of Charlie's outgrown clothes to the worthy vicar's wife who ran the jumble sale at the church hall, so Felicity had jumped at the chance to be alone with Brook. Now that he was to be in London for a week, she thought angrily, it would be at least seven days before she would see him again.

However, she had no intention of wasting her entire morning. She needed to see Ellen, who she expected to bring her up to date with the ongoing relationship between Brook and Harriet. With Harriet absent in the village, she was able to do so without any delay. Ellen, however, had only bad news for her, namely that Brook had spent the previous night in Harriet's bed. Knowing that marital relations had been resumed between the couple left her white-faced and shaking as she returned home.

Harriet's few commitments in the village, meanwhile, did little to lessen her shock and unhappiness at Brook's cruel behaviour the previous night. When she went up to the nursery to see Charlie on her return, Bessie, seeing Harriet's white face, the dark rings under her eyes and her shaking hands, looked at her in dismay. Harriet said that she had not slept well, an inadequate excuse for her condition.

Bessie was not convinced and suggested that Harriet might be sickening with the onset of the dreaded influenza, which the baker's boy had reported that morning was afflicting several people in the village.

When Harriet had gone downstairs for breakfast that morning, she had dreaded the thought of seeing Brook. It was a huge relief to her, therefore, when Fletcher reported that he'd been told to tell her that Brook had gone to London with Hastings 'on urgent business'.

Harriet went into the morning room where she sank grate-fully into one of the armchairs by the window. Try as she might, she was unable to put memories of the previous night from her mind.

Was it possible, she wondered, that Brook had left because he was ashamed of himself? Bessie had described to her how degraded she'd felt when she had been violated. She, too, now felt the same. Her whole body ached and there were bruises on her arms where he'd gripped them to subdue her struggle to free herself. Could he have intended to hurt her in retaliation for the way she had hurt him?

Harriet now relived the events which had led up to her decision to produce Charlie as Brook's son. At the time, it had seemed as if Fate was determining she should do so to compensate Brook for the bitter disappointment of her past miscarriages. Even more compelling had been her need to have a living baby in her arms.

Not for the first time, Harriet wondered if Fate had predisposed the meeting with Mrs Bates, with a mother who did not want her baby. And at a time when it had been possible for her to establish that the baby was hers?

Harriet lent back against the cushions, her eyes closed as she recalled Una's unquestioning assumption that she had given birth to Charlie. Nor had it been doubted by her old nanny, or Una's children, who had been so thrilled with their new 'cousin'. As she stared out at the cold, wintry garden, her thoughts were not on Hunters Hall but in Ireland. Without difficulty, she could recall the children's questions:

'What are you going to call your baby, Aunt Harriet?'

'May I hold your baby, Aunt Harriet?'

'Your baby looks just like you, Aunt Harriet!'

'What have you called your baby?'

No one had ever suspected that Charlie was not her child.

Even before the time of her return home eight weeks later, she had almost come to believe the baby was hers. Her only doubt had been that Brook's reactions might not be the same as hers. She had convinced herself that he would be thrilled with a son of his own, that he need never know that the baby was not of his conceiving. As she had hoped, he'd taken Charlie to his heart.

She was forced now to face the fact that she'd had no justification for deceiving him in so vital a matter: to lie to him, to let him love another man's child believing it to be his own. Her actions, she now saw, had been in answer to *her* need, not his.

She'd known from the start that if she'd asked him to let her keep the baby, he would never have permitted her to do so.

Harriet now rose from her chair and paced the room restlessly as she tried to marshal her thoughts. Brook loved children and would almost certainly have told her that she must place the unwanted baby with some kind, motherly person – someone in the village, perhaps; someone with whom the child would have been well cared for, that he would pay for his upkeep had that been necessary. But . . . he would not have let her keep Charlie and pass him off as theirs.

Close to tears, Harriet was now thankful that Felicity had not called to see her. Good friend though Felicity was, she could not bear to tell her how humiliated she had been by Brook's assault upon her. She knew Felicity was a very great admirer of Brook.

It had always made Harriet proud to think that other women found her husband as attractive and loveable as she did, and she had no wish to disillusion Felicity as to Brook's unfailingly kind, courteous behaviour. Were Felicity to have visited today, it would not have taken her long to extract at least some of the details of the previous night's horrors. Moreover, knowing of the reason for the current rift between her and Brook, Felicity had started to suggest that it might be best for them both to live apart. Harriet had been finding it harder and harder to explain to Felicity that despite Brook's indifference, his coldness towards her, the withdrawal of his love and now, awful as it had been, last night's drunken assault, she knew she would rather bear it all than have to live apart from him.

'I know Brook can't forgive me,' she had said often enough to Felicity, 'that he may never be able to love me as he once did, but whilst he allows me to go on living here, I can still hope, can I not? There are times when I raise my head and see him looking at me as if . . . as if he didn't hate me . . . as if . . . it's silly I know, but I think he does need me, needs things between us to be as they once were. He would have told me to leave long ago, would he not, if that was what he wanted? I cannot leave him, no matter how unhappy I am.'

Whilst Harriet was grappling with these distressing reflections, Felicity had been riding home with her groom. She, too, was trying to come to terms with the fact that, according to Ellen,

Brook had spent the night in his wife's bed and the couple were, presumably, reconciled. The thought was intolerable and was followed by another – Brook still loved Harriet; he still wanted to make love to her. Why else would he have suddenly returned to her bed if he had not forgiven her?

By the time Felicity reached home there was a cold, hard place where her heart should be. This was the first time in her life that she had not been able, by some means or another, to get what she wanted. As a child, she'd only have to name it for her doting father to provide it whether it be a gown, a toy, a party, a horse – even her own phaeton. She had been allowed to eat only the foods she liked, attended only the lessons that interested her, to rise or to sleep only at the times she wanted. Even her brother, Paul, had come second in her father's adoring eyes. Finally, although Paul thought the man she had married, Matthew Goodall, was unsuitable in many ways, not least because the fellow was even older than their father, the marriage had seemed to be a happy one, doubtless because the man indulged her in the same way her father had done. His untimely death had left Felicity an extremely wealthy widow with most of the world's pleasures at her disposal. Thus it was that throughout the years of her life, she had had every desire fulfilled. All but one – she had not been able to get the man she wanted.

Throughout the ensuing long afternoon and evening, Felicity gradually came face-to-face with the fact that, despite her patience and her efforts to become part of the couple's lives, her employment of Ellen to spy on them and report any discord to her, Brook and Harriet were now reconciled. If she were not to face final defeat, she must risk one last chance of success.

It was long after midnight when Felicity Goodall was ready to go to bed, by which time, she had finally devised a way to achieve her desire to win Brook Edgerton for herself.

EIGHTEEN

February, 1869

'It has to have been something in the food she's eaten, Mrs Barker,' Harriet said to her cook when it had been reported that Annie, one of the maids, had been vomiting all night. The sixteen-year-old girl had, even more worryingly, lost control of her bowels.

'If she is not better by teatime,' Harriet continued, 'I will ask Doctor Tremlett to call after surgery. It sounds to me very much like food poisoning.'

The cook's cheeks grew red and she drew in her breath before saying indignantly, 'If that good-for-nothing girl stole something she wasn't supposed to, it wouldn't be anything I've cooked, madam. I'm most particular as to my cooking and . . .'

'I know, Mrs Barker, nobody is questioning the hygiene in your kitchen,' Harriet broke in quickly. 'It's just that I was wondering if Annie had found something leftover that you had put aside for Cripps to use for compost.'

Slightly mollified, Cook said, 'If'n she did, madam, she didn't oughta have. She ate two helpings of the leftover cold veal-and-ham pie we all had for our tea yesterday, and then two slices of bread and treacle after. Eats like a horse, she does!'

Harriet nodded. 'Maybe it's not food which has caused her upset,' she said. 'Perhaps you can get one of the maids to take up a jug of cordial for her, Mrs Barker. The doctor always recommends fluid to stop his patients becoming dehydrated.'

She did not stay long enough to explain the meaning of the word, but hurried up to the nursery to reassure herself that Charlie and Bessie were in good health. She need not have worried, for they were putting on their outdoor clothes ready to go down to the lake to feed the swans.

Harriet now suspected that Annie must have secreted something from the larder and, always hungry as she was, hidden it and not eaten until several days later, by which time it would have turned bad. However, when Harriet visited the girl again mid-morning, Annie vigorously denied doing such a thing, the words coming in a whisper between groans of pain as she clutched her stomach and finally vomited into the chamber pot beside the bed.

Harriet went back downstairs to the morning room, wishing even more fervently than usual that Brook had not ceased to converse with her. He only ever did so now when a reply in front of the servants necessitated it. Since his return from London after a week's absence, he'd made no reference to the night he had gone to her bedroom. He'd offered no apology, and behaved as if nothing had happened. Nor had there been any change to the distant relationship he had imposed upon them.

The second half of the morning passed with a tiresome call from the vicar's wife, who wanted her opinion on how the church should be decorated for a forthcoming wedding. She then made a polite request for any unwanted clothing or objects for next month's jumble sale, and finally asked if Harriet would act as judge for the best flower display at the village fête in the spring.

When at last she had departed, Harriet was approached by the footman saying that Thomas was waiting in the drive with the horses, and had she perhaps changed her mind about riding over to Melton Court?

Harriet caught her breath. 'Oh, dear, I'm afraid I had forgotten all about it, Albert,' she said. 'Please ask Thomas to give my apologies to Mrs Goodall. I will not be needing him again after all.'

As a rule, she tried to ride out at least three times a week for exercise, more often than not doing so in company with Felicity. It made a pleasant way of passing the morning until luncheon, which they would eat together. Brook frequently absented himself on some pretext or another, only appearing briefly for the meal if Felicity was there.

On those occasions he would converse almost entirely with Felicity, and would depart afterwards to his study, or to engage in some other private activity. He seldom reappeared until dinner time. Quite often now he stayed up in London, and Harriet was growing accustomed to eating on her own.

A ride this sunny morning with Thomas would have been welcome in other circumstances, she thought now, but this morning she was feeling distinctly queasy and wondered whether she had caught the same infection as young Annie. Alternatively, it might simply be because seeing someone vomiting always made her nauseous. Even on the rare occasions Charlie was sick, she had to leave the room for fear of being ill herself.

Harriet now decided to miss luncheon and go to her room to lie down. When she felt better she would write a long letter to Una, who had spoken in her last missive of coming to visit with the entire family at Easter, to make up for the disappointment of not being able to visit at Christmas. Easter was only five weeks away, she reminded herself, and she would have to think of an excuse, as she had at Christmas, to prevent her sister coming. The very last thing she wanted was for Una to see how very far from well the state of her marriage was. Una would want to know the reason why, and she could not bear to hear her sister's reproaches for keeping secret from her the truth about Charlie's parentage; for allowing her to assume the baby had been born in the convent and was hers.

What a hopeless mess she had made of her life, Harriet thought unhappily – yet how could she wish she had never adopted the little boy she cherished? Was it possible that Brook, who had been so devoted to Charlie, was hoping if he forced her to choose between him and Charlie that she would send the little boy away? Surely he could not be so cruel . . . not only to her but to the little boy he had once loved?

Annie's condition worsened as the day wore on. When the doctor came, he informed Harriet that her indisposition was almost certainly caused by some form of poisoning. On hearing that Harriet, too, had been feeling unwell, he gave instructions that no uncooked food in the larder must be eaten, and that all drinking water must be boiled lest the well water had become contaminated.

The following day, Annie seemed slightly better, but Harriet could still not eat any breakfast. Felicity came to spend the morning with her and comforted her with the news that one or two of her own household were also laid low. This seemed to prove to Harriet that, despite what the doctor suspected, there must be an infection flying round the neighbourhood in much the same way as the recent measles epidemic had spread.

As had become Felicity's custom, she never came empty-handed, and this morning she brought a pretty little circular box of violet cream chocolates tied with a violet ribbon. 'It's the very least I can do seeing how often I enjoy your hospitality!' she said when Harriet protested at the frequency of her gifts. Settling down together in front of the fire in the morning room, she continued, 'I managed to find these in Fortnum and Mason last week when I was in London. They come from France where they crush real violets for the flavour, which is what makes them rather special. I'm sorry the box is so small, but they did not have a larger size.'

Harriet untied the ribbon and opened the lid. The smell of chocolate and violets filled the air around her. 'Felicity, my dear friend, how kind you are!' she gasped, trying to quell the onset of nausea. 'If I may, I shall indulge myself after luncheon.'

'Are you still feeling ill?' Felicity enquired. 'It certainly does sound as if you have the same infection as your maid. Fletcher told me when I arrived that the girl seemed to have turned the corner and was feeling a little bit better.'

She put an arm round Harriet's shoulders, adding: 'Now promise me, dearest, that you won't go handing round these chocolates to anyone else. I know how generous you are and I would really be most upset to learn you had shared them with others. The salesman in Fortnum's told me that they were hand-made, and they could not guarantee they would be able to obtain them again, so they are a little special.'

As the little circular box they rested in was only large enough to contain six chocolates creams, Harriet understood Felicity's persistence that she should not share them.

At luncheon, Harriet could eat only a fraction of the venison pie Cook had made before the feeling of nausea returned. Excusing herself, she went up to her bedroom, leaving Felicity to be entertained by Brook who had appeared, belatedly, in time for the meal. Soon after it was over, Felicity went up to Harriet's bedroom to announce that she and Brook were going to ride over to Melton Court to look at a newly born colt.

For a brief while, Harriet slept, but whilst Charlie was having his afternoon nap, Bessie came down unexpectedly to see her.

Standing at Harriet's bedside, she looked at her white, exhausted face in dismay. 'Oh, Miss Harriet!' she said. 'I do hope as how you haven't caught Annie's sickness! Has Doctor seen you? I doesn't like to see you like this!'

Harriet felt like crying. Bessie's sympathy was undermining her resolve not to give way to depression. It *was* depression and not jealousy, she told herself, but it did upset her a little bit to observe how enthusiastically Brook responded to Felicity's amusing banter: laughing at her jokes, his face alight with smiles. Harriet could not remember how long it had been since he had smiled at her.

Time and again, she found herself wondering if it was Brook's intention never to forgive her: to continue living with her in this limbo, acting only when they were in company as was expected of a husband. She hated the thought that he had told Felicity the truth about Charlie – about his subsequent rejection of the child and his alienation from herself. He had done so, Felicity had admitted, one evening when he had imbibed a little too much brandy.

According to Felicity she had done her best to make Brook see things differently; had told him he should make allowances for the fact that Harriet had acted as much to make him as happy as herself.

That conversation was the very reverse of what Felicity had actually said to Brook – namely that Harriet had thought she could get away with her lies, and had totally disregarded his feelings in order to satisfy her own desires; that such behaviour was not that of a loving wife but of a self-centred person wanting the best of both worlds. She had further suggested that Brook should tell Harriet to get rid of the child. He could then forgive her and all would be well between them again. If Harriet truly loved him, Felicity had remarked, she would get rid of the child she had tried to force upon him.

Unaware of these damaging suggestions, Harriet felt increasingly grateful to the woman who was such a good friend, acting as a mediator in what had seemingly become an impasse. Felicity was nearly always a very welcome companion who helped to occupy her time, who was always ready to try and jolly her out of her depression. Another reason why she valued Felicity as a friend was because she was always amazingly kind to Charlie, spoiling him with toys and books and games, never arriving empty-handed. If she were in Harriet's shoes, Felicity said, she would never dream of parting with such an adorable little boy.

Harriet was aware that her devoted Bessie did not share her esteem for Felicity, although Bessie never revealed her feelings in words. It was not that Felicity was ever disagreeable to her when they encountered one another in the nursery. Perhaps, Harriet thought, Bessie sensed that Felicity considered it unwise of her, Harriet, to treat Bessie more as an equal than a servant. It was also possible that Bessie was a little jealous the amount of time she spent with Felicity, as a consequence of which she had far less time in the nursery.

Harriet turned now to regard her servant, who was clearly concerned for her health. 'I'm sure I'll feel better tomorrow, Bessie, dear!' she said reassuringly. An idea suddenly occurred to her. She reached out to the table and lifted the little violet-beribboned box. 'Bessie, I would like you to take these,' she said. 'Mrs Goodall gave them to me this morning and I promised I would taste them after luncheon, but . . . well, I simply can't face chocolates, or any other sweetmeat at the moment. I was asked not to share them with anyone as they are so special, but I simply can't eat even one. If you would now take four of them for yourself, if Mrs Goodall comes upstairs again and looks in the box, she will presume that I have eaten them. I'm anxious not to hurt her feelings because she went to quite a lot of trouble to buy them for me. They were made in France.'

Bessie nodded. 'You can be sure I won't say nothing, Miss Harriet. Now you look after yourself, seeing as I can't do so what with that Ellen being your maid now . . .'

'Shush, Bessie, I know you don't like her, but she does her job very well so it wouldn't be fair of me to dismiss her,' Harriet said, not for the first time. She added truthfully: 'Not that I don't miss you very much, Bessie!' She sighed and then added: 'All the same, I wouldn't want anyone else looking after Charlie. I know he loves you, and I couldn't ask for a better nanny.'

Looking happy with the compliment, Bessie took four of the chocolates from the box, tucked them into the pocket of her apron and, promising to come in again that evening after Charlie had been put to bed, she left the room.

At the foot of the staircase leading up to the nursery floor, she encountered Hastings. Making sure there was no one in sight, the valet planted a quick kiss on her cheek.

'Wish it was tomorrow!' he whispered, knowing that they both had their half day off and there would be time then for a lot more kisses when he walked her up to the empty sheep-shearers' sheds.

'Me, too!' Bessie whispered back. 'Here . . .' She took one of the chocolates from her pocket and gave it to him. 'Came all the way from France, they did!' she confided. 'Poor Miss Harriet couldn't eat them. Right poorly she is! If she's not better by morning, I shall go myself to see the master and ask him to fetch the doctor to her.'

For a minute or two neither spoke, then Hastings said, 'As you know, Bess, I've never been one for talking about the master's affairs, nor anyone else's come to that, but I do have to say that I don't care for what's going on 'tween him and the mistress. 'Twas all right when she first came back from Ireland with Master Charlie, but it's different now.' He drew a deep sigh. 'The master won't tell me what's up 'tween them. With just the two of us – him and me – when we wus in Jamaica he treated me almost like I was a friend – not that I ever overstepped the mark, mind you. He's the master and I'm his servant, and nothing can change that.'

He drew a long sigh. 'Maybe the mistress will tell you what's up between them, Bess. The master's not only right strange with her but with Master Charlie, too. Was a time when he couldn't spend enough time with the little'un. Now . . .' He broke off, giving a puzzled sigh.

'I don't get to see Miss Harriet that much these days,' Bessie told him, 'and when I do, well, that Ellen who I can't abide – she's always there in Miss Harriet's room. Then, with me up on the nursery floor and Miss Harriet downstairs, it isn't often we come across each other. I know as how she does spend time in the nursery with Master Charlie, but we can't talk private like in front of the boy. If'n I do get a chance, Hastings, I'll see if I can get her to tell me what's wrong 'twixt the two of 'em.'

Hastings was about to reply but they both heard footsteps

further along the passage, so he planted another quick kiss on Bessie's rosy cheek and they went their separate ways.

Upstairs on the top floor, Bessie met the nursery maid, Jenny, about to come out of the nursery with the empty dishes from their lunch. 'I wus comin' to find you, Nanny,' she said. 'Master Charlie's been asking where you was. I gotta go down now else Cook will have me guts for garters!'

Bessie thanked the good-natured nursery maid who had been keeping an eye on her young charge whilst Bessie had been downstairs. She rewarded her now with one of Mrs Goodall's chocolates, saying, 'Made with real violets, they are!' she said. 'The mistress gave me them.' She hustled the girl on her way, waving aside her thanks.

When Bessie went back into the nursery, Charlie came hurrying towards her wanting to know where she had been. Seeing Bessie take the chocolate out of her pocket, he demanded to have one.

'No, you can't, young man!' Bessie said. 'They's not to your liking. You can have one of them humbugs out of the sweetie jar seeing as how it's not yet time for your tea.'

Not too sure whether she would fancy a chocolate tasting of a wild flower, Bessie put the remaining two chocolates into an empty sugar bowl and placed them on top of the bookcase where Charlie wouldn't find them. She then promptly forgot they were there.

Downstairs, having admired the colt and enjoyed an exhila-rating ride with Brook that afternoon, Felicity was sitting with a glass of sherry with Brook in the drawing room. She was engaging Brook in plans for a large party she and Paul intended to have. It was to celebrate her brother's engagement to the pretty French mademoiselle, Denise Etoile, who he intended to marry the following year. Paul's house in London was not big enough for the kind of entertainment he had in mind, and he wished also to be able to accommodate his future relations, of whom there would be at least fifteen, if not more. Melton Court was capa-cious enough to receive them and any other French friends who might wish to attend. All they would need, Felicity told Brook, would be extra staff.

'I'm hoping, Brook, dear, that as I am without a husband to act as host, and Paul will probably be busy with his future in-laws, that you would be very kind and assist me when I need an extra hand. There will be so much to think about – the food, which of course I will see to, but the drinks and an orchestra and suitable valets for the gentlemen guests. I thought Hastings might vet some applicants for me . . .'

A little surprised but pleased to be thought so necessary, Brook smiled. 'My dear Felicity,' he said, refilling her sherry glass, 'I will be only too pleased to assist you in any way I can, but won't your Paul want to oversee all the details himself?'

Felicity shook her head. 'No, Paul has too many business affairs to see to in London to spend the necessary time up here. He seems to think that I can quite well manage on my own, but . . .'

Brook interrupted her. 'I will happily assist you, Felicity, my dear,' he repeated, 'in whatever way I can. Do you have a date arranged as yet?'

Felicity nodded happily. 'I have suggested three months from today, and Paul and Mademoiselle Etoile have agreed. I told Paul I was going to seek your help and he was delighted, so May the fifteenth it will be.'

Brook stood up. 'I expect you will wish to say goodbye to Harriet before you go, and I have to meet my bailiff at six o'clock so I shall have to leave you. You must let me know immediately when you need my help.'

He reached for Felicity's hand and, lifting it, merely brushed it with his lips.

As he turned to leave the room, he did not see the rush of colour flooding Felicity's cheeks. Her eyes followed him to the door and, when he closed it behind him, she pressed her own lips to where Brook's had touched her hand. Her heart thudding in her breast, she gathered up her gloves and left the room.

She now made her way slowly upstairs, her fevered brain racing. Soon . . . soon Brook would be hers! Soon it would not be just her hand he kissed, but her mouth, her eyes, her breasts. Although he never spoke of love, she was convinced that he felt more than mere liking for her. There were times when she had seen him looking at her with what she believed to be desire, and felt her body throbbing in response with feelings such as she had never experienced with a man before.

Brook and she belonged together, Felicity told herself. She

had no doubt of that now. As soon as Harriet was out of the way and Brook was no longer restrained by his sense of duty to his wife, he would be free to claim her. No other woman could have such a consuming love for him as she did. There was nothing she would not do to be with him, near him, loving him, for the rest of her life.

Upstairs, Felicity encountered Ellen leaving Harriet's bedroom with an armful of towels. Seeing the look on the maid's face, she whispered a quick apology that she had not paid her any money for the past month. It was a bad oversight. The woman had far too much knowledge of her intentions were she to decide to betray her. Whispering a promise to bring the money with her the following day, she escaped into Harriet's room.

Harriet was sitting in a chair by the window, a shawl round her shoulders and a rug over her knees. She looked deathly pale.

Felicity went to stand beside her. 'Are you still feeling unwell, dearest?' she enquired. 'You are very pale!'

Harriet sighed. 'I wish I knew what was wrong with me,' she said, not far from tears. 'I feel so ill all the time and I have a horrible pain here!' She put her hand below her ribs. 'You know, Felicity, I have been wondering if Doctor Tremlett is right and our well water is contaminated. He said an animal could have fallen in and drowned and that would be enough to have polluted it.'

She drew a shaky sigh. 'First that unfortunate girl, Annie, nearly died, and Ellen tells me that Jenny, the nursery maid who shares her room in the attic, has retired to bed crying because she's in such pain. She is being sick, too, just like Annie. I am in little doubt now that I, too, am suffering from the same infection.'

Felicity bent and gently stroked Harriet's cheek. 'You must take better precautions, dearest,' she said softly. 'You must not drink the water if there is a chance that it could be to blame. You had no lunch, so it is no surprise that you are feeling weak. I will call tomorrow and see if you are feeling better. If you are not, I shall insist Brook sends for Doctor Tremlett despite your insistence that you don't need him.'

Harriet's pause was only fractional, and then she nodded. She usually enjoyed Felicity's company but there were times, such as now, when she found it almost exhausting.

'I'm so sorry I am such poor company,' she said. 'Please do not feel you must visit me every day. By tomorrow I shall be quite all right, I promise you. I'm sure you have better things to do with your time.'

'Darling girl, you know I love coming here!' Felicity said, 'and I'm not happy about you being on your own. It's not as if Brook . . .' She broke off when she saw tears welling in Harriet's eyes. 'I shall pop up to the nursery now and pay a quick visit to that dear little boy of yours.' She paused before adding: 'Harriet, forgive me if I'm being too intrusive, but I've noticed Brook does not see as much of little Charlie as he used to do. Has he really taken against him? I know you confessed that Charlie is not his son, but surely he cannot mean to reject him completely?'

Harriet was now even closer to tears as she replied in a choked voice: 'I sometimes think Brook would be happier if I left him; if I took Charlie away, out of his sight. My poor little boy is too much of a reminder of my lies, my deception.'

For a single moment, Felicity's heart soared. If Harriet left with the child . . . there would be no further barrier to prevent Brook turning to her. He could obtain a divorce and she . . .

She broke off as Harriet said, 'But I can't leave him, Felicity. I love him too much! Unhappy as he makes me with his silence, his withdrawal of all we once meant to each other, I do at least see him every day. I get to be near him. I can still hope that one day he will find it in his heart to forgive me. Just very occasionally I feel that he wants to forgive me but his pride will not allow himself to do so. I pray it may be possible!'

Felicity turned aside so that Harriet could not see her expression as her heart twisted painfully at Harriet's suggestion Brook might still love her. Although, as far as she knew, Brook had not spent another night in Harriet's bed, it was perfectly possible, she well knew, that a man could desire a woman without loving her, and he might wish to demand his marital rights again.

Suddenly, a smile returned to her face. It didn't make any difference what Harriet's hopes were for a reconciliation. If she had another chocolate, by tomorrow morning – if not tonight – she would be beyond realizing her hopes.

Upstairs on the shelf above the fireplace, the bowl containing the remaining two arsenic-filled chocolates grew steadily warmer from the heat of the nursery fire. By evening they had all but completely melted. Finding the congealed mess the following morning, Bessie decided that they were in no state to be eaten, tipped the lot into Charlie's chamber pot and gave it to the maid to throw away.

NINETEEN

1869

For the second time within the past few weeks, Brook awoke with a throbbing in his skull and the shafts of daylight visible through the curtains stung his eyes. Through the fog clouding his brain, he slowly became aware of the cause behind his blinding headache as he recalled the previous evening when he had visited Melton Court. He had drunk far too much of the vintage wine which Felicity's father had imported from France.

Brook now had a vague memory of voluptuous white breasts spilling out of Felicity's low corsage: of her husky voice begging him to make love to her. Had he done so? he wondered now. There had been times . . . quite a few times when he had been tempted to do so, but despite everything – the cruel way Harriet had betrayed him, it was still Harriet's body, her kisses and her touch that he craved.

Hastings, who had finally learnt the truth about Charlie from Brook, had now become accustomed to his master's eating habits on mornings such as these, and was unsurprised when Brook pushed away the breakfast tray. He needed no bidding to pour out a cup of strong coffee. The look he gave his master was not sympathetic. It was not only that he – and indeed all the servants – disliked Mrs Goodall, it was that they had suspected for a while that the motive behind her ever-increasing number of visits to the house, ostensibly visits to their mistress, were in fact to attract their master.

It was, of course, common knowledge amongst the staff that

there had been a breakdown in the marriage, and that Mrs Goodall was intending to set her cap at him.

At first, Hastings had supposed Felicity wished to become Brook's mistress, but now something a great deal more serious was happening; he and Bessie were convinced that she intended to become not just his mistress, but his wife.

When Bessie had first told him of her suspicions that her beloved Miss Harriet was being poisoned, he had instantly rejected such a crazy notion. Then, last week, Bessie had repeated her accusation. Her voice trembling and her eyes full of tears, her young mistress, she wept, had lost so much weight that she was becoming a wraith! She could keep no food down her, and she was always far, far worse after Mrs Goodall had visited her and encouraged her to eat the hot-house fruit or the delicacies she had bought for her.

Finally, Bessie had told Hastings she had determined to test her suspicions, and on her last afternoon off, had gone down to the farm with some of the fruit and fed it to one of the young goats. Next morning, the kid had collapsed. Its life was only saved by the farmer who dosed it with a whole bottle of paraffin oil, which he kept for the animals should they have picked up and eaten something poisonous.

Hastings had dismissed such a conclusion – the animal could as easily become ill by eating evergreens instead of grass or hay, he argued. Since then, however, his master's even more frequent visits to Melton Court had made him wonder if, after all, there could be some truth in Bessie's allegations. He would, he decided, speak to Brook, alerting him to their concerns.

This morning, he now thought, would be a good moment to do so whilst his master's senses were weakened by too much alcohol, and he would be unlikely to dismiss him before he could finish saying what he must. Inadvertently, Brook made it easier for him to do so by saying with a sigh: 'I wish you wouldn't stand there looking at me with that unpleasantly disapproving expression, Hastings. My God, man, if you hadn't been in my service for so damn long, I'd tell you to pack your bags and be off before I wipe that look off your face.'

There was an infinitesimal pause before Hastings said very quietly, 'I am very sorry to have to say this, sir, but I must take the risk of my dismissal and say what has to be said.' He turned away from the look of disbelief on his master's face, and continued, 'I think you know, sir, that I would lay down my life for you. Having no family of my own, I have been more than content to serve you and your family. I have never wanted otherwise! But now . . . now I cannot stand by silently and watch you destroy your life . . .'

Brook sat up, still with a terrible headache, a look of disbelief on his face as he tried to clear his mind. Despite the long years of intimacy between him and his valet, Hastings had never once overstepped the boundary between them.

'What in heaven's name are you talking about, Hastings?' he said. 'Have you gone off your head? Spit it out, man! We have no secrets between us, so say what you will.'

Hastings paused, his heart sinking as he realized that his beloved master might well send him packing if he said what he felt was necessary. His voice quiet but steady, he began at the deep end.

'Bessie and I believe that Mrs Goodall is trying to get rid of madam.'

Disregarding the look of utter disbelief on Brook's face, he proceeded to relate Bessie's story of the poisoned kid; of the unexplained sickness of the mistress, of some of the staff including himself. Before Brook could interrupt, Hastings continued, 'Ever since you found out that Master Charlie wasn't yours and you took against madam for deceiving you, Mrs Goodall has increased the number of her visits to this house to such an extent that some of the downstairs servants have said that, with her coming and going as she does without invitation, as she isn't family she must now be your mistress. There has even been talk that you might be going to divorce madam and marry Mrs Goodall. They all know, you see, sir, that you've taken against madam and Master Charlie . . .'

He broke off, unnerved by the scowl on Brook's face and his unaccustomed silence. Finally Brook spoke, his voice unnaturally quiet as he said, 'Well, get on with it, man! I can see you have more to say.'

Hastings hesitated before continuing quietly, 'I know it's just downstairs gossip, sir, but both Albert and the parlourmaid have

remarked that Mrs Goodall didn't seem to mind the times when
they opened the drawing-room door and saw her standing right
close to you. They say she's a comely woman and the men servants say they understand you wanting her, 'specially as you no
longer share madam's bedroom.'

He heard Brook's sharp intake of breath as he listened to
Hastings relating such a shocking account of what was being
said in the servants' quarters. Seeing the expression on his
master's face, Hastings now expected to be dismissed immediately, but having started to say what had been on his mind for
so long, he would not now be stopped.

'It isn't just Bessie and me as is sorry for madam,' he said.
'None of the staff can understand how you've turned against
young Master Charlie. There isn't one of us as isn't fond of him
– always smiling, laughing and singing, lovely little voice he
has. You can hear him singing to himself those Irish songs young
Maire taught him. "A ray of sunshine!" Cook calls him. Only
time he hasn't got a smile on his face is when you come upon
him and turn your back. He can't understand it, and . . .'

'You can stop there, Hastings!' Brook interrupted sharply.
'You know damn well he isn't my child. How in God's name
do you think I feel? It cuts me to the quick every time I hear
him call "Papa" when he sees me. *He isn't my son – the son I
wanted, and never will be!*'

There was such pain in his voice that Hastings felt a moment
of pity for him. Then he said quietly, 'I'm a lucky man then,
aren't I, sir? If your father hadn't taken pity on me when I was
newborn, I'd have been in an orphanage same as those unhappy
children in Mr Dickens' books. That's where Master Charlie
would be if'n madam hadn't taken pity on him.'

For a brief moment, Brook's expression was one of uncertainty,
but then he said harshly, 'It's none of your damn business,
Hastings, but it isn't just the boy – it's that I can't forgive my
wife for deceiving me! How could I ever trust her again? For
nearly *three whole years* she let me believe a lie . . .' He broke
off, his throat too constricted to continue.

Hastings sighed. 'And if madam had told you, sir? Can you
say on your oath that you would have said, yes, we will keep
him and bring him up as our own? I dare say none of this would

have happened if madam had had children of her own, but she'd just lost one – another one, and women need children.'

He broke off once more, Brook's unexpected silence unnerving him. Then, gathering the remnants of his courage, he said, 'Bessie and I think Mrs Goodall is determined to be part of your life, sir. If that's the way you want it, and you divorced madam, then I'm sorry I spoke.'

'Of course I don't want that,' Brook said sharply, 'and Mrs Goodall is aware I will never go to such lengths.'

Hastings shook his head as he said urgently, 'Don't you see then, sir, that that is the reason Mrs Goodall wants madam out of the way? That is why she wants to kill her.'

'*Kill her?*' Brook shouted. 'You are out of your mind, Hastings!'

'I fear not, sir,' Hastings said quietly, 'and before you tell me again that it is impossible, I must repeat what Bessie told me, that madam always complains of pain in her stomach after eating the fruit and sweetmeats Mrs Goodall gave her; that madam has lost a lot of weight and looks far from well.'

Try as Brook wished to ignore Hastings' ridiculous accusations, he could not quite do so. It wasn't so much that he thought them absurd but that Hastings, his trusted valet, should dare even to suggest such things. Had any other servant said a fraction as much he'd have dismissed him on the spot. No matter what he might think, Hastings obviously believed what he was saying.

It struck him suddenly that Harriet indeed did not look well: there were dark shadows under her eyes, and she was often to be seen walking strangely, as if in discomfort. His coffee had grown cold. And the pounding in his head was even more painful than before. He wanted to be left alone in the darkness to sleep off his hangover. He'd had far, far too much wine – so much that he simply couldn't remember anything about the last few hours he had spent with Felicity at Melton Court. Nor did he recall how he had managed to climb into the cabriolet and allow the horse to find its way home. He did recall Felicity begging him to make love to her, insisting no one would know and he remembered, too, reminding her that he was a married man; that despite his estrangement from his wife, he wished to remain true to the vows he had made at his wedding. He vaguely remembered

Felicity laughing as if she didn't believe him. He remembered, too, holding her in his arms, her perfumed, seductive body soft and inviting in his embrace, but there his recall became hopelessly confused. He'd wanted to give way to the temptation to possess her, but had he actually done so?

He looked up at Hastings, the valet who had been his faithful, caring servant for over twenty years. Inappropriate as it might be, he had treated Hastings almost as a confidant, if not a friend. Never once had Hastings taken advantage of this relationship, and now he, Brook, was having difficulty reconciling himself to the fact that Hastings was not only questioning his behaviour, but even more outrageously, accusing Felicity, who had become both a companion and a friend, of trying to murder his wife!

'Dammit, man, you are not making any sense,' he said harshly. 'I thought better of you, Hastings, than to be heeding the servants' ridiculous gossip. No one could have been more caring or more attentive to the mistress than Mrs Goodall has been. I find it unbelievable that you are standing there accusing her of trying to poison my wife. Have you completely lost your senses?'

Hastings shook his head. 'No, sir, I wish I had done so.' And he repeated Bessie's tale of the kid's illness.

Anger now cleared Brook's mind sufficiently for him to say, 'Pull yourself together, Hastings! It's not like you to be so . . . so fanciful . . . letting Bessie put such ridiculous ideas into your head. What exactly are you expecting me to do? Jump on my horse, ride over to Melton Court and tell Mrs Goodall she is to stop trying to murder my wife! Pull yourself together, man!' he repeated, 'and take this damn tray away – yourself, too.'

His voice softened a little at the expression on Hastings' face. 'I'm sure you mean well but I don't want to hear another word on the subject. I mean it, Hastings! Mrs Goodall is not only a good friend to the mistress, she has proved a great comfort to me since . . . since our estrangement. We enjoy many activities together – hunting, backgammon and so on, so kindly keep your silly notions to yourself in future and tell Bessie to do likewise. I will do my best to forget this whole ridiculous discussion. Away now, before I change my mind.'

Quietly, Hastings approached the bedside and removed the untouched breakfast tray, his heart full of misgivings. He was certain that his master was being drawn into a terrible tragedy, and that it might soon be too late to avoid it.

Taking the tray down to the kitchen, he resolved to discuss the matter once more with Bessie in the hope that she might have a further suggestion as to what might be possible for them to do for the two people they loved.

TWENTY

1869

Paul Denning was worried. There was something about his sister's behaviour which he could not define. He was aware that she enjoyed entertaining and had welcomed with enthusiasm the opportunity to arrange his engagement party, but her present euphoria seemed quite out of proportion judging by the amount of time she was devoting to it. There would be no more than two hundred guests and possibly eight house guests. Simkins, the family butler, was unconcerned about the numbers. With the extra staff employed for the weekend, he'd assured Paul, it should all run smoothly.

Felicity, however, had insisted that Brook Edgerton should be involved in the planning. Paul did not dislike Edgerton. On the contrary, they enjoyed each other's company, sharing interests not only in shooting but in the new industrial technology and, of course, the railways. However, Felicity's insistence that Brook Edgerton should be present on such an occasion did seem unnecessary.

There was something indefinable in Felicity's behaviour when Edgerton was around which concerned Paul – a heightened vivacity, perhaps, or a change of her tone of voice. Her manner with Brook had always bordered on flirtatious, but harmlessly so. Now he found himself wondering if her changed behaviour did not disguise something a great deal more serious than he'd supposed.

On one of his recent evenings with Felicity she had told him that the Edgertons had quarrelled and were barely talking to each other: that the quarrel had to do with their child. Paul was astonished. No couple he had ever met had seemed as devoted as Edgerton and his wife. In fact, he had actually delayed his own proposal of marriage to his future bride, uncertain as he had been that they were as close in spirit as the Edgertons were.

He put such speculations to the back of his mind as he made his way to his father's study, and gave his attention to the list of guests he wished to invite to his engagement party.

After Matthew Denning's death his personal effects had been sorted, and his study was locked up and remained unused. Felicity had her own writing desk in her dressing room and, other than for a yearly spring cleaning, the study remained unoccupied.

Paul now decided to make use of his father's old mahogany cylinder desk. He rang the bell for the butler and asked him to bring him the key. Apparently it was in Felicity's possession, Simkins told him, but he believed there was a spare one in the housemaids' pantry. He left the room to see if he could find it and returned shortly after, bringing the key with him.

Paul now unlocked the study and sat down at his father's desk. He found some writing paper, slightly discoloured with age, in one of the drawers, and then, as he closed it, his eye was caught by something shiny. It was a small bottle with a label on it which he read with a look of utter astonishment on his face. ARSENIC. CAUTION.

The words jumped in front of his eyes and questions flooded his mind. What possible use had his father had for such an unpleasant poison? And why he not seen it when he'd disposed of all his father's papers after his death?

Quite suddenly, another question came into his mind. Did Felicity know the poison was here? Was that the possible reason she had the other key, as Simkins had told him? The only place where arsenic was kept that he could recall from his youth was in the padlocked gardener's shed used by the old man for killing vermin. As children he and Felicity had been warned never, ever to touch it if they found the shed door open because it could cause death . . .

He picked up the bottle a second time and unscrewed the top. It was by no means empty. Quite suddenly, a frightening memory flashed into his mind – how his young sister had attempted to poison the governess she disliked with poisonous berries. Only a little older than Felicity, he had heard his father and the doctor's raised voices, and disbelieved what they were saying.

He pushed the bottle hurriedly back into the drawer, as if putting it out of sight would put it out of mind, and telling himself it was he, not his sister, Felicity, who was deranged; that he must be insane even allowing himself to wonder – still less suspect – that his sister might now be trying to kill someone . . . Edgerton's wife.

Paul felt sickened by the way his mind was working – Felicity, a widow, doting on Edgerton . . .? It was a horrible possibility.

He wanted to get up and leave the room, shut the door and forget he had ever gone in there, but he could not even raise himself out of his chair. Memories were returning to him like angry bees in his brain: all too clearly he could hear Felicity telling him that Harriet and several of her staff had recently been laid low with an unexplained sickness. She had related some time ago that Harriet, Edgerton's wife, had deceived him and was not worthy of his devotion: how she was needed to keep the peace between the two and do her best to distract Brook from the unhappy state of his marriage. Paul had yet another memory – to add to Felicity's heightened colour and her vivacity when Brook was in the room, Paul now recalled her insistence that he was needed to help organize the party when clearly he was not.

Paul glanced at his timepiece. It was twenty minutes to four o'clock. Felicity was out riding with Brook and they were due back at any minute for afternoon tea. He realized that he must leave the study and get back to the drawing room – and sanity – before they returned. Edgerton, he told himself, was a thoroughly decent chap: he would never cheat on his wife the way some husbands of his acquaintance did. His manner with Felicity seemed to be similar to his own – protective, jocular, teasing by turn, and solicitous, but never overly flirtatious.

As Paul settled himself in the drawing room, the writing of the guest lists forgotten – his heartbeat slowed and he started to see more clearly. It was utterly absurd, he reflected, even to have thought for a moment that it was Felicity who had hidden the arsenic in the study for some nefarious purpose. However unlikely, it could have been left there by a member of staff who had seen mice in the empty room.

Paul glanced once more at his watch. It was now half past the hour. Frowning, he rang the bell and told the footman that he would not wait for them and to bring him tea.

Whilst he awaited its arrival, his thoughts were still in turmoil as he continued to dwell on his sister. Despite the social life she had led ever since she had been out of mourning, Felicity had been quite lonely before the Edgertons had come to live in Hunters Hall. He had hoped then that she would meet a suitable man and marry again. She was an attractive woman, and men rather liked her somewhat masculine personality. She did not simper or titter or play the helpless little woman as some young women did. Nor did she have the vapours or flutter her eyelashes behind a fan. Yet for all that, she was still attractive to the opposite sex. Two of Paul's unmarried friends who had met Felicity in London had demanded to be invited to Melton Court in order to get to know her better. That nothing had come of such encounters had been of her choosing, not theirs.

Paul might have succeeded in putting all such fears to the back of his mind had not Edgerton, when the couple finally joined him for tea, talked of the illness that had been affecting Harriet and three of their servants. The doctor, Brook told him, had suggested that an animal might have fallen into the well and contaminated their water supply, but he himself had not been infected.

'At one point,' Brook elaborated, 'one of the young maids nearly died.'

Paul was gripped once more with frightening doubts. There could be no reason for Felicity to harm a servant, he told himself, but had she been trying to divert any suspicion that Harriet was her target? Again he fought against his irrational fear for his sister's sanity – something which he knew had once been questioned all those years ago. He tried to argue against such thoughts, telling himself that if Edgerton wished to be free to marry Felicity, then he had only to divorce his wife. As for his ongoing relationship with Felicity, he had only ever shown a friendly affection for her.

Quite suddenly Paul was stuck by a frightening thought. *Was this where the trouble lay?* Felicity had always craved those few things in life denied to her. If her desires were not fulfilled, she had flown into ungovernable rages. As a child when he had refused to give her one of his possessions she had flown at him, swearing, hitting him, even biting him in the hope of making him hand over what she wanted. Such tantrums had continued until their doting father promised to buy her whatever she wanted which, as often as not, she ceased to want once it belonged to her. Could Edgerton's unavailability have aroused that dangerous, obsessive determination to fulfil her desires?

Paul's uneasy speculations continued into the night, preventing sleep. Something, he knew, needed to be done before anything dreadful could happen: but what? Would he be able to entice her to go abroad with him? Could he take her on a prolonged holiday during which there would be time for her passions to cool? Fortuitously, his fiancée was about to return to France to see her parents after their engagement was made official, partly to visit her many relatives but also, he suspected, to give her time to ascertain that she had made the right choice of husband.

The following morning he put the idea of a holiday to Felicity. 'You never did take that steamship passage to America you promised yourself,' he said, 'and I have been thinking that once my dearest Denise and I are married next year, I will not be available as I am now to escort you. Or, if you preferred, we could do a tour of Europe or, perhaps more exciting, travel to Egypt and see the pyramids.'

Felicity shook her head. 'I don't have the slightest wish to go anywhere, Paul,' she told him, 'though I thank you for the offer. I have a number of plans for the next few months which will occupy me here.' And she changed the subject.

Paul stayed on a further two weeks longer than he had planned in order to visit the Edgertons with Felicity, in the hope of reassuring himself that his suspicions were totally unfounded. Although he thought that Harriet seemed quiet and rather pale, Brook seemed reasonably attentive to her, much as any normal husband might be, and there was no indication of any serious discord between them, although there had been a certain coolness, nonetheless. He was further reassured when a servant arrived at Melton Court with a letter from Brook saying he would not be able to meet up with Paul for some time as he had just learned he must sail at once to Jamaica where there had been another serious outbreak of trouble at their plantation.

If, Paul had told himself, Felicity had been planning in some way or another to tempt Edgerton into an affair, she would have no opportunity for some time to come. As for any intention to harm Harriet, he had convinced himself that he'd been out of his mind even to have entertained such an idea. Furthermore, he'd spoken to Simkins about the arsenic, and the butler had suggested that one of the maids cleaning the room before it had been closed up might have found it and locked it safely away.

It was, therefore, in a far calmer frame of mind that Paul returned to London.

If Felicity was devastated by the news of Brook's sudden departure, Harriet was even more so. She was now reasonably certain that the cause of her sickness was that yet again she was pregnant. She knew exactly when she must have conceived – the night Brook had come to her bed and wordlessly, without love, forced himself upon her.

She had been waiting for the right moment to tell him of her condition, hoping desperately that the news might heal the dreadful rift between them. On the contrary, when Brook told her his father expected him to take responsibility once again for their plantations, he had said in a cold, hard voice,

'I trust when I return home this time, Harriet, that you will not have another unacceptable and unwelcome shock for me.' Without looking at her, he'd added, 'I shall be taking Hastings with me, of course, and I have informed Fletcher not to expect me back for at least two, if not three, months.'

Two days after his departure, when Felicity came to see her, Harriet gave way freely to the tears she had been too proud to shed in Brook's presence.

'I have made up my mind,' she told the woman she considered to be her best friend and confidante, 'to go away myself. I cannot stay here in this house watching the days pass slowly by waiting for Brook's return. I am leaving next week with Bessie and Charlie to stay with my sister in Ireland. It will make up a little for the disappointment we both felt when I was unable to receive her at Easter.'

Felicity regarded her in dismay. 'You cannot go away . . .' she began and added quickly, 'that is to say, you have not been well and . . .'

She broke off as Harriet interrupted with a wan smile. 'Dearest Felicity, I have not had an illness,' she said. 'I am certain that I am pregnant. I only realized it when I missed the second time.'

Mistaking the look of disbelief followed quickly by anger on Felicity's face for one of concern, she added: 'I know I lost my last baby on that fateful journey to Ireland, but I shall not go unprotected this time. I shall take one of the footmen with me, armed if he thinks fit. Believe me, I shall be quite safe as it is another six or seven months at least before I have this baby . . .'

She broke off to take hold of Felicity's hands. 'I now have hope, dearest! Don't you see, I can hope that the arrival of his child will soften Brook's heart. His absence may also do so, and we shall be reconciled. I shall get well in Ireland with my sister, regain my looks, I trust, and when I return, I shall hope you will see me looking my old self again.'

It was only with huge self-control that Felicity managed to conceal her desperate dismay. She declined to stay for luncheon, summoned her groom and as soon as she could decently do so, she rode home. Once there, she gave way to her fury, shouting at her staff, trashing the drawing room and turning the meal her cook had prepared for her upside down on the table. It was not the behaviour of a gentlewoman, but Felicity did not care. Only later, as she grew calmer, did she decide that whilst both Brook and Harriet were away she might as well accept her brother's invitation to take her travelling. His fiancée was conveniently away visiting relatives in France, and after the engagement party Paul would not be seeing her at least until Christmas.

Harriet, she told herself, should make the most of these extra weeks of life whilst she was travelling with Paul. It was only the time of her death which had had to be postponed.

TWENTY-ONE

1869–1870

Felicity's enjoyment of her European tour in Paul's company had been tempered by thoughts and dreams of Brook. Wherever they visited, there was always something which reminded her of him – a man's tall figure crossing St Mark's

Square in Venice; the sound of a similar voice to his in a restaurant in Paris; a stallion in Vienna identical to Brook's favourite mount.

She was tormented, too, by her failure to succeed in poisoning Harriet, although not altogether surprised. She had read in her father's medical directory that arsenic was sometimes administered medicinally, but in the book the amount to be used was obscure. She did learn that if a person had been given a regular amount and it was suddenly ceased, it could be very dangerous, but because she had not been able to visit Harriet on a regular basis, she'd had no chance of administering it daily. Moreover, before leaving England, she had been forced to face the fact that she could not use poison again when she returned home. Paul had told her he'd found the bottle of arsenic and disposed of it. He had not overtly accused her of secreting it in the desk, but she'd had the impression he believed it to be so. She wondered uneasily if he suspected her of using it, although it had occurred to her that this was the reason he had persuaded her to accompany him on the lengthy holiday abroad. Newly engaged as he was, with an engagement party in a few months' time, it had struck her as strange.

Sometimes, on a wakeful night, she would question whether Harriet had ever suspected that the fruit and sweetmeats she had given her were contaminated. Why else would the other members of the Edgerton staff have fallen ill unless Harriet had sent some of them untouched down to the kitchen? On those sleepless nights, Felicity also had doubts about Ellen – whether she'd guessed that she, Felicity, was responsible for Harriet's occasional bouts of sickness.

During the daytime, it had been possible with so many new sights, new people and new countries to occupy her mind – for her to forget the precarious position she would be in if Ellen were to betray her; but in the early hours, unable to sleep, she realized that she had laid herself open to blackmail. When she had first decided to use Ellen to spy on Harriet and Brook, she'd banked on the maid's obsessive wish to improve her sister's situation. However unnerving though this thought was, Felicity's longing to see Brook again invariably pushed such anxiety to the back of her mind.

As the weeks of the holiday passed, Felicity's unease grew in proportion to her compelling desire to go home. Moving from place to place as she and Paul were doing, they'd had no contact with home other than when Paul telegraphed his office in order to update himself as to the firm's current affairs. As far as Felicity knew, Harriet was still in Ireland, but surely, she thought, both Harriet and Brook must return home soon, if they had not already done so.

In the meantime, Paul had not only grown tired of his sister's company despite their interesting surroundings and changes of venues, but he was anxious to return to his fiancée in London. He knew Denise would have finished visiting her family and be wondering where he was. Although he had sent her postcards from every place he and Felicity had visited, he wanted his pretty French fiancée back in his arms. He made no objection, therefore, when Felicity expressed her desire to go home.

Felicity would have been even more desirous of returning to England had she known that Brook, too, was on his way home from Jamaica. He had sent a telegram to Fletcher advising him of his imminent arrival so that the staff had the house in readiness. He was unaware of whether Harriet was still in Ireland with her sister, but his pride forbade him telling Fletcher to alert Harriet of his homecoming.

Fletcher assumed his mistress would likewise have received a similar telegram from the master, but having had no instructions from her he thought he should enquire if there were any particular preparations she might wish him to make. A telegram in reply to his arrived by return from Harriet saying she was about to leave Ireland and wished him to instruct Jenkins to have the carriage waiting at Clarence Dock to meet the ferry from Dublin in three days' time.

Thus it was that three days later, with Bessie and Charlie beside her, Harriet's coach approached Hunters Hall. The cold winter months had given way to spring, and as Jenkins turned the horses' heads into the driveway, she could see the delicate green of the beech trees in the surrounding woods of the Edgerton estate, and a few minutes later the lovely red bricks of the house, glowing in the sunshine, came into view.

Her heart filled with a mixture of excitement and fear. Was Brook already home? Would he be pleased to see her? Or would he still be as unforgiving as when he had departed to Jamaica?

Despite the heart-warming company of Una and her family, he
had been constantly in her mind. As if mirroring her thoughts,
beside her Charlie was now demanding excitedly, 'Is Papa home?
Shall we see Papa? Can I show him my new clockwork monkey?
Will he see how I am growed?'

Bessie removed his hat from his brown curls and smiled at
Harriet. 'I'm sure I don't know where he gets his energy from!'
she remarked, smiling. 'You'd think as how he'd be tired after
all that long journey!'

Harriet returned Bessie's smile and replied to her son, 'If Papa
is not out riding, or visiting Grandfather, I expect we shall see
him.' Her heart was beating furiously in anticipation as the coach
pulled up outside the front door and Fletcher came out to greet
them.

Harriet lifted the little boy down into Fletcher's waiting arms.

'We are expecting the master back this afternoon, madam,'
Fletcher told her as he followed her into the house. 'We had a
telegram from him saying their ship had arrived on time; that
Hastings was hiring a coach and they hoped to be home before
dark.'

Following Fletcher into the house, Harriet reflected happily
that she would have time now to change from her travelling
clothes into something pretty. Una's dressmaker had made her a
lovely sky-blue Princess gown, and Ellen would have plenty of
time to iron out any creases.

An hour later, feeling entirely refreshed after her holiday in
Ireland, despite the long journey, Harriet went down to the
drawing room to have tea and await Brook's return. She had
finished her tea by the time she heard the sound of horses' hooves,
and she hurried to the window. The carriage drew to a halt by
the front steps, and with Hastings following him, she saw Brook
spring down from the coach, cross the terrace and disappear
through the front door.

Suddenly shy, a confusion of pleasure and fear engulfing her,
she remained at the drawing-room window, not going into the
hall as she would have liked to do. She longed to be able to
throw herself into his arms but knew she must not. It was now
eight long weeks since she had set eyes on him, yet it seemed
a lifetime. Although she had been happy at Una's house, which

in many ways had become almost a second home, she was always haunted by the look on Brook's face when he had accused her of lying to him, and cheating him; she knew that he would never trust her again, perhaps never learn to love Charlie again.

It was now her hope that, because of the baby she was carrying with no sign whatever of a miscarriage, he might relent when he knew she was going to be able to give him his own child. Surely, she'd told herself, he would forgive her now?

Three miles away at Melton Court, Felicity sat reading the note Ellen had sent her via one of the stable lads informing her that Brook was home. In it, she reported the fact of Harriet's condition.

Felicity's heart contracted painfully with fear. This news meant that it was more probable than ever Brook and Harriet would be reconciled; that any hope she might have had of winning Brook's love for herself may have gone. The thought filled her not only with fear but with a devouring anger. *IT MUST NOT HAPPEN.* She would not let it happen. Feverishly, her mind searched for a way – any way, to prevent it. Paul was back in London and she was free to do whatever she wished without worrying about his intervention.

After half an hour, taut with excitement, she thought of a better way to kill Harriet than her risky attempts to poison her; a way where no suspicion would lie at her door; a way even Ellen could not prove was of her doing. A way without risk to herself.

As Harriet had feared, Brook did not hold out his arms to her when he entered the drawing room. Taking advantage of Hastings' presence, he greeted her politely. If he noticed her pregnancy, he made no comment but followed Hastings upstairs to change from his travelling clothes, saying he would be down in time for dinner.

During dinner, he was not silent as he had been in the past, but his conversation was entirely impersonal and he did not enquire after Charlie. Not entirely without hope that Brook's attitude towards her had softened a little, Harriet resolved to emulate him, addressing him only impersonally in the presence of Fletcher and enquiring about his activities in Jamaica. That night he returned to his dressing room.

The next morning Harriet gave Bessie instructions to keep Charlie as far as possible out of Brook's sight. She could not bear the thought of the little boy's distress if Brook gave no sign of pleasure in seeing him.

At first there was no sign of Felicity so Harriet sent a letter to her via her groom advising her friend of their return home. Three days later, Felicity arrived shortly before the lunch hour. She was on her way home from Melton Mowbray, she explained, and had not intended to leave so late or she would have called by earlier. Harriet instantly invited her to stay for luncheon, during which Brook encouraged Felicity to tell them all about her visit abroad with Paul.

During the course of the meal, Harriet remarked on how well Felicity was looking and Felicity returned the compliment, glancing as she did so at the lace flounces falling in delicate folds down the front of Harriet's bodice, concealing her increased girth. Had she not yet told Brook of her condition? she asked herself. Was Harriet trying to hide her pregnancy from Brook? Was it possible he knew nothing of it as yet? On the other hand, his manner towards Harriet and the tone of voice he used when addressing her were considerably less abrasive, far gentler than before he had gone abroad. *Not that it would matter if her plans were to succeed,* she told herself.

Her heart thudded with excitement as Brook smiled at her, remarking how well she looked and how beneficial the holiday had been to her health. They must go riding together as soon as he had cleared the backlog of problems on his estate which had arisen whilst he had been abroad, he told her. He had greatly missed their outings. Harriet's account of her holiday with Una and the children had followed but the child, Charlie, was not mentioned by either her or Brook.

Felicity felt a sudden stab of anxiety as she pondered the possibility that Brook and Harriet might be on the brink of a reconciliation and that the plan she had devised might not, for some reason, work. The birth of the child Harriet was obviously carrying would almost certainly restore their relationship at least to some degree. Any doubts she, Felicity, had had about the timing of her plans now vanished entirely.

The meal over, Brook excused himself, saying he could not stay for coffee as he was meeting their estate manager, Banks, at two o'clock. Bidding them both goodbye, he left the room. As soon as she had finished her coffee, Felicity stood up, announcing that she, too, must leave. As she did so she gave a little cry, saying that she had inadvertently put the heel of her button boot through the hem of her petticoat – 'Such a silly thing to have done,' she elaborated, as it could now so easily trip her and cause her to fall.

Harriet immediately rose to her feet and went to the bell rope to summon Albert. He was to find Ellen, she told him, and tell her that Mrs Goodall needed her assistance immediately upstairs in her dressing room.

'We'll go straight there, and Ellen shall pin the hem back in place for you,' she said solicitously.

Felicity's reply was instantaneous. 'There is absolutely no need for you to accompany me, dearest.' She added with a smile: 'I should know my way there by now, should I not?' She looped the skirts of her dress together with the undamaged petticoat over her arm and, reassuring Harriet a second time that she need not go with her, she made her way upstairs.

Ellen was waiting for her.

'Close the door!' Felicity said sharply, and as soon as Ellen had done so, she added: 'Now listen to me.' She took a letter out of her pocket and handed it to the maid. 'You are to give this to your mistress tomorrow morning immediately after breakfast. You will ensure that there is no one – *no one at all* – who sees you do this. Do you understand? It is vitally important that you carry out my instruction implicitly. Moreover, you will not mention it afterwards to anyone – *absolutely no one else*. Do you understand?' she repeated.

Ellen understood perfectly but made no reply. Although she had no idea what was in the letter, she gauged by Felicity's tense expression and tone of voice that her holiday had done nothing to lessen her desire to disrupt her employers' marriage, and that this letter must be yet another ploy to do so.

'Did you not hear what I said?' Felicity demanded sharply.

'Shall I not give it to madam tonight?' Ellen enquired ingeniously.

Felicity was not deceived by what she perceived were delaying tactics. Ellen was after more money. Angry though she was to be held to ransom by the servant, she had neither the time nor the inclination to barter.

'You will do exactly as I say, Ellen, and if all proceeds as I intend, there will be a very handsome bonus for you – a VERY handsome one. I might add that it could put you in a position where you could leave domestic service and live in comfort with your sister. But understand me, Ellen, there must be no word whatsoever about this letter – that I gave it to you or that you did as I requested and gave it to your mistress.'

She paused to draw a deep breath before adding: 'Bear this in mind, Ellen: if you were ever to speak it to a living soul, I have the means to ensure that not only you but your sister would suffer the consequence. Do you understand me?'

Ellen understood Felicity perfectly well. She also believed what she was saying – that she had adequate means to harm her and her beloved sister. The woman was rich – rich enough to hire criminals to carry out whatever she was prepared to pay for – robbery, assault, even kidnapping: money could buy anything short of murder.

The slight tremor of fear which now passed through Ellen was quickly ignored. Two days previously she had learned that her sister was in hospital with a chest infection. When Susan came out, she would need to have special care, delicacies to whet her appetite and aid her recovery, and sea air. A nursing home on the Sussex coast would be expensive. The money she had so far managed to save – Felicity's hush money – would cover such necessities but would eat up all the money she had put aside to buy the seaside bungalow. Whatever else her paymaster might be guilty of, Mrs Goodall had never failed to pay her for her services. She need have no fear that this latest request would be as well rewarded as she'd promised.

Ellen was not particularly interested in the contents of the letter and locked it away in her suitcase beneath her bed. The following morning, however, she decided she should know the contents, lest she was somehow implicated. However, when she tried to open it imperceptibly, the flap split suddenly so it had become obvious the letter had been tampered with. For a few moments, Ellen felt sick with anxiety. Then, with an effort, she pulled herself together and considered what she could do.

As her racing heartbeat slowed, it occurred to her that there was a simple, more-or-less safe way out of the problem. The spoiled envelope had only Harriet's name on it. She, Ellen, could take one of the plain white envelopes from the desk in one of the guest rooms, seal the letter in it and write Mrs BROOK EDGERTON in capital letters on the front. Harriet would have no reason to question it if, as Felicity had instructed her, she told Harriet that it had not come by post but had been delivered by one of the Melton Court grooms early that morning.

Satisfied with her decision, Ellen drew the single sheet of paper out of the torn envelope, and began to read Felicity's hurriedly written script.

> *Dearest Harriet,* she read, *I would not ask this favour but I am quite desperate and am urgently in need of your help and support. I have a woman coming to see me at eleven o'clock on Tuesday morning who I fear has reason to wish me harm. She is aware I live here alone and I am certain is taking advantage of the fact.*
>
> *You may think it advisable to bring Brook with you but I have a very good reason for begging you not to do so. It is a matter for female ears only and I do assure you that I am quite certain there is nothing he could do to help. You being here as a witness will suffice to make my adversary think twice about threatening me again. It is verbal and not physical damage she can inflict, but will not do so if I have a witness present.*
>
> *I am counting on your help, my very dear friend.*

The letter Ellen had given Harriet after breakfast that morning, which she'd just finished reading was unsigned. At first Harriet wondered if it had been intended for someone other than herself. She could not begin to imagine that the self-sufficient Felicity was unable to deal with a verbal difficulty by herself.

She now set aside her untouched breakfast tray and glanced at her bedside clock. It was already half past eight. If she was to be at Melton Court by eleven o'clock it was time she got up, she told herself. Felicity had specified particularly in her letter that she must come on her own so, she now decided, she would drive herself in the gig. Although the pathway between their two houses was no more than three miles long, she would be driving slowly because of her condition. There was no way, she told herself, that she would risk another miscarriage. All her hopes for a reconciliation with Brook now depended upon her giving him a son of his own making. She must therefore depart for Melton Court in plenty of time.

Turning to Ellen, who had just entered the room, she told her to find Albert and tell him to go straight to the stables and give instructions that she would need the gig to be ready at the front door by ten o'clock; that she wished to drive herself and would therefore have no need for a groom.

'When you have carried out those instructions, you can come back and assist me to dress, Ellen,' she told the maid.

'If anyone asks, am I to say where you are going, madam?' Ellen asked.

Harriet looked at her sharply. 'Certainly not! What I do with my time as you should know by now, Ellen, is my business and no one else's. Now be off!'

As she struggled into her petticoats, it suddenly occurred to Harriet that it was a little strange of Felicity to have left it until this morning to request her help, although she was unlikely to be elsewhere other than at home, at so early an hour. Felicity's concerns must have evolved quite suddenly, she thought as she stooped to put on her boots, but could not be of any great magnitude as she had specified she had no need for Brook to be involved.

Pulling her dress over her head, Harriet decided that it was only moral support Felicity needed: a witness to what was being said. By now, Ellen had returned and set about dressing Harriet's hair, buttoning up her boots and taking her outdoor cloak and bonnet from the wardrobe. When finally Harriet descended the stairs, Ellen carrying her gloves and cloak, Fletcher was in the process of opening the front door.

Seeing the post boy standing there, a new lad who obviously had not been told to use the tradesman's entrance, Fletcher instructed him quite sharply to do so. Looking slightly apprehensive, the lad remained where he was because, he said, he'd been told not to leave without obtaining a signature from a Miss Ellen Reed saying she had received the letter he was holding.

Realizing the boy did not know that Ellen was a servant and seeing her in the hall with the mistress, Fletcher said more gently, 'If madam has no objection, Ellen, you can sign for the letter here.' Taking the remaining letters from the post boy, he sent him smartly on his way.

Ellen put the envelope in her apron pocket, and when Fletcher had assisted their mistress up into the driving seat of the gig and seen it disappear down the driveway, she hurried back upstairs to her bedroom. She had seen by the postmark on the envelope that it had come from the seaside nursing home in Worthing, where her sister was being cared for. The matron reported the patient's condition to Ellen once a fortnight; however, it was barely a week since her last report, so as Ellen sat down on the hard iron bedstead, it was with a faint feeling of unease that she opened it, fearing news of a delay in her sister's recovery.

The words blurred as she started to read:

> '. . . *died very suddenly last night. We sent at once for the doctor but Miss Reed had had a heart attack and there was nothing that could have been done to save her.*
>
> *We would have sent you a telegram with this sad news but knowing how devoted you were to your sister, and as there was nothing you could do for her, Doctor thought it would be less stressful for you to hear of her sad passing by letter.*
>
> *As you will be coming from some distance away, we will be very willing to accommodate you . . .*'

Ellen stopped reading. Her heart thudding, her hands trembling, she tried to come to terms with the horrific fact that her beloved sister, who she had believed to be recovering well from a bout of pneumonia, had suffered a heart attack and died.

The shock was so intense, so heart-breaking, that for several minutes Ellen was paralysed. Then her mind began working at a furious speed as the initial shock gave way to anger. *How could God have allowed this to happen?* Her sister had never in her life done anything wrong. She'd been a gentle soul, suffering ill health without complaint as she had suffered the impoverished conditions in which she lived. Now, just when she, Ellen, was acquiring the necessary money to transform Susan's life, God had taken the opportunity from her.

Ellen scrunched up the pages of the letter and let them drop to the floor where it lay at her feet; then, anxious to read it once more, she stooped to retrieve it. As she did so, the letter from Mrs Goodall to Harriet, which she had stolen from her room whilst fastening her boots, fell from her skirt pocket on to the floor beside that of the matron's. As she stared at the two lying side by side, she was struck suddenly by the thought that this could be prophetic: that Susan's untimely death was God's way of punishing her, Ellen, for knowingly complying with Felicity's evil intentions. What better way was there of showing her she had been selling her soul to the Devil in order to achieve what she wanted?

For a moment, Ellen feared she might faint as she faced the fact that assisting to commit a sin was as wicked as perpetrating it. There was no denying that she had suspected Mrs Goodall of intending serious harm, if not death for the wife of the man she wanted. She, Ellen, had closed her mind to what had become a certainty last night when she'd read Mrs Goodall's request for Harriet to visit her secretly and alone.

Although not overtly religious, Ellen attended church every Sunday and did not doubt the existence of an omnipotent God nor indeed of His counterpart, the Devil. She now caught her breath as her mind, distorted by shock and grief, envisaged Mrs Felicity Goodall as Satan in disguise. The Devil had closed her mind to the suspicion that the fruit and sweetmeats had contained poison; the Devil who had directed her to give Brook the stolen letter revealing the child's origins, knowing full well that it could bring about the disintegration of a hitherto idyllic marriage.

Throughout Susan's childhood, her favourite book had been one containing Bible stories which she had had to read to her again and again. If any living person knew right from wrong as a result, she did; but she had chosen to sell her soul to the Devil and ignore those teachings. Was it now to be wondered that if God had chosen to remove the most precious thing in her life as a punishment? That he was giving her one last chance to redeem herself?

Her hands trembling, Ellen smoothed out the page containing Felicity's instructions to Harriet. Eleven o'clock Harriet was to be at Melton Court. Was there still time to prevent what she feared might be about to happen? If she could show God that she wished to repent, might He forgive her so that she could be certain to be reunited with her beloved sister in Heaven when she died? It was only with the certainty of seeing Susan again that she could even begin to face life without her; to accept that she would never hear her voice again, never see her lovely smile . . .

Ellen rose stiffly from the bed and, drawing a deep breath to steady herself, resolved to carry out what she now had no doubt must be done. She looked once more at the hands of her watch and saw with dismay that even now it could be too late to prevent the disaster she suspected – a disaster it must surely be when the letter made it so clear Harriet must go to Melton Court on her own. The master must see the letter: hear her confession that she was in Felicity's pay, and that she was convinced of her evil intent towards his wife.

She grabbed the letter in one hand, her crumpled skirt in the other, and hurried down the main staircase, praying with every step that the master would be in his study and that her confession would not come too late.

TWENTY-TWO

1870

For some time now, Felicity had been standing behind some trees in Badgers Wood, a dark cloak covering her dress and helping to conceal her presence. Confident that Ellen would have given her letter to Harriet that morning, she was in no doubt that Harriet would pass that way to Melton Court within the next half hour. Had Harriet been unable to come, she reasoned, she would have sent word to say so. All her planning now depended upon Harriet's kindly nature ensuring she answered Felicity's appeal for help. The only possible danger she could envisage was if, for some reason, Brook came with her. But she had even thought of a way to deal with such a contingency. If Brook was accompanying Harriet, she would be obliged to reveal herself as soon as they came into sight, pretend that she had fallen from her horse on the way to meet Harriet, and allow them to conduct her to Hunters Hall to recover. In due course she would insist upon returning home alone, which would afford her the opportunity to dismantle the trap she had set.

Felicity had no fear that any other person might come this way. The road, if such it could be called, was no more than a cutting between the dense forest of trees that lay between their adjoining estates. Only a trespasser ever came this way or a poacher, and they would keep well hidden off the beaten track.

It was a mild, sunny morning and squirrels were scampering about in the beech trees beneath which Felicity was standing. A rabbit ran past her motionless figure unaware of any danger. Apart from the rattling of a woodpecker calling to its mate from a nearby tree, there was no other sound to distract her apart from that of an approaching horse's hooves. Stretched across the bridlepath, almost completely concealed by last winter's leaf fall, lay a tripwire.

Many years ago, when she and Paul were children, he had proudly explained to Felicity his newly acquired knowledge, imparted by the gamekeeper, of how to make snares for rabbits. At the same time he had described various aspects of nature, one of which was the fact that wild animals nearly always frequented the same paths through the undergrowth. This knowledge, he said, had come in handy in the war when tripwires were laid across routes in forests known to be used by the enemy's horses pulling their gun carriages. All too frequently the unfortunate animals broke their legs and had to be shot.

Now, whether Harriet came in a carriage or on horseback – this unlikely in her condition – the wire she had stretched across the bridleway would at the very least unseat her. If the fall did not kill Harriet, then she had beside her a stout branch which would complete the job, and would explain the resulting injury to Harriet's head.

Back at Hunters Hall Hastings was in the hallway, the look of anxiety on his face deepening when he saw Harriet descending the stairs. He stepped forward quickly and, apologising for halting her progress, he said, 'Pardon me, madam, but the master thought as how you had departed about half an hour ago. He has gone after you. He said if he wasn't back within the hour, I was to go to Melton Court.'

Harriet looked at the valet curiously. Hastings was what Brook called a rock, always quiet, dependable and unflappable. He was now quite clearly in a disturbed state.

'I did leave, Hastings,' she said, 'but I went first to the hot-house to pick up a plant for Mrs Goodall, and the heel of my boot came loose. I've just been upstairs to change. I am a trifle late, so I must hurry now. But you sound worried, Hastings. Your master had no need to follow me. Do you know why he has done so?'

'Yes, madam, I am concerned,' he said. 'The master did not even change into his riding clothes. Nor would he wait for me.' Hastings caught his breath. He could see no reason why the truth could not be told – it would be bound to surface sooner or later.

'Ellen came downstairs to speak to the master,' he said as calmly as he could. 'She warned him that you were in danger, madam; that you were on your way to see Mrs Goodall and must be stopped. The master did not even wait for me to fetch his hat and coat but went himself to the stables to fetch Shamrock and, without saddling him, went galloping off down the driveway.'

'What danger, Hastings? I don't understand,' Harriet said, her heart quickening in anxiety. 'Are you trying to tell me that it is my husband and not I who is in danger? If so, why aren't you with him, Hastings? No matter what orders he gave you?'

'Because he forbade me. He said I might hold him up,' the valet replied simply, 'as I'm not able to ride without a saddle as he can. He . . .'

'Then we must go and tell him that I am perfectly safe!' Harriet said. 'Besides which, I am due at Mrs Goodall's house at eleven o'clock and I should be well on my way by now. The gig should be waiting outside,' she continued. 'We will go together, Hastings, and if, as you seem to think, my husband is anticipating some kind of trouble, you will be on hand to take care of it.'

A few minutes later, as she set off in the gig with Hastings, down the driveway and into the woods leading to Melton Court, she tried to fathom what possible reason Ellen might have had to see Brook that had disturbed him sufficiently to follow her to Melton Court.

Never having liked Ellen, she had consequently not mentioned to her that she was visiting Felicity alone that morning. Even had Ellen seen her depart alone in the gig, it was not her business to relay the fact to Brook.

It was time she got rid of Ellen, she told herself, as Hastings urged the horse into a faster trot. She would have dismissed her years ago, had it not been for two reasons – one, that Ellen was extremely efficient, the other that Ellen had no family other than the invalid sister for whom she was solely responsible. Pity had outweighed her antipathy for her.

At first, all they could hear above the muffled noise of their horse's hooves on the rough ground was the harsh cawing of the rooks as they flew off in alarm. Then suddenly there was the sound of gunshots. A moment later they turned a corner and a horrifying scene came into sight. Hastings reined in the horse as they drew nearer. A man in rough clothing, holding a gun, was standing looking down at a dead horse. Beside him was a man's body with a woman crouched over him, cradling his head in her arms and keening.

In a flash, Hastings had jumped out of the gig and was running towards them. Only as he reached them and the woman raised her head did Harriet realize that the sobbing female was Felicity. A second later, horrifyingly, she caught sight of the man she was holding: it was Brook, and the dead horse was Shamrock, his precious stallion.

Hastings was now trying to pull Felicity away from Brook's body, but she clung to him with astonishing strength. As quickly as she could, Harriet struggled to climb down from the gig. The man with the gun, who she now recognized as Tyler, Paul Denning's gamekeeper, came hurrying over to her, saying, 'Best not go near them, Mrs Edgerton, not 'till your man's got hold of her. Reckon as how the poor lady's off her head!' He scratched his chin in bewilderment. 'Don't make much sense to me, her carrying on like that, not seeing as how it were she what set the trap for him – leastways, that's what I'm thinking!'

Seeing the look of incomprehension on Harriet's face, he continued, 'When I came this way last evening, I saw that there wire, coiled up like, behind that tree. I reckoned t'was one of them dratted poachers were about as have been after the pheasants. So I thought as how I'd keep an eye on it. When I comes back this morning, there was the wire fastened to that tree across the path and . . .'

Harriet was only half listening as she stared at the dreadful scene in front of them. Brook's inert body lay only a few feet away from the dead horse. Resisting Hastings' attempt to lift her, Felicity was cradling Brook's head, rocking to and fro. She had stopped moaning and was whimpering, her words barely decipherable as she protested over and over again that she loved him and had not meant to harm him; that he mustn't die because he belonged to her; she needed him. Harriet only half heard the gamekeeper's voice as he continued to relate what he'd seen.

'Weren't no one about that early,' he was saying, 'but the deer often comes this way and I reckoned that them poachers were hidden somewhere's awaiting for one of 'em to come by and break its leg like that poor horse. Had to shoot 'im, I did!'

Seeing that he now had Harriet's attention once more, he continued, 'I didn't see his rider, Mr Edgerton, at first, and next thing madam comes running out of t'other side of the path and . . .'

He broke off as Hastings finally managed to pull Felicity away from Brook's body. Disregarding her screams, he was restraining her with his belt as he twisted it round her waist, securing her to a nearby sapling. As Harriet ran forward to Brook, Hastings turned his back on Felicity and came over to kneel down by Brook's side. Harriet watched him, her heart pounding as he put his ear to his master's mouth.

After what seemed to Harriet to be an interminable time, he looked up at her, saying, 'He's alive, madam, but only just. We need to get the doctor fast.' He turned to the gamekeeper. 'You stay here with madam and I'll take the horse and ride to the village to fetch Doctor Tremlett.' He took off his jacket and covered Brook's body as best he could. Then, rising quickly, he hurried over to the gig and took the two cushions off the seat.

With great tenderness, he put one under Brook's head and the other on the ground beside him.

'If you stay here with him, madam, Tyler can keep an eye on Mrs Goodall. I'll be as quick as I can. Are you sure you'll be all right?'

'Yes, of course, Hastings!' Harriet told him. 'Please hurry!' she whispered as she forced herself to look at Brook's ashen face. There was a smear of blood coming from a gash on his forehead, and his breathing was slow and frighteningly uneven.

Tears filled her eyes but remained unshed as she stroked his cheek, whispering words of endearment and begging him not to leave her. So concentrated was she that Felicity's screams as she tried to free herself went unheard.

Thus it was that with her head bent over Brook's body as she willed him not to die, Harriet was unaware when Felicity suddenly managed to extricate one arm from the belt securing her body to the tree. Tyler, walking back to pick up his gun from where he had placed it by some trees, turned as he heard a sudden piercing scream, and saw Felicity hurrying towards the couple. She stopped momentarily to pick up a stout branch of wood lying by the dead horse. Then she reached Harriet's side and, screaming hysterically that Brook belonged to her, raised her arm ready to bring the branch down on Harriet's head. Her hair was now in a wild tangle about her face, which was distorted with hatred. Even from some distance away, Tyler could see that her eyes were blazing like those of someone demented. In that single moment, he was in no doubt whatsoever of the mad woman's intent. Simultaneously, he realized he could not cover the distance between them quickly enough to prevent the blow being struck. He reached instinctively for his gun, pulled back the safety catch, and took aim.

Seeing him do so, Felicity gave a wild laugh and raised the branch still higher above Harriet's head. 'He's mine! Mine! Mine!' she screamed, and was still screaming when, believing he had no other alternative, Tyler pulled back the trigger and fired.

TWENTY-THREE

1870

I t must be all of twenty-four hours ago, Harriet thought, that she had gone into labour. Bessie had sent for the midwife who had come up from the village and examined her, and gone away saying Harriet would have to wait a while yet before her baby arrived. To Bessie she confided that she intended having a word with Dr Tremlett as she feared things were not as they should be with Mrs Edgerton.

Not really frightened by the intermittent pains, Harriet had no wish to be left on her own and was happy to have her faithful Bessie sitting with her.

There was no sign of Brook. He had been in a coma for over a month before he had regained consciousness, and it was a further eight weeks before Dr Tremlett had pronounced his complete recovery. However, he had not regained any memory of the accident. According to the doctor, this was not unusual and he had assured Brook that he might recall events in the future.

To Harriet's distress, there had been no change in Brook's attitude of indifference to her or to Charlie. Hastings, Brook was told by the doctor, had been instrumental in saving his life by his prompt action following Brook's fall. As a consequence, his valet had received a generous recognition in the form of a gift of one of the cottages in the village for himself and Bessie when they were married the following summer.

The gamekeeper, Tyler, had also received recognition for saving Harriet's life. Surprisingly, it was not from Brook but from Paul Denning. Paul had not put in an appearance at Hunters Hall but had written to Brook apologising unreservedly for what had happened. Felicity, he wrote, was now safely locked up in secure accommodation in an asylum, there to remain until the doctors in charge of the mentally-ill patients declared it safe to release her. His sister owed her life, such as it now was, to their gamekeeper who had aimed at her arm rather than her body in order to prevent her carrying out her intention to harm Harriet. He wrote further that he was temporarily in England in order to arrange the sale of Melton Court as he was to live in France with Denise, now his bride, who he had secretly married shortly after he had dealt with Felicity.

Brook had not commented on Paul's letter when he had handed it to Harriet. Nor had he shown any interest in the inquest which had followed the shocking discovery of Ellen's body washed up on a south coast beach. The matron of the nursing home where her sister died had given evidence that Ellen was seen by one of the nurses to jump off the end of the Brighton pier and drown; that she herself had thought Ellen had appeared unhinged with grief when attending her late sister's funeral. The coroner had, therefore, not hesitated to give a verdict of suicide.

'Best not think about such things, Miss Harriet!' Bessie had said. 'The master may not have said so but there ain't no doubt it were Ellen as stole your letter you wrote to the lady on the ferry, and showed it to him. As for Mrs Goodall's letter setting that trap for you, the master told Hastings that Ellen had showed it to him and confessed she was being paid by that wicked woman to spy on you. Good riddance, I say!'

It had been a huge comfort to Harriet when Bessie had replaced Maire. So devoted was she to the little boy, she made no demur when Harriet was obliged to employ a new lady's maid. Being as close as they were, Bessie had mirrored Harriet's hopes that the baby Harriet was expecting – Brook's baby – would bring about their reconciliation. The previous day, however, Doctor Tremlett's visit at the request of the midwife had given cause for concern. Not only was the baby in the wrong position, he told the midwife in Bessie's hearing, which was going to make the birth a hazardous one, but he could only detect a very faint heartbeat.

It was not until early the following morning that Dr Tremlett had finally managed with the aid of the midwife to extricate the lifeless baby from Harriet's womb. It had been no compensation for her to be told that even had the baby – a boy – survived the birth, he would not have lived for long.

Such was Harriet's distress that she could neither weep nor

sleep. Her distress at losing the baby was overshadowed by the knowledge of the consequence; that there was no longer a reason for Brook to forgive her. The loss of the baby meant the loss of hope.

Regarding her anxiously, the midwife said, 'You must be very tired, madam. You should try and have a little sleep . . .'

She broke off at the sound of the bedroom door opening, then Harriet heard Brook saying, 'It's perfectly all right, Nurse. Doctor Tremlett said before he left that we might pay a brief visit to the patient. Now you may go and kiss Mama, Charlie, but no jumping on the bed.'

The next moment, the little boy was at Harriet's bedside, standing on tiptoe so that he could kiss her cheek.

'Nanny let me wear my new sailor suit so I'd look special when I saw you, Mama,' he said. 'Do you like it, Mama?' He paused for a moment and then reached up his hand and touched her cheek. 'Why are you crying, Mama? Did you hurt yourself?'

Harriet managed a smile as she replied that yes, she had hurt herself but he was not to worry, she would be better soon.

From the foot of the bed, Brook stood looking at her, an expression on his face she had never seen before – a deeply serious expression which made her catch her breath. Then he turned to look at Charlie.

'Run along now, Charles,' he was saying and, turning to the nurse, added: 'Tell the new nanny she may bring the boy down to say goodnight to his mama this evening . . .'

Looking at Charlie once more, he said, '. . . but only if you are a very good boy.'

With a last anxious look at his mother, Charlie left the room with the nurse and Brook came over to sit on the chair beside Harriet's bed. He was staring at her, his dark eyes deeply thoughtful as he said, 'I want you to forgive me, Harriet. When Doctor Tremlett told me he could save only one of you – you or our child, and that I must tell him which it was to be, I knew instantly that I could not bear to live without you. I have been all kinds of a fool, Harriet – a stupid, selfish, inconsiderate husband unworthy of you.'

He paused to take a handkerchief from his pocket and wipe the tears on Harriet's cheeks. His eyes never leaving her face, he said, 'I took out my disappointment on you when I discovered Charlie was not my child, when I should have thought of you and how unhappy you must have felt losing yet another baby after your ordeal in Liverpool. All women need to have children, and I should have understood how you felt when that woman left her baby in your care. Without thought of your feelings, I told you to give him to someone else – that I didn't want him in my house.'

He took Harriet's hand in his and held it between his two. His voice was husky as he continued, 'I didn't want to forgive you! I thought if I hardly saw you or Charlie, I might be happy again without the constant reminder of what you had done. I fought very hard against the need, the longing, to have you back in my arms. Oh, Harriet, my love. When Doctor Tremlett told me last night that you might die, I realized I would not want to go on living if I lost you. Forgive me, my darling, please?'

It was several minutes before Harriet could find her voice through the lump in her throat. Scarcely able to believe that she was hearing the words she had prayed for for so long, she whispered, 'Didn't Doctor Tremlett tell you, Brook, that I can never give you the son you want – never? I can never be the wife you had hoped for when you married me.'

Brook leaned over and, releasing her hand, touched his fingers to her lips and said, 'My darling, you have never failed to give me all a man can ask for: your love even when I didn't deserve it. As for a son, I thought when I found out Charlie was not of our making, that if I was able to avoid him . . . and he was made to spend his days in the nursery with Nanny, where I did not have to see him, I could force myself to tolerate his presence in the house. But then . . . well, I would come upon him on his walks with Nanny, who would say, 'There's your Papa, Master Charlie,' and he would come running over to me, his face alight with pleasure, or he would be helping Baldwin to water the greenhouse flowers with his little watering can and, seeing me pass by, would come running to me . . .' He broke off, his voice husky when he resumed speaking.

'Harriet, my darling, I won't go on. The fact is, Charlie so much wanted me to love him the way I did before I learned the truth. I tried so hard not to do so! But I did, I do! I love him very much although . . .' he added with the glint of a smile, '. . . nothing like as much as I love you. Say you still have a little love left for me. Say it is not too late!'

Harriet had no need to speak through her tears. She simply took his hand in hers and pressed it to her lips. He stayed with her until at last, exhausted, she fell asleep.

When she awoke, it was nearly teatime. Bessie was standing looking out of the window. Hearing Harriet move, she said, 'So you're awake, Miss Harriet! It's been a beautiful day. Nurse said not to wake you. The master has been out riding and has just returned. He just looked up at the window and waved his hand. I think he thought it was you standing here. He looks right handsome on that new black horse of his and Charlie quite the little man on his pony. The groom is just going to lift him down . . . but no, his papa has dismounted and he is doing so. I just wish you were well enough to come to the window to see them, Miss Harriet. Such a very happy picture they make!'

Harriet didn't need to go to the window. She guessed that this was but the first of many ways Brook intended showing her how deeply he loved them both.